I0658634

SNAFU

Glen C. Allison

YOKE
PRESS
United States of America

Copyright © 2013 by Glen C. Allison
Published by Yoke Press

All rights reserved. Except for brief quotations in critical articles or reviews, no part of this book may be reproduced in any manner without prior written permission from the publisher, except as provided by U.S. copyright law. All inquiries should be directed to AllisonDigital, 883 Mt. Vernon Rd., Tupelo MS 38804.

Cover design: Kris Zediker
Cover photo: Derek Courtright
Page design: Peggy Carlton Jones

Printed in the United States of America

ISBN 0971810559

To

the Twenty.

Rest, angels, rest.

"You never really know your friends from your enemies until the ice breaks"
— Eskimo Proverb

Chapter 1

Any other night, the man in the stained bandana might have pitied the bikers, their reflection tinted yellow by the nicotine glaze on the mirror above the bar.

Tonight, however, he wasn't in the mood to regret the ass-whipping they were about to receive, thank you very much.

Bandana sat at the bar on the last stool next to the wall. The wall-sized mirror showed everything to be seen in the room: A dozen men in motorcycle jackets like the one he wore — three at the bar, the rest sprinkled in groups of two and three at tables. All of them drinking. None of them so drunk yet that they couldn't be trouble.

He could easily imagine a hundred other places he'd rather be instead of this dive, this joint that clung to the edge of the French Quarter like a worn-out whore on the arm of a drunken john, its pores saturated with decades of grease and idle danger.

He had seen more disgusting joints. Just not recently. He hated being here, surrounded by whiskey fumes and cigarette breath. Not that the stench and the clamor bothered him. What annoyed him most was how natural it felt after five years of sobriety.

The man sighed and scratched his head through the black do-rag. Duty calls.

A big guy guarded the door in the back, assuming there was actually a door behind him. It wasn't visible. He wore a genie-style ponytail on an otherwise slick head. His arms, scarred and littered with jailhouse tats, were neither flabby nor cut with the kind of vanity muscles made by celebrity workout machines. He wasn't drinking, he wasn't idly joking with anyone, and he wasn't ogling the frayed back pockets of the barmaid's tight jeans.

The gorilla was calm but not too relaxed. He shifted his weight back and forth slightly so that his legs wouldn't go numb from standing so long. His head swiveled slowly to avoid staring at any one person too much.

The big man was alert. But he wasn't watching Bandana Man too closely for too long a stretch of time. Good sign.

For all appearances, Bandana was just another dusty biker. The jacket hid his strength well. His face was set hard enough that the others left him alone. Like many of their kind, the bikers had chosen a tough life a while back, long enough to sense that the man at the bar was not some accountant who'd bought a shiny Harley to bolster his ego. They knew the man on the stool wasn't one of their regular crowd. But as a pack of wolves sensed the strength of a loner wolf, these men knew Bandana was comfortable with violence, if provoked. At the moment, they chose not to provoke him.

The man tipped his mug to himself in the mirror and drained it. To his left, the barmaid was drying a shot glass. He held up his beer mug and tilted it at her. She continued to dry for a beat, then carefully set the glass on the narrow shelf below the mirror. She walked over to the jukebox in the corner, punched a button. Then she finally walked back toward the bar as the first tentative chords of "Little Martha" drifted through the smoke.

She sported a black ponytail and a gymnast's body which, even in her 40s, drew leers from the patrons. A lanky biker snaked a hand toward her rear as she passed. Without breaking stride, she snapped the man with a dish towel. The bikers at the table cackled.

Then she was at Bandana's elbow.

"That storm is angry out in the gulf," she said.

"Weather talk. Huh. Nice," he said. He tipped his drink back again. "This fake beer sucks."

"Anybody ever say you got some strange yellow eyes, cowboy?" she said.

He answered without turning. "Anybody ever say you got a strange white streak in your hair?"

"That ain't the only streak I got," she said.

"Stubborn one?"

"Mile long."

"Comes in handy at times, don't it?" He checked the room behind him in the mirror. Everything was calm again after the attempted booty grab. "Good move on Mr. Hands over there," he said.

She made a puffing noise and he could feel her breath on his face. "He wasn't nearly fast enough."

He swiveled a quarter turn on the bar stool. Her face was expressionless except for a wee sparkle of challenge dancing somewhere in the back of her brown eyes. "Is anyone that fast?" he asked.

"Not since I stopped being a nun." She abruptly turned and went behind the bar. She poured him another drink.

He sat and listened to the Alman brothers play their acoustic guitars until the last harmonics died. The lanky biker got up and punched another button on the jukebox. The intro to "Magic Carpet Ride" crackled across the room.

Just as the first driving, syncopated chords of the song kicked in, the genie guard stepped away from the door at the back. It opened. Genie took a step to his left so that the door was now visible.

Nothing changed in the actual physics of the room, far as the yellow-eyed man at the bar could tell. The bikers kept up their good-natured swapping of insults. The bartender continued streaming another round of beers from the tap. Steppenwolf kept riding their carpet.

Yet the room seemed different as the back door swung open. The air was heavier. The walls had moved a foot closer to the center of the room.

Bandana deliberately avoided turning his head toward the opening door. But he was already picking up his mug, using peripheral vision to take in every detail.

The person who opened the door was not a biker. Probably no taller than the barmaid, he was three times the width. More broad than fat, he casually lifted his hand and motioned to the bartender, who picked up a plate of sandwiches from the end of the bar. The barmaid finished filling up a tray of beer mugs for whoever was in the back room.

The Wide Man blocked the view of the interior of that room.

On the back of the door hung a pink sweater.

The yellow-eyed man slid off his bar stool and stepped toward the jukebox.

From the corner of his eye, he saw the barmaid set the last mug of beer on the tray. She fell in step with the bartender as they hoisted their trays and walked toward the back door.

When the pair reached the opened door, they handed their trays to the Genie and the Wide Man.

At that point, several things occurred almost simultaneously. And violently.

The barmaid smiled at Genie as he grasped the tray in his oversized hands. Then she kicked him hard in the groin.

Bandana covered the ten feet from the jukebox to the bartender as if by magic. He tapped the bartender's head with a lead-filled sap. The man went down.

A half-second before that, a small metal object had dropped from Bandana's hand. If the music hadn't been so loud, the bikers might have responded to the flash bang grenade before it exploded.

Genie dropped the tray of food the barmaid had handed to him. He was in the process of doubling over when she hit him with 10,000 volts. The stun gun melted the Genie into a spasming pile on the floor.

Bandana kicked the tray of beer up out of Wide Man's hands. Before the liquid showered down, he punched the Wide Man hard, twice, once in the solar plexus, once on the jaw. The man went down.

The pair of attackers swept through the pile of bodies and broken glass into the back room, the man high, the woman low. Both had guns in their hands now.

Three seconds had elapsed since the first kick.

The back room was ten feet square, with a metal door on the back wall and four battered file cabinets next to it. A slender bathroom door was on the side wall.

A dented metal desk had been shoved in the corner. A long-haired man was half-bent over three lines of white powder on the desktop, his face twisted into a mask of surprise and fear.

The woman immediately zapped him with the stun gun. The man groaned and flopped face down on the desktop.

In front of the metal door was another man in a black coat. He was covering his left ear with his left hand. With his right hand, he was pulling a .357 magnum revolver from a shoulder holster.

The door behind him exploded. He went down and stayed down.

The woman scurried behind the desk. A girl of sixteen was huddled there, both hands over her ears. She wore a man's undershirt and purple pajama pants with green frogs dancing. White dust rimmed her nostrils. She was handcuffed.

Another man pushed open the shattered back door and stepped into the room from outside. He wore a black tee-shirt with the words "When Nothing but Forte Will Do" on it. He held a 12-gauge sawed-off shotgun.

The woman scooped the girl up into her arms. She began to step toward the back door.

The man with the yellow eyes held up a hand. Everyone froze. He hand-signaled for the woman to back up, then stooped low and tapped on the bathroom door with the barrel of his pistol.

A shotgun blast from inside the bathroom decimated the door.

Yellow Eyes stuck his pistol around the door frame and shot three times. He waited. The song still pulsed from the jukebox in the next room. A body fell to the bathroom floor.

Bandana nodded at the man with the tee-shirt, who stepped to the door of the bathroom, looked in. "He's down and hurting but not dead," the man said. He stepped past the others and yelled into the bar, "Keep your butts on the floor or I'll shoot them off." A few moans came from the bikers.

Bandana took the .357 magnum from the grip of the unconscious man on the floor. He stuck it in his waistband. He took the girl from the arms of the "barmaid" with the white streak in her hair.

From outside the building came the howls of at least three ambulance sirens. In the alley were two large men wearing shirts that read "Forte Security."

Bandana said, "Nice job, Jackie Shaw."

"Likewise, Al Forte," she said as she untied her barmaid apron.

In the alley, one of the Forte Security men carefully laid the girl on an ambulance gurney. He took a key from his pocket and unlocked the handcuffs. The other covered her with a blanket. They pushed the gurney around the corner to an ambulance. The girl's parents hovered nearby, anxious to see their stolen baby.

From around the front of the bar came the raucous growls of big motorcycles cranking up.

The man with the "Nothing But Forte" shirt, the one who had blown open the back exterior door of the bar, stepped out into the alley.

"Mr. 'Nomatter' Jones," said Al Forte. "How many Forte shirts do you have?"

Nomad shrugged. "The shirts ain't my idea. Ask the PR lady about them."

Forte sighed. "She's driving me crazy with the slogans."

Jackie Shaw unbuttoned her shirt and took off a Kevlar vest. Beneath it she wore a black tee-shirt.

On it were the words "Need Some Forte Force?" in big white block letters.

Forte looked at the shirt, then at her face.

She grinned.

"Has a ring to it, doesn't it?" she said.

Chapter 2

I'm a little mousey, mousey, mousey.

The tune was mostly inside Freddy's head but he caught himself whispering it. He forced himself to stop. For one thing, he was seven years old and that nursery rhyme was old-school for big kids like him.

Plus, if he sang it out loud, the men might find him.

He peeked around the chipped edge of the rusty dumpster. No sign of the men anywhere down the alley.

The fumes almost gagged him. His fear made him stay put, so completely quiet that all he could hear now was the *huh-huh* of his breathing and the quick thudding of his heart.

He swallowed hard. His throat was tight, as if it were dammed up against the flood of sobs so close to the surface. He willed himself to look around the dumpster again.

Still nothing moving.

Running through the housey, housey, housey. Freddy closed his eyes and saw his baby self and his daddy half-giggling their way through their made-up song as they chased each other through the old upstairs apartment on Julienne Street. Just the two of them. Just two boys playing, that's what you is, his grand mama would say.

He wished he could blink his eyes and be back there at that unpainted house with its creaky floors and faded wallpaper and mildew stink.

A vehicle rumbled along a distant street. Freddy stopped and listened. Was it nearby? Would someone in the vehicle see him if he made a run for it?

He wished he had not crossed Canal after running away from the men in the French Quarter. The narrow streets and noisy music of the Quarter made for a much better place to evade two grown men. True, one of the men, the one in the baggy shorts and basketball jersey, was faster than most adults Freddy had known. The jersey-ed man was probably close to his dad's age – early twenties maybe. The older guy in the wrinkled blue golf shirt was another story. He had been left holding his big belly, bent over gasping back on Royal Street. Freddy had easily zigged and zagged through the Saturday night crowd after he had twisted free from the fat man. He had glanced back twice to see the younger pursuer's eyes, white and frantic against the shiny blackness of his skin. "Freddy, baby, don't run away, baby!" The man's tone was pleading, like that of a favorite uncle trying to protect the boy.

Freddy knew the opposite was true. The men were out to hurt him. And they may have already hurt his daddy.

A stab of heart pain hit him when he thought of his father. He had last seen his dad an hour earlier. To celebrate the last week of summer, they had spent the day together. Visited Audubon Zoo. Rode the St. Charles streetcar. Clapped for the jugglers at Jackson Square. Taunted the sharks at the aquarium. After a long day of eating muffulettas and pralines, they had been strolling through the crowded Quarter as they listened to the jazz flowing out through the clubs. They had stopped at a souvenir shop. Freddy had been waiting on the sidewalk for his dad to come out. That's when the men grabbed him.

Now he felt wetness on his cheek and wondered if another summertime shower had started to fall. Then he realized it was a tear.

The boy swallowed hard. *Tighten up the tough part of you, tighten up,* he told himself, remembering his dad's commands to him when he wanted to give up on his homework or basketball practice or run from the taunts of the other kids at school.

I'm a little mousey, running through the housey...

The whoop-whoop of a police siren echoed through the alley. But it, too, was distant. The siren died and the boy again listened hard. A faint rustling came from within the dumpster. Freddy tried not to the think of the rats and roaches just on the other side of the pockmarked metal container wall.

If he could just make it back across Canal Street, he could make it back to the Quarter. He would be safe there.

He carefully raised himself to a running position. He checked the alley again. Empty.

Then he ran.

The brightness of Canal lit the entrance of the alley ahead.

He glanced behind him.

Nobody was chasing him. He was free.

He slowed at the sidewalk before stepping out of the alley. His view was narrow from where he stood. But everything seemed normal out on the big boulevard that funneled traffic into downtown New Orleans in the middle of the night. A few cars were passing. People were walking along the sidewalks on their way to the upper French Quarter.

Freddy took a deep breath and let it out, the relief flooding over him.

He stepped out on to the sidewalk.

A hand clamped his shoulder.

Freddy screamed.

"Hold still, punk," said the fat man in the golf shirt.

Freddy twisted from the man's grip and kicked him hard on the left shin.

The man cursed and loosened his grip on the boy's shirt.

Freddy thrashed hard and felt the shirt tear.

He was free again.

A streetcar buzzed somewhere from around a corner. The thought flashed through his mind: Maybe I can jump on it and get away.

From behind him the fat man yelled, "That kid stole my wallet. Stop him!"

A man and woman in evening wear backed away, pressing against the glass window of a drugstore as the boy *whooshed* past. Freddy took in the shocked look on their faces and kept running north on Canal.

A grizzled man with a cane stepped out from the bus stop ahead. He waved his walking stick at the boy to stop him. Freddy feinted toward the street. The man lurched in that direction. The boy easily went around him on the side closest to the storefront.

The fat man was still rumbling after him, his shouting punctuated with wheezes now.

The nose of the streetcar edged around the corner of St. Charles ahead.

Foot traffic was sparse at this time of night. Only a handful of people were still out on the streets, most of them having wandered out of the Quarter for a walk down the boulevard. A group of four woman wearing name badges were standing at the corner of the St. Charles intersection ahead. One of them was pointing across Canal toward Royal Street. Two of the others were on their cell phones.

Freddy zoomed past them. "That man is trying to steal me!" he shouted.

He turned right where the streetcar tracks came out of St. Charles and curved on to Canal.

When he looked back, he could see all four ladies on their cells now. The fat man was yelling at one of them.

Honk! Freddy almost stumbled as a taxicab came screeching to a halt. Even in the summer heat he felt a chill at how close the car's bumper was to him. He put one hand on the asphalt to keep himself from completely falling to the ground.

Then he regained his balance and kept running.

The streetcar was bearing down on him to his right.

Just need to make it back to the Quarter.

He propelled himself across Canal Street's wide, cement median, past a few people standing wide-eyed as they waited for the streetcar, and sprang over the tracks just inches ahead of the advancing trolley.

The car slowed to a stop behind him, blocking the view of the fat man's pursuit.

Freddy dashed straight across Canal, ignoring the honks from cars in the opposite lanes.

When he was across, he looked back. The younger man in the jersey was nowhere to be seen.

Where are you, Jersey Man?

He darted into the darker confines of Royal Street. The streets of The Quarter were so narrow after the broadness of Canal, it was like guiding a canoe into a jungle stream after floating along the Mississippi River. The sounds of a street musician came from the next corner, where a police car was parked.

A tall cop leaned against the car.

Freddy nearly slumped to the pavement with relief.

A crowd of a dozen businessmen with name badges and party hats rounded the corner, catching him in their flow and jostling him back toward Canal.

Between the laughing, singing drunks, he could see the cop car.

When he tried to break free of the moving party, one of the men grabbed his shoulders and twirled him in a mock dance. He spun, trying to get his balance. His feet got tangled and he went down, banging his head on the pavement. A flash of light passed over his eyes.

Then darkness.

When he regained consciousness, he was floating through the air. So pleasant. Not walking. Just drifting along.

He realized he was being carried in someone's arms.

A feeling of dread slowly came over him. He opened his eyes.

The Jersey Man was carrying him.

Chapter 3

Al Forte stood atop the French Quarter levee. The leather jacket he had worn at the biker bar was folded and hung over the back of a bench beside him. He gazed across the dark water at the West Bank and thought on his city.

New Orleans is a two-sided Mardi Gras mask: One side of the mask is for those who come to visit. That side is a flirty one, a face with sparkle and scarlet lipstick and a built-in calculator to tally the gratuities.

The other side of the mask is for those who live here. It is not unattractive but it has no glitter. Instead, this side of the mask is lined with small wrinkles of wisdom and worry for those who make their livelihoods here. It is the face of vigilance that scans the river for any signs of high wind and water.

The violence at the bar was just part of Forte's business. By now, the adrenaline had drained from his system, yet he felt no need to sleep. This liquid summer night wasn't over for him yet.

A voice came from behind him.

"So, how many years since you lost her? Seven?" said Nomad, the one they had always picked for point man in their SEAL days when blunt harsh action was needed. The Naval Special Warfare teams – for Sea, Air and Land – were trained for unconventional warfare. Nomad relished the unconventional parts. Others might be gifted in the more intricate art of violence, operating like scalpels. Nomad was a sledgehammer.

Forte said nothing to his old friend for a moment as he held his vigil of contemplating the big water in front of him. The low profile of a coal barge creased the Mississippi, herded along by a tugboat.

"Yes," said Forte. "Seven."

Nomad faced away from the river, toward Jackson Square. His head was rotating back and forth methodically. He stopped and glanced back over his shoulder at Forte. "What?"

The man with the yellow eyes said, "Expecting company?"

"Hopefully."

"They are all locked up."

"Not the bikers."

"They are long gone."

Nomad's eyes were shadowed, back lit by the lights of the park. "I can always hope," he said. "Next time, it's your turn to stay out in the alley with the explosives." He walked down the steps of the levee. "You had all the fun."

Forte followed him. "Whatever you say."

No one dangerous seemed to be watching for them at the bottom of the stairs or anywhere in the open plaza next to Cafe Du Monde. They took a table close to the sidewalk. A Vietnamese waitress took their order and sped off.

At 2 a.m. the outdoor tables were half full at one of the most famous outdoor cafes in the world. College students with New England accents filled the three tables closest to the two men. Two of the girls, one light-skinned and one dark, giggled when Nomad passed by. They stifled their laughter when he glanced at them. When they noticed the white powdered sugar from the beignets on the tips of their noses, they erupted into guffaws again.

A group of men and women in business suits and name tags had pushed two tables close together under the covered pavilion area attached to the century-old stucco-sheathed building. A family of five huddled around a table, the third-grade daughter chattering away while her two teen brothers looked bored, iPod wires hanging from their ears.

"People really can smell a storm coming?" Forte said, the words not really a question.

Nomad focused on the people out on the sidewalks, couples hand in hand, groups of three or four enjoying the final moments of a night out on the town. "You gonna get us killed one day, coming to this place," he said.

Forte shrugged. "Not a bad place to die."

"Oh, here we go with the shrugs."

Forte shrugged again. "So, answer me about the storms. About smelling them."

"You can't smell it?" Nomad asked.

"I can smell something. Don't know if it's a storm."

Nomad stopped surveying the surroundings and focused on Forte.

"I remember these moods you used to have."

Forte raised an eyebrow. "What moods?"

"You know what moods."

"I don't know what the hell you are talking about."

"See, it always starts like that."

Forte cursed sharply. The girls at the next table swiveled toward him, eyes wide. "Sorry," he said to them.

Nomad chuckled. "I'm just BS-ing you, buddy. You've always been a moody individual. Tonight's no different."

Forte looked at his friend hard.

Nomad covered his mouth with an elaborately fake yawn.

Forte gave a tired smile. "I get it. You'd rather have me pissed than sad."

Nomad resumed scanning the crowd. "You so smart."

Forte grunted.

Nomad stretched his arms high then moved his head in a circle to loosen his neck muscles. "Thought you might be in a better mood after the fun we had at the biker bar. Rough up some bikers. Blow up a door. Shoot a drug dealer. Rescue a kidnapped girl. Good times, good times."

"Not even sure she was kidnapped. She probably went willingly with those guys," Forte said.

"Maybe so. But her parents wanted her back."

Forte grunted.

"And they paid extra for it."

"I guess."

"Oh, that's right, the money means nothing to you."

"Comes in handy. Bills to pay."

"Yeah, but that's for Forte Security; you'd do it for free. See, that's the difference between you and me."

"Right. I forgot. You do it just for the money. Old friends and loyalty and stuff mean nothing to you."

Nomad lifted his chin as if in deep thought. "Only if they have money."

"Should've left your ass for dead in the jungle."

"Those Nicaraguan women would never have allowed that."

Their unsmiling waitress arrived after weaving her way through the metal tables in the courtyard of the café. From the tray, she produced two thick mugs of cafe au lait and two plates of beignets. Nomad pulled out a bill for twice the amount of the cost of the food and drink. He whispered to the woman in Vietnamese. Her eyes widened as she glanced at Forte out of the corner of her eye.

It wasn't exactly a smile that played across her mouth. But her face seemed less passive than before.

She bustled over to two other waitresses. A spirited round of chattering ensued, punctuated by a few *hee-hee*'s and *ahhh*'s. One of the other women cocked her head, appraised Forte, and nodded smugly.

Nomad tipped his mug back and studied the statue of General Jackson and his horse as carefully as if he expected them to gallop down Decatur Street any moment.

Forte said, "Don't guess you're going to tell me what you said to her, huh?"

Nomad set the cup down and daintily picked up one of the powdered donuts. He shook it gently to send the powdered sugar back to the white china plate. He took a tiny bite off one corner of the square doughnut. He took another sip of the coffee then dabbed at the corner of his mouth with a napkin. "It was a compliment, I assure you, Mr. Forte."

Forte squeezed his eyes shut and pinched the bridge of his nose between the forefinger and thumb. He began to reply when his eyes focused on someone across the street. A woman.

She was walking away from the cafe, alone on St. Ann halfway up the block of the pedestrian walkway toward Chartre. From the back, she could have been any age between 20 and 40. Her brown hair fell to her shoulders and hid the top straps of the white sundress she wore. Square-shouldered and slim, her natural sway seemed at once athletic and alluring.

Then she reversed and headed back toward him. Forte slowly set down his coffee mug. All the chattering at the surrounded tables faded away from him now.

She passed through the shadows cast by the streetlamps along the fence that bordered Jackson Square. All the umbrellas that shaded the street artists during the day were collapsed for the evening. The woman, a stranger to him, wasn't looking at the park, however. She was looking straight ahead.

Forte wondered if she was looking directly at him.

He remembered how *she* would look at him, back then.

In his mind, he heard the song faintly, then stronger.

Something in the way she moves... and looks my way and calls my name... it seems to leave this troubled world behind.

22

Chapter 4

10 years earlier

Forte stood at the abundantly stocked bar in the corner of the room listening to the lyrics of "Something in the Way She Moves." He had always liked that song. *If I'm well, you can tell, she's been with me now. And she's been with me now, quite a long, long time. Yes and I feel fine.*

One of the richest men in New Orleans had volunteered to honor the Navy SEALs with a small but tasteful reception at his mansion in the Garden District. Forte surveyed the room as the bartender mixed his rum and coke.

He glanced toward the door just as a young woman entered the room. She was attractive, not glamorous. She wore a simple knee-length black dress with a single strand of pearls around her neck. Her chestnut hair fell naturally to her shoulders.

What struck Forte was her expression. It was one of both amusement and curiosity.

He found himself wondering if she was accompanied by a man.

Another young lady in a short red dress strolled in through the 10-foot doors of the ballroom of the mansion. She stopped and spoke to the girl with the pearls. They both laughed.

Hmm. Forte picked up his drink as he scrutinized the women. He was just raising the glass to drink when he felt a sharp poke in his ribs.

"You scoping her out, huh," said his fellow SEAL, Michael "Nomad" Jones. His nickname had started out years earlier as "Nomatta." That had been his unfailing answer when asked to complete the most audacious of missions: "No matter what." As is the case among men and boys on a team, the nickname had been cut to "Nomad" pretty quickly.

Forte observed his squad mate, who was dressed exactly as he was: In dress whites. Nomad's face held an expression Forte had seen in a wide variety of settings all over the world. It was a mixture of wolf and Labrador, both cunning and inviting.

"Scoping who out?" Forte said.

"Red dress. Long legs. Stiletto heels," Nomad said.

"I think she has a head, too."

"Oh yeah. But just to make sure the legs move."

"You are one romantic bastard."

Nomad drained his drink. "Launch sequence initiated," he said. He handed the glass to Forte and walked directly toward Red Dress. The crowd of five men surrounding the woman parted. Nomad held out his hand, gently pulled her out to the dance floor. Soon they were swaying to an instrumental version of "It's a Wonderful World."

Forte let his attention wander back to the woman in the black dress. She was smiling and shaking the hands of three men in dress whites.

He took another sip of his drink as the men jockeyed for position. He wandered out to the sun room adjacent to the big ballroom where the hundred-or-so guests drank and danced and drank some more.

The sun room was empty of people. Tropical plants filled most of the spaces not occupied by heavy rattan furniture and oriental chests and tables. Floor lights, hidden throughout the room, illuminated the area just enough for navigation but not enough to sharpen the details. A large glass case full of horsemanship trophies lined an entire wall of the room. Through the floor-to-ceiling windows Forte could see a stone patio with candles lining the decorative concrete railing.

"Not much for crowds, huh? Me neither, actually." The man's voice came from behind him. Forte turned to face a tall man in a panama suit, a tumbler of clear liquid hanging from one hand at his side. He had a hooked nose that was balanced by a wide smile. His stance was one of a man accustomed to deference.

"We've met before. I'm Brock Randall," he said. "I wanted to thank you for attending my little party."

Forte stepped forward and shook the man's hand. "My pleasure, Mr. Randall. It's a nice honor for the SEALs." He had heard much about Brock Randall over the years. The man's grip was strong. Up close, his eyes were like black bullets.

"I especially wanted to talk to you, Al," Randall said. He waved a hand around the sun room. "These plants come from Central America. Most beautiful place in the world. Beautiful flowers. Beautiful people." He sipped his drink and looked down at Forte. "You have been there before, right? I'm sure you agree."

"I didn't take the scenic tours much. But I know there are good people there."

Randall chuckled. "My company does a bit of business there. We could use a good man like you."

"I appreciate that, Mr. Randall, but I already have a …."

"After you muster out of the Navy, I mean, son."

"I'm hoping that will take a while."

The tall man tipped the tumbler back and drained his drink. "Never can tell. People change, Al." He held out his hand again. "Just keep it in mind. Enjoy the party."

Randall had always reminded him of a type of commanding officer he had known in his military career. They were few and far between, but those commanders were the types who made a show of supposedly caring about the men under their command but, in the long run, merely cared for their own agendas. By contrast, Forte remembered bitching about a squad leader who rode his men hard and rarely praised them. Then, one day, in a mock operation, one of his men broke his ankle while dangling from a rock wall during training. The captain personally rappelled down and rescued the man.

Randall was far from that type. He would have taken a moment to calculate the cost of training another man to replace the one with the broken leg.

Forte spoke up suddenly. "I don't think so," he heard himself say. "I mean about working for a private security company. I just don't see myself doing the kind of things you do." He wondered why he felt the need to be so blunt. It had often caused him problems, his inability to sugarcoat a message.

Randall faced the younger man. For maybe a half-second, something like pain crossed his face. Then he smiled again. "Well, if you ever change your mind, let me know."

Forte shook his head. "I won't."

"I see." The older man sauntered back out to the main ballroom.

Forte had known about Brock Randall for a while. Rumors had floated among the ranks about the possible types of activities his companies conducted in Central America. But he had always been generous toward the SEALs and those surrounding them.

"Enjoy the party," he said aloud to himself.

Forte walked out through the French doors and found himself alone amid the flickering lights.

The back yard was bordered by an eight-foot concrete wall that had been stuccoed carefully to match the house. The entire yard was filled with plants, everything carefully and tastefully landscaped so that visitors could easily be herded to three or four separate seating areas complete with benches and water features. Forte compared the foliage in the back yard to what he had encountered recently on a top secret mission to Nicaragua. He spied a type of palm tree that he was sure he had seen a sniper tumbling from. He stepped out on to the crushed gravel path leading away from the patio.

"So, this is your idea of a party?" It was a woman's voice. Forte resisted the impulse to about-face quickly.

It was the woman in the black dress. Her face was mostly back lit from the light spilling from the ballroom. Forte couldn't be sure whether she was smiling or not.

The tone of her voice, however, was what piqued his curiosity. The question was less inquisitive and more teasing. Her voice was low and non-threatening, yet it was laced with provocation. *Who is this woman?*

He moved a step to his left in order to catch the flickering reflection of the closest candle. When he did, he could see that her face was totally impassive. Except for the eyes.

If not for the eyes, she could have been a school teacher calmly asking for an explanation from an errant schoolboy.

The eyes, however, were full of mischief.

She spoke again. "Obviously, they teach you SEALs to use strategic silence."

"Apparently you didn't attend that class yourself," Forte said. He added, "Ma'am."

"Ah," she said. "Such unexpected wittiness from a man who is comfortable with death. But I suppose I deserve it."

He stood squarely before her now. "How do you know I'm comfortable with death?"

"I just assumed it, based on the stories of your friends inside."

He shrugged. "It's our job. Some guys like to run their mouths about it."

She cleared her throat. "And some don't."

"And some don't care for small talk," he said.

Although they were outside, Forte felt as if the universe had shrunk to the size of the patio on which the pair stood.

"And some guys run away from women," she said.

He snorted. *What the hell?!* "I didn't run away. I just wanted a breath of fresh air."

"Right."

"I didn't notice you lacking for attention."

"Yes, I noticed you noticing."

"Like a pack of wolves."

"Unlike you, huh, Mr. Forte?" She pronounced it correctly. *For-TAY.*

He said nothing.

She stepped closer and peered at him. "They really are yellow."

"You came out here to see if my eyes really *are* yellow?"

"I thought they were, from across the room when you were trying to act like you weren't ogling me so much."

"I barely glanced at you," he said.

He noticed her eyes were green. She was more attractive up close.

Chapter 5

Once he realized they weren't going to kill him, Freddy relaxed a little.

Okay, maybe that's pushing it. All he really knew was that they weren't going to kill him immediately. He had almost peed himself when the man in the jersey first grabbed him. He had started to struggle, but the pain had shot through his skull where he had hit the pavement. For a minute, he thought he might vomit from the hurt.

Then he was in the back of the van on the pile of blankets. The fat man was in the driver's seat shooting mean looks at him in the rear-view mirror. Freddy just closed his eyes against the glare of the naked bulb in the top of the cargo compartment of the van. The lights clicked off and they were rolling.

Freddy could tell they were winding through the streets of the city, never traveling fast or straight for very long.

The Jersey Man perched on a plastic milk crate next to him, his legs splayed wide to brace himself against the sharp turns of the vehicle. After checking the boy's head to make sure it wasn't bleeding, he ignored Freddy. His total focus was forward, as if he were actually driving the van remotely by his thoughts.

Freddy inched his way to a sitting position and craned his neck to see out the front window. Jersey Man looked sharply at him.

"Get down and stay down, boy," he said.

Somehow the lack of emotion in the man's voice frightened Freddy more than if he had screamed at him.

He sank into the pile of stinky blankets in the back of the van. They weren't totally gross; his laundry basket at home smelled as bad. He sniffed. They smelled like his dog's bed, except stronger. He remembered going to the stables on a field trip with his class. *Horses.* Neither of the men seemed like horse people. Freddy wondered what they were doing with horse blankets.

Then his thoughts spun backwards like a Yo-Yo. His dog, Callie, was home alone. He knew his dad would not be going back to the apartment any time soon while his son was still missing.

"My dog," Freddy said aloud. The sound of his own voice startled him.

Jersey Man swung his head a quarter turn toward him but still kept his attention on the road ahead. "What?"

"My dog. She needs her food. And water."

"Your dog?" The man's voice sounded amused.

"I need to call someone to feed Callie."

The man grunted.

"She'll die if I don't." Freddy heard his own voice stretching thinner. "I can't let her die. My mother gave her to me before she ..." A sob blocked the rest of his words.

"Boy," the man said, "we ain't calling nobody about no damn dog. Now lay down and shut up."

Freddy pressed his face into the smelly blankets and tried to muffle his crying.

Daddy, where are you?

* * *

The trombone player was extraordinarily proficient on an instrument that was easy to play badly. The young dad had to nudge his way through the small crowd of tourists gathered around the street musician.

He had just stepped out of the souvenir shop on Bourbon Street to tell Freddy "no luck" for a tee-shirt for kids. All the shirts were emblazoned with funny but crude remarks. He could just imagine the phone call he'd get from Freddy's school.

Raising the boy by himself was tough enough without the teachers ragging on him. He knew Freddy would give him a hard time about not getting a shirt, but it was just how it was. It blipped through his mind how the fears of being a father had faded with each passing year of his son's life. He had been so young himself, just a teen, when his youthful irresponsibility had brought so much trouble on himself. He regretted many things he had done back then. But Freddy wasn't one of them. Once he held that little brown baby in his arms, the world had changed for him. And it didn't matter that he would eventually be a single parent.

He wasn't too alarmed when he saw that his son was not standing right next to the door of the shop. The boy was adventurous and the pair had been out in the Quarter many times.

The young dad casually scanned the couples and trios and quartets of people flowing along the thin street like boats on the river where he worked the docks.

No Freddy.

He felt the first mild tingle of alarm in his head.

He pushed his way closer to the trombone player.

"Did you see a little boy right here?" he asked.

The man kept playing, his head rolling back and forth on his shoulders, his dreadlocks dancing Medusa-like.

The dad felt the panic rising now.

He walked 20 feet in one direction then 20 feet back, quickly. He kept his focus low, about four feet off the ground as he searched for that small head among all the adults crowding through the street.

The trombonist revved up his playing.

The young dad increased his range to 50 feet in both directions from the souvenir shop.

No Freddy.

The dad cupped his hands around his mouth. "Freddy!" he yelled.

His voice was lost in the cacophony of the bawdy street.

He felt as if the sin-stained air of the Quarter would suffocate him if he inhaled it too deeply.

"Freddy! Freddy!" he screamed into the din.

He whirled and ran toward the gaping front door of a strip bar. Electronic music pounded through the doorway. A huge red-haired man barred his way. "Come to see the dancers?" he said.

"My little boy... is he in there?" The young dad's voice was strained.

The bouncer shook his head. "No minors in there."

"I need to look. He's my son. I can't find him."

The muscled man began to shake his head again.

The young dad let his shoulders droop then darted past the red-haired man.

Only neon lit the room. A circular bar centered the club. Booths sprinkled with tipsy couples and noisy college kids lined the walls.

The dad ran past the bar to back of the room.

Behind him he could hear chairs being knocked out of the way.

The back of the club featured a wide stage where three women danced under a black light. The two on the sides were further back in the shadows. The middle woman was closer to the front of the stage where a dozen or so conventioneers were waving paper money.

The dad pulled chairs away from the tables.

"Freddy!" he screamed.

One of the men pivoted to block him.

"Did a little boy come in here? My little boy!" Freddy's dad yelled in his face.

The man's mouth formed the word "Whaaaaaaa?"

The dad felt a big hand grab his shoulder.

He twisted free and pushed through the crowd of men lining the stage.

A table tipped and beer glasses crashed.

The woman on the stage froze, her sequined bikini top in mid-twirl above her head.

"Fredddyyyyyyyyy!" the young dad screamed.

Then he was suddenly weightless, floating above the room. He could see the mouthed *Oh*'s on the dancer's faces and the men with their name-tags pointing up at him.

He realized the bouncer had grabbed him. He was held aloft above the bruiser's head as he moved toward the door.

Then he was sailing out into the street.

He cursed the fact that the human mind was so fast at processing that he could feel the dread of how hard the pavement would be during the half-second before he hit.

He hit and rolled until he came to a stop in the middle of the street. He lay still for a moment, assessing any damage. He groaned as he pushed up to a sitting position. A drunk in a business suit offered to help him up. He waved the man away and struggled to his feet. *Got to find Freddy.*

Somewhere nearby a phone was ringing. He stumbled over to the sidewalk across the street and propped against it. The dread was rising inside him. He knew the boy would not just wander away.

The phone kept ringing, a raucous electronic twitter. He found himself wanting to scream "Somebody answer that!"

Then he realized the noise of the phone was coming from his pocket.

He pulled out a phone he had never seen before. Just as it stopped ringing.

He opened the throwaway phone. No calls had been made. Only one number was listed as an incoming call. He hit the dial button to call it back.

A man answered. "So, you finally are paying attention."

Freddy's father winced as he twisted slightly to put the phone to his ear. "Who is this?"

"We have your son," the voice on the other end said calmly.

The man almost dropped the phone as he slid down the wall to a sitting position.

"Hello? You there?"

When he spoke, his voice was a croak. "Yes."

"I'm going to give you some very specific instructions." The voice droned on for a moment.

The man on the sidewalk listened then suddenly sat up straight. "No!" he shouted. "You are crazy. I can never do that."

There was silence on the phone. "Yes," said the man on the other end. "You can do it and you will do it. Or your little boy will die."

"Let me talk to him, please," the boy's father pleaded.

The line was dead.

Chapter 6

Seven years earlier

The guitarist was out late for a street musician in the quarter. The daytime tourists that mobbed the Square were gone, replaced by couples and infrequent bands of revelers on their way to somewhere else in the Quarter.

Something in the way she moves. The street singer launched the James Taylor song with more sensitivity than expected. Most street players went for volume because noise usually equaled tips. This one probably had his loud moments but for now he played softly. Maybe he was playing mainly for himself at the moment. His voice carried the song well, not pushing too hard, letting the lyrics ride the melody comfortably.

"He's good," Ruth whispered.

"Yes," said her husband. "He is."

She raised up on tiptoe and kissed him. "What a special day."

Ruth loved to come here late at night, to stroll around the outside of Jackson Square when it was relatively free of people. The buildings can speak to you then, she told him. Sometimes they spent hours walking and pausing, scrutinizing some detail of a building. Occasionally, she would bring her small drawing pad and sit on the nearest bench and capture the way the stucco had faded from the bricks on a wall or how a particular gargoyle proudly displayed his stone menace.

Al would sit and peek at his wife as she concentrated, her eyes going back and forth between the object of her drawing and the pencil making all those precise movements. Back and forth. Over and over. Her teeth tugging at her bottom lip.

She was a social worker, not an artist, she told people who admired her talent. Forte figured that somehow his wife was frightened away from actually drawing or painting unless she saw it as something for which she wasn't totally responsible.

He understood that way of thinking. He felt somewhat the same about what he did for a living. Even though he had spent hundreds of days in training as a Navy SEAL, he took little personal responsibility for his special skills. In a way, he felt he was born with the ability.

Sometimes she would talk to him about the light and dark, the shadows and how they looked different in the light of the old streetlamps compared to the sunshine. Or about the texture of rocks or leaves or trees or the blades of grass in the park.

And he would listen carefully. As long as he could. Then his eyes would glaze over. And eventually he would reconnect with the conversation and she would be saying something like, "and when I go to paint the Sistine Chapel next summer" or "sometimes I use that number 464 pencil that is big as a baseball bat." And he's nodding pleasantly the whole time.

Until he hears the real words. "Busted," he would say.

She never got pissed about it, though. She just moved on.

...and looks my way and calls my name.

The singer on the sidewalk seemed oblivious to them now. His head bobbed slightly as his fingers glided through the instrumental lead-ins for each verse. When he sang, he flung his head back and long blond hair flipped away from his face. Eyes closed, he let it come out as if he couldn't stop it.

Forte knew now that the man was playing for his own enjoyment, that it didn't matter if the couple was listening. This slab of warm concrete in the muggy evening air was the man's personal stage for an audience of one.

But it's also for us tonight, this song, Forte mused. *A night of celebration.*

Peripherally, he saw his wife's hand slip into her purse. She pulled out a small pad and flipped it open. She began to draw.

* * *

The four teens slouched against the side of a brick building in the night heat. They had been careful to gather in the shadows away from the insect cloud around the streetlight instead of directly beneath it. Though it was after 2 a.m., the air was as steamy as a laundry. In a couple of hours, it might cool by 10 degrees or so, just before the sun appeared again and reminded everyone how wonderful New Orleans in August could be.

The boys were unaffected by the heat. It's all they had known during their young lives in the less glamorous parts of the Big Easy. Anyone who whined about it was slapped down quick and teased for a while afterward. The boys endured the heat the same way they endured the hopelessness of their welfare-ridden existences. They created their own cool just the way they'd conjured their own hope: by sticking together.

The leader of the boys flipped open the cylinder of an old revolver. He spun it, making the brass cartridges go by. He flipped his wrist and the cylinder clicked back into place. His three followers leaned in close to look at the gun. In the yellow light of the streetlamp, the gun looked worn and grimy. But it would do.

"Where the hell is Marty?" the leader said, irritated. "He want to do this or not?"

The other boys said nothing and carefully avoided the eyes of the bigger boy. They had seen his anger become dangerous rapidly many times. The smallest boy pulled at the sleeve of his oversize black tee-shirt and mumbled something under his breath.

The leader looked directly at him. "What you say, boy? Don't be mumbling, Zeebo."

Zeebo let his arms hang straight at his sides and looked up at the larger boy. "He gone to a party, Chug. His birthday party."

Chug snorted. "Today his birthday? Dayum, well, this will be a fun little memory for him, won't it?"

None of the three responded. They stood in the damp heat as the bugs hit the streetlights like kamikaze pilots, casting stringy shadows.

Chug slapped the gun against his leg. "I said 'won't it,' y'all."

Yeah Chug, sure Chug, cool Chug, they said at the same time.

The leader's face tightened. "None of y'all told Marty about this tonight, did you?"

The boys stepped back involuntarily, eyes wide. The two smallest of the crew shook their heads vigorously. The other spoke up. "No, Chug. We swear. We ain't told him nothing about it."

Chug held his stare a beat longer. Then he put the gun in his waistband and covered it with his shirttail.

Two blocks down, Martin Bailey jogged toward them, having just crossed Esplanade from the east.

At age 15 he was almost as tall as Chug but not as bulked with muscle. His gait was graceful as the long distance runner he was. Like the others, his head was shaved. Unlike them he had no tattoos. Yet. Those would come later after he'd proved he was worthy of the gang. He came to a stop and smiled at the three followers, then fist-bumped each of them.

Chug leaned against the brick wall of the building and studied the slim boy. "Well, Mar-TAY been to the par-TAY." He cackled at his own remark and the others laughed nervously. "So, they give you some birf-day cake, boy?"

The newcomer squatted and tied his shoe before answering.

Chug repeated his question. "You eat some cake, boy?"

Marty straightened up and regarded the leader for a moment. "Yeah, Chug. I did."

Chug moved closer so that his face was only inches away from the other boy's. His voice was low now. "You want to be part of this?"

"Yeah."

"You sure?"

"Yeah, why not?"

"You know you gonna have to show how much you want it," said Chug. A wicked smile came over his face. The other boys chuckled quietly.

Marty looked around at the others, then back at the leader. "How?"

Chug surveyed the street north and South. A car full of low-riders from a Hispanic gang flowed past them in a wave of Los Lobos music. He motioned to the others to follow him around the corner. In the alley, they huddled around him.

The big boy pulled the revolver out of the waistband of his baggy jeans. He held it up to catch the tainted light from the streetlamp.

Martin Kennedy Bailey felt ice between his shoulder blades despite the 90-degree heat. He was sure all the caramel color of his face had drained away like a baseball glove left out in the rain.

Chug studied him carefully as he waved the gun in front of the other boy.

"You ever shoot one of these, boy?" he asked.

Marty opened his mouth but no words came out. He swallowed and tried again. "I...Chug... I... can't shoot anybody."

The boys surrounding him maintained their dead-pan gang expressions for a beat. Then they burst into laughter.

The leader clapped him on the back and mimicked him in a high-pitched voice. "Ch..ch..chugggg… I cain't shooooot nobody!" The other boys hooted and cackled even more.

Chug held up the gun to Marty. Thumbed the release latch to open the cylinder. "You ain't gonna shoot nobody. See these bullets? They blanks." He clicked it shut with a flip of his wrist. "You gonna scare somebody, though." He leered at Marty. "We all had to do it. Now it's your turn."

He handed the gun to the younger boy.

* * *

"What are you thinking about?" Ruth had paused with the drawing pad on her lap, the sketch of the guitar player half finished.

She had the pencil poised above the pad, a quizzical look on her face.

He focused on her. "Oh, nothing."

"Right," she said. They both laughed easily.

"You were thinking about this song, the first time we met, weren't you?" she said.

"Something like that."

She reached over with the pad and herded his head closer to her. She kissed him.

"You were so tough."

"You were playing so hard to get."

She swatted his rear with the pad. "If I'd left it up to you, I'd be here right now with one of those true Neanderthals."

"Instead of a fake caveman like me, huh?"

Someone gave a couple of pseudo-coughs nearby. It was the street musician, packing up his guitar.

Forte took out a twenty and dropped it into the ragged fedora next to the man's guitar case. "You're good. Thanks for the songs."

The musician bowed dramatically. "Merci, monsieur."

Forte took his wife's hand. "Let's walk around for a little while."

* * *

The pistol felt like heavy cold death in the waistband at the back of Marty Bailey's jeans. He and Chug were walking down Royal into the heart of the Quarter. The other three boys slunk ahead of them, their voices pitched high with the thrill of the night.

They walked down the middle of the narrow street. At 2 a.m., few cars were driving through this part of the Quarter. Parked cars lined the street next to apartments that opened directly onto the sidewalk. The boys made a show of ignoring the one taxi that slowed at the intersection of Ursuline and Royal. The cabbie leaned out his car window and cursed at the boys in Cajun French. The smallest of the three ahead of Marty gave the man a rude gesture with his hand. The cabbie revved his engine and lurched forward.

Chug glanced at the cab. The man stopped the vehicle. He rolled up the windows.

The leader of the small gang spoke to Marty. "You can't let them make you a bitch."

Marty opened his mouth to respond, then closed it. He knew what the other boy meant when he said it, but when he searched his own mind, he just didn't feel the anger and resentment that must be inside the muscled boy. Not for the first time, he asked himself what he was doing lurching through the streets of the Quarter with a gun in his belt.

On each side of Royal were shops and apartments that had come to life in the centuries-old buildings. Some of the structures were two or three stories high with balconies strewn with ferns and trailing vines. A thin woman stood on one high to Marty's left, smoking a cigarette as the boys passed beneath her. Marty couldn't see her face, just a mass of curly hair back lit by the lights of her apartment. From the open door behind her came the scritchy-boom of a rap song the boy didn't recognize. She flicked the glowing cigarette butt out into the street. It made an orange streak to the ground then was trampled under the boys' feet as they continued their journey toward the center of the Quarter. The rap song faded until the boys could no longer hear the *boom-boom-bahhh-boom* of the bass.

Marty wished he were safe up on that balcony. Or back at his house. Or anywhere but out here on this crazy mission. He realized that Chug was talking to him.

"Thing is, nobody gonna look out for us but us. That's what gang means."

Marty felt the heat of the other boy's annoyance even as the group kept walking.

Chug spoke again. "You listening to me, boy?"

"Yeah. I hear you."

"I 'member my first time messing somebody up. All I had to do was scare the man but he freak on me. Had to bust his ass." He made a rattling noise deep in his throat that Marty recognized as a chuckle.

"I got tired of his whining, so I took the barrel of the gun and I ..." His voice kept on trickling out words in the humid gray of the New Orleans night but Marty couldn't make them out. It felt like the tightness in his throat had spread to his ears.

But he heard the last question.

"You want to live the life, or not?" Chug asked.

Marty realized that the barrel of the gun now felt like it was searing his hip where it rested.

"What?"

"Live the life. Be a banger," the leader said.

The group of five continued to walk west on Royal. But Marty felt as if the oil-stained asphalt had cracked open and swallowed him.

Do I want to be in the gang? Marty thought of the grimy hallway of the tenement building where he and his mother, grandmother and a thousand or so cockroaches lived. He thought of his track coach who had believed he could be a long-distance champion until he caught him smoking in the locker room and dissed him in front of his friends. He heard the voices and saw the looks of the guests at the fancy hotel where his mother worked as a maid.

He was about to answer Chug when the older boy raised his hand and hissed. The three in front stopped.

They were behind St. Louis Cathedral, peering down Pirate's Alley toward the river.

A man and a woman were walking through the alley.

* * *

Forte felt his wife's hand slip through the crook of his arm. He knew this was one of her favorite places, the alleys around the cathedral. She had never been to Europe but she imagined that it was like this one – clean, historic, bum-free.

He had been in alleys all over the world and knew they were never like this one unless they had been protected by some history society.

It was a ritual of hers, though, to walk this alley. So they did.

In the darkness, he pulled her to him, breathed her hair, kissed her neck.

"Your lucky place, huh," she whispered. She giggled.

Forte didn't notice the boys in the alley until they were right on him.

"Now ain't that sweet," said the leader of the pack of five boys.

Forte immediately positioned himself between the boys and his wife.

As he had done dozens of times in worse situations, he assessed the threat. The oldest looked to be 18 to 20, pumped up and wild eyed. He was flanked by a slim boy who looked scared. The three others were spread out behind the first two. They were shorter. They seemed jittery and expectant.

Forte spoke calmly. "Just relax, gentlemen. We will lay our money down and leave."

"Do it," said the strong boy.

Forte took his wife's purse and removed the folding money there. He did the same with his wallet. He laid it on the the worn bricks of the alley and stepped back.

One of the boys stepped forward. "Want me to pick it up, Chug?"

The lead boy grunted. The other boy picked it up.

Forte was annoyed at losing the money. He knew he could kill the boys easily with a quick grab of the Glock at the holster in the back of his waistband.

But they were just gang boys. He had seen much worse. Better to let them go.

Then he noticed the look on the muscled boy's face. He had seen the expression before on the face of older, harder men. Men about to become violent.

He tensed.

Chug said, "Do it."

The slim boy next to Chug jerked a big pistol out of his pants.

As the boy swung it around, Forte twisted to grab for his own gun.

The boy's gun boomed in the narrow alley. It bucked in his hand.

His face was suddenly twisted with horror.

Forte felt the bullet pass between his side and his arm as he yanked his pistol.

He immediately centered the sights of the Glock on the boy's chest. He didn't pull the trigger. The twisted shock on the boy's face stopped him from firing.

In another fraction of a second, Forte focused on the older boy, Chug.

His look was one of awe and fear.

Forte began to pull the trigger. He felt his wife pull away from his back, her fingers trailing down his back as she fell.

He turned.

And saw the blood.

Chapter 7

Present day

The digital clock on the wall showed 1:49 p.m.

Forte stood just beyond the tangle of cables in a corner of the interior courtyard. He drank the chicory coffee from a heavy porcelain shaving mug as the video crew finished setting up their equipment.

Four portable halogen lights were positioned around two folding chairs in the center of the courtyard. One of the crew sat in a chair with a white card in front of him. A camera on a tripod was trained on the card, a camera operator peering into the viewfinder. "We are now white balanced," he announced.

A woman with headphones pointed at the man in the chair. "Give me a sound check," she said. The man ran through the testing-one-two-three-four routine until she nodded.

Beyond the video setup, but still in line with the camera, were two children playing on a geodesic climber. A swing set and merry-go-round filled the rest of the small playground area. Flakes of green rubber provided clean and safe flooring for the children. *Recycled, no doubt.* Forte had little interest in most of the details of the organization he had founded years earlier.

On the interior balcony three stories up, a pair of burly men in black Forte Security shirts stood guard. Above them was the reinforced, vaulted ceiling with bulletproof skylights. At mid afternoon, only gray sky seeped into the room.

Forte noted the skylights and wondered if the storm would hit New Orleans hard. He pushed up his shades and rubbed the bridge of his nose between his left forefinger and thumb.

A woman's voice came from behind him.

"Just wake up?" asked Jackie Shaw.

She stood just behind him and to his left. Forte noticed that she was in the perfect position to both attack – or defend against – a right-handed opponent. She was barely more than an arm's length away but close enough to have kicked his legs from beneath him. She wore a Forte Security shirt and black chinos that fit with less cling than the jeans from her barmaid role in the early hours of the day.

A clipboard hung from her right hand. Her eyes seemed weary.

"I'll take that as a yes," she said.

Forte finished the rest of his coffee, still watching the video crew rushing around. "We about to start this circus?"

Jackie checked her watch. "Any time now."

Forte grunted.

"Rough night, huh?" Jackie asked.

"Just a night," he said. "And how long is this supposed to last?"

Jackie tapped the clipboard against her leg three times. "Look, I know you don't like this whole thing, but it's just part of the big picture." She faced him. "The more information we get out there, the more kids will be helped."

Forte had yet to face the woman at his side.

She touched his arm. "I know this is a bad time for you, Al. The anniversary of her death."

He finally rotated his head slowly to the side and downward toward her face.

47

His expression was devoid of emotion, as if a perfect robot replica of Forte had been smuggled into the building. When he spoke, his voice was flatter and softer than she had remembered ever hearing it.

"It is just a day," he said.

She took in his features – the amber eyes, the x-shaped scar on his eyebrow, the close-cropped black hair, the strong jaw. He was a man who neither realized nor cared how attractive he might be.

"Yes," she said, "it's just a day."

The director for the TV crew waved them over.

Jackie took three steps toward the video area before realizing that Forte wasn't following her. She looked back to see him standing in the same position, same look on his face. "You going to be okay?" she said.

His look went through her and past her and beyond the walls of this heavily protected place. Once again, he said nothing. He set the coffee mug on the floor and began walking with her toward the crew.

"You read the script right?" she said.

"I glanced at it."

"Just answer the questions with some kind of feeling and we'll be fine."

He gave her the least sincere smile she had seen him deliver. "I'll be Mr. Cheer."

After brief and perfunctory introductions, the crew hooked up the mics and positioned Forte and Jackie under the lights. The director of the video shoot waved at the children in the background. "Just keep playing, kids. You look great."

The woman reporter leaned forward in her chair and said. "Let's roll."

Jackie glanced at the owner of Forte Security in the chair next to her. He looked perfectly calm. Only a longtime friend would have seen the underlying sadness behind his eyes.

The reporter began to speak. "We are here today with Al Forte and Jackie Shaw of Forte Security. And this," she waved her hand in recognition of the room in which they sat, "is called The Refuge. Some consider it the safest place for endangered children in the world." She turned toward the two people being interviewed.

Her voice changed from broadcast to personal as she gave her best smile. "This isn't a live feed, so we will edit everything together for the interview show. So, just relax about your answers." Her voice changed gears again.

"Mr. Forte," she said, "exactly what gave you the idea to start Forte Security and The Refuge?"

He gave the same forced smile he had given Jackie Shaw a moment earlier.

"I just figured it was better than doing drugs," he said.

The atmosphere in the room changed. The man operating the camera raised up slightly and peeked from around a monitor. On the walkway above, the security guards halted their rounds.

The interviewer squinted slightly but maintained her smile. "It was after your wife's death, wasn't it, Mr. Forte?"

"Yes," he said, "it was."

She waited for him to continue. She knew that most people could not endure silence more than a few seconds when engaged in conversation. She knew that the other person, the one being interviewed, would usually take it upon themselves to fill the quietness with words.

Forte, however, knew how to be patient in a way most people didn't. He knew how to crouch in perfect stillness under a pile of jungle loam, being gnawed by unseen insects, while men with guns intent on his demise skulked within inches of him.

A few moments on-camera? Piece of cake.

Finally the interviewer spoke. "It was today, seven years ago, wasn't it, Mr. Forte?"

The room became so still now that the faint hum of the air conditioner vents sounded like a roar. Every person in the room was focused desperately on the man being interviewed, as if they were witnessing a train wreck.

Forte realized that everyone near him was holding their breath.

Then he began talking softly.

About the murder.

About the boy who had claimed it was a gang prank gone horribly wrong and that he was told the gun was loaded with blanks.

About his wife's love for children and her work as a social worker with kids very much like the gang members that night.

About his decision to start The Refuge, a place where kids who had been threatened by very bad people could be protected.

About his realization that he would always use his formidable skills at search and rescue to save children, and not adults.

About the children he and his crew had rescued all over the world and the people who had died opposing him.

His voice never wavered nor cracked as he spoke of the crashing descent into drugs he had taken after he washed the blood of his dead wife off his hands.

Jackie noticed that the room was perfectly quiet during his interview. But this time the quietness held no fear. Everyone hung on every soft word that came out of the mouth of the man in the center of the room.

As she listened to him wrap up the on-camera interview, Jackie noticed one of the guards at the top balcony motioning to her. He was pointing to his cell phone.

She stepped away from the video lights and switched on her cell. During the few seconds it powered up, she idly watched Forte stand and shake hands with the woman who had interviewed him. He moved with a kind of deadly athletic grace as he shook hands with all the crew members.

The beep of her phone notified her of two text messages.

She opened the first. It read: "Please call your doctor immediately."

Then she opened the second text message.

"Call the governor's office. He wants Forte."

She slipped the phone back into her pocket.

She stepped back toward the video crew and scanned the room. No Forte.

A cold knot began to form in her core.

She jogged toward the back exit and down a narrow hallway. She pressed her thumbprint onto a scanner at the first door. "Go go go," she hissed at the door.

It clicked open and she banged through it. Running now, she approached the exterior door that led to the alley behind the building. She scanned her finger again and banged twice on the door.

She pressed the intercom button that would allow her to hear any noises out in the alley.

A motorcycle kick-started into a roar.

The door clicked and she slammed against it with her shoulder.

She half-tumbled out into the alley.

A motorcycle was rumbling around the end of the alley.

Forte was gone.

Chapter 8

The Bourget is a motorcycle out of Arizona that caters to lovers of customized high-performance bikes. They get a lot of admiration for their stylized frames and extended front chopper-style forks.

Forte rode a Bourget Fat Daddy, a gift from a retired Marine who'd decided the two-wheeler had more power than he felt comfortable straddling.

Forte had no such misgivings about the bike. He roared past an 18-wheeler on I-10 heading west, gripped the handle-bars hard, and muscled through the buffeting of the wind wash from the big truck.

The speedometer showed 85 miles per hour.

He twisted the throttle further.

To his left, the sky was dark with the incoming tropical storm. It was still 18 hours away and would achieve hurricane force long before it hit land, the forecasters said. To his right was a great inverted half-bowl of azure and cotton puffs of clouds.

Same world. Two different experiences.

Ordinarily he would have taken the two-lane roads out of the city to shake off the claustrophobic grip of the concrete and brick boundaries. He would have wanted to smell the swamp air and see the cranes picking their way around the cypress roots. His pace usually would have been casual enough to read how much the roadside Cajun merchants were charging per pound for the crawfish in the back of their rusted pickup trucks. Eventually he would be riding slow enough to see the welcoming spark in the eyes of raven-haired beauties with their wild locks and their challenging swagger as they walked bare-foot on the side of the road.

Today, however, all he wanted was speed. And a lot of it.

He'd be lucky if he could read the writing on the side of the long vans.

He nudged the Fat Daddy up to 95 and kept going west toward Baton Rouge. At this rate, it wouldn't take long to be past the capitol city of Louisiana.

He came up on an SUV full of kids. A car top carrier was strapped to the top. Three preteen girls were struggling to hold up a homemade poster board sign as he bore down on the vehicle. The girls were giggling and tugging the sign into place as he roared past them. It read "U R A Hottie!!!"

He bumped the bike up to 100.

The hot air blasted against his face, scouring it. He wore no helmet but he had tinted goggles strapped to his head. Definitely not a poster boy for safety.

He approached a long curving bridge just before Baton Rouge. He leaned slightly to the left to balance the weight of the motorcycle. He could feel no vibration in the front forks. The muscles in his forearms, however, were taut with the strain of holding the bike steady on the curve.

You could fly now. The thought edged into the foggy despair of his mind. *Just let go of the handlebars.* He let the bike drift a few inches closer to the concrete and steel railing of the bridge. *No more pain, no more struggle, just peace.* He let his mind test the plunge, tasting how it would be soaring out over the rail, no restraints, no sorrow, completely free and unbound. His forearms ached now. He could see the veins pronounced now.

He could see the place where a needle had first delivered the cocaine. He hadn't used a needle many times on his arms before finding other places on his body and other ways to get the high he desperately needed to blot out the pain back then.

But he remembered the first time.

He had spent the first month after the funeral drinking his way through every bar along the Gulf Coast. Phone calls from friends went unanswered. Bills overflowed his mailbox. His temporary leave from the Navy became a permanent discharge. He didn't care. He was driven by the need to drown out a pain that would not go away.

Then one night he found himself at impromptu party with four others at a beach house in Pensacola. The blonde on his left kissed him and he offered his face to the redhead on his right who did the same.

"How do you know me?" he asked, his tongue sluggish from liquor.

"Oh baby, we know you," said the blonde.

The redhead whispered, "And we are about to know you better."

When he looked back to the left, the blonde had tied his arm with a strip of terry cloth towel and was twisting it. As he turned to his right for another kiss, he felt the vague prick of a needle sliding into the bulging vein on the inside of his elbow. Within moments he felt no sorrow. Only wonderment that he had never noticed how the waves on the shore murmured such wonderful truths to him.

The whispering slowly increased in volume until it became a roar in his mind.

It was the roar of his motorcycle.

His right handlebar was three inches from the highway railing.

It took all his willpower to resist jerking the bike away from the railing. At this speed it would have sent the bike tumbling. Instead he steadily steered away from it until he had reached the end of the bridge.

He let the heavy bike slow to a stop as he pulled over to the shoulder. He dismounted and hung the goggles from the handlebars.

He stumbled down the grassy embankment to the edge of the swamp bordering the highway.

All strength left him. He fell to his knees and dropped to all fours. He vomited into the mud and rotted undergrowth.

Then he screamed.

A group of birds fluttered up from behind a gnarled stump about twenty yards out in the water.

Forte let his anguished cry roll into the air above and around him, letting it mix with the *whump-whump* of the traffic on the highway. Like an animal dragging a claw trap on its mangled leg, he let out the pain of loss and suffering and failings in a sustained shredding of the peace around him. He picked up a bleached stick next to him and pounded the marshy ground around him, splattering himself with water and dirt.

He let it all out until it became a strangled remnant of its former fury.

Day by day by day by day by hour by hour by minute by minute. He felt his limbs loosen, their strength ebbed. He flopped face down in the mud.

For several minutes he lay there letting the past haunt him and the future terrify him. Bugs crawled over his neck. The calls of seagulls punctuated the air. The traffic still zoomed to destinations of hope and purpose.

He spit to the side. Gathering what strength remained, he pushed himself back up to all fours.

Then he saw the alligator.

It lay six feet straight ahead, its body and tail straight out behind it.

It was looking straight at Forte. Its mouth hung open slightly in the kind of grin that precedes a meal.

Forte felt his strength returning. He smiled back at the animal. *Lord, thanks for letting me know it was time to quit my whining.*

He figured that gator had been floating out in the swamp as it soaked up the Louisiana sunshine. It had probably been attracted to the noise and thrashing of the crazy human at the water's edge. It had drifted closer to investigate. Closer and closer.

Forte knew that the smallest movement would trigger a charge from the huge *Alligator mississippiensis*. He had seen the speed at which they snagged prey with those teeth and dragged them under the murky water.

He kept perfectly still as his adrenaline level spiked.

He knew that a few shots with the Glock into the mouth of the charging animal would probably slow it down. Probably.

The problem was the full second of time it would take him to yank the pistol out and start firing. By then he would be an appetizer.

Direct offensive action was out.

His only hope was misdirection and escape.

His hand clenched around the scrap of wood he had been pounding into the mud.

He took a deep slow breath, his eyes still trained on the alligator.

With a flick of his wrist he tossed the stick about four feet to the right of the big reptile.

He did not immediately move. Almost the full second passed as the stick twisted in slow motion through the thick air on its way to splashing in the brown water.

Then everything exploded into fast forward.

The alligator launched itself toward the flying stick. Amazingly quick, the 15-foot long animal snagged the piece of wood in its jaws. Its tail whipped through the water sending a spray taller than a man.

Then the gator lunged toward Forte.

But his quarry had not conveniently stayed put.

Forte was rolling to his left, away from the attack. His boots were slipping in the mud, trying to find traction. He had been facing the alligator. Now he was trying to turn and head back up the hill.

His feet slipped. He splat face first in the mud.

Go Go Go. His right boot found solid ground.

At the edge of his vision, he could see the gator swinging around toward him.

He pushed hard with one foot, then the other while clawing at the clumps of swamp weed in the mud.

Then he was moving.

He scrambled diagonally up the embankment. The animal followed him for a dozen steps then stopped, observing him with the same unmoving malevolence as before.

Forte gained the top of the embankment. He kept his focus on the alligator until it turned and slid back into the swampy water.

Then the man flopped down on the gravel of the highway shoulder.

He could feel the small sharp stones digging into his back and lodging themselves into the mud that caked him. He could hear the cars whooshing past on the other side of the guard rail, vehicles full of people with their own joys and worries and pains and excitement. He could smell the natural rotting of the swamp on his clothes and the fumes of the cars and hot asphalt a few feet from his head.

And he could feel the glorious sun as it began its mission to dry him.

He started chuckling softly to himself. Then louder. Then full-bore laughter poured out his throat and mixed with the hot wet air and the fumes and the searing sun. For a full minute the guffaws racked his body, his eyes closed as he let the emotions seize him and comfort him.

When he opened them, a motorcycle cop was looking down at him.

"Sir, are you okay?" the cop said.

Forte just lay on his back as the giggling subsided.

"Sir?" the patrolman said.

Forte sat up and put out his hand. The cop grabbed it and helped him to his feet.

Pieces of gravel fell from his mud-covered back.

"Just another day in the life of a maniac," he said.

The cop contemplated the mud-smeared man before him. Then his face changed from one of official sternness to genuine awe. "You're Forte, aren't you? The guy who rescues kids."

Forte said, "No, but I get that all the time. He's much uglier than me."

He climbed over the rail and walked back to the Fat Daddy.

"Nice bike," the cop said. "Nice tag."

Forte looked down at the vanity tag his assistant had ordered for him as a joke.

It read "FORTE" in bold letters.

He looked back at the cop and put a finger to his dirty forehead in salute.

He mounted the bike, kicked it into action, and sped off.

Chapter 9

The campground was a cross between a trailer park and a carnival. Travel trailers filled every slot and most of them were surrounded by families grilling burgers, flinging Frisbees, and enduring the heat. A swimming pool overflowed with grade-school kids splashing water on the teens trying to wring the last rays of summer sun. Kids on bicycles and skateboards had overtaken the tennis courts behind the motor homes. Moms pushed babies on the swing sets. A family huddled around a television under an awning. On the lake beyond the playground a speedboat was in the process of slinging two skiers across the water.

Moving only fast enough to keep the motorcycle from stalling, Forte steered the Fat Daddy through the middle of camper city.

Everyone stopped and stared at the muddy intruder and his growling chopper.

A group of men were gathered around the last motor home in the temporary village. Three were pointing at various parts of the engine while the other two held up the hood.

Forte stopped next to them and clicked the big bike into neutral. Over the chug-chugging of his idling motor he asked, "Are the cabins close by?"

One of the men, lanky with an unapologetic mullet, pointed in the direction Forte was already traveling. "Around that bend and over to the other side of the lake," he said. "Nice bike." He looked

Forte up and down. When he spoke again, his Cajun accent was more pronounced. "Partner, you look like you tried to catch them crawdads with yo' teeth."

"Is there any other way?" Forte said. He rumbled away.

A tunnel of pine trees led the way to the levee next to the lake. The road took him to a group of cabins hidden by trees from the group of travel homes. A beach area had been formed of white sand hauled in from somewhere else. Next to the beach was an outdoor bath consisting of a rusty shower head on a plain iron pipe. Forte veered off the road and pulled the Fat Daddy under the shower. Without dismounting, he blasted the mud off the motorcycle, then pointed the shower head to spray on his head and let the cool jets of water blast the grime from him, clothes and all.

Soaked but cleaner, he started the bike and tooled back to the road.

The cabins looked occupied, from the looks of the towels and flip flops decorating their rustic porches. Nobody was in sight, however.

Around a curve he spied a covered pavilion. A group of 30 people sat in folding chairs arranged in a semicircle. He parked the bike and walked down to the pavilion on a path covered with pine needles.

A slight man with an unruly shock of white hair was speaking to the group as he paced the concrete floor of the open-air meeting place. A dog lay in the shade of a weeping willow just outside the group.

"Back when I was a drunk but not admitting it," Manning Laird said, "a lot of people in my church were being hurt by it. But sometimes I think I caused more pain by letting everyone believe that being good was the best goal. It wasn't."

The preacher looked directly at Forte but showed no surprise at his unexpected appearance at this retreat.

The crowd, a mix of men and women from their 20s to their 60s, was listening intently.

"The goal was to have no goal except to admit I would never find meaning and peace and love inside myself." Forte could see the blue of his eyes from where he stood at the edge of the pavilion. "But where I failed, that's where I found victory. When I was powerless, then I found what power really meant.

"Look at us. We are all messes. We are drunks and addicts and liars and cheats." He considered the small group, none of whom shifted in embarrassment. "But we are thankful, or should be, because we can never find *up* until we admit we are *down*."

Forte felt the wind kick up behind him. He looked up at the dark clouds which were slowly encroaching on the blue sky to the north and west. On the far side of the lake a small shirtless boy was struggling to launch a kite. After three attempts, the kite darted upward and soared over the lake. *Good job.* He hadn't realized how much he was rooting for the kite until it flew.

"I bored you into a coma, I see," Manning Laird said. He was standing at Forte's elbow. Though he was a foot shorter and sixty pounds lighter, the older man's presence almost made Forte take a step back.

"Never, friend," Forte said. He embraced the older man. "Sorry about the wet shirt, Manny."

The preacher just grinned. He turned and waved at the others who were folding up the chairs, gestured to Forte to have a seat at a nearby picnic table. "I'm sure there's a story as to why you show up here soaking wet but still smelling faintly like swamp mud."

Forte sat at the table and told the story.

By the time he was describing the look on the highway patrolman's face, Manny was doubled over laughing, tears streaming. Some of the retreat helpers glanced in his direction, amused curiosity on their faces. He waved them away as he wiped tears.

He finally regained his composure. "Nice license tag," he said, setting off the laughter again. He guffawed and slapped the table top.

"Well," Forte said, "I forgot I had that tag on there."

Manny held up a hand as if warding off evil spirits and gasped "Stop" in between his laughs. Finally he calmed down. He dabbed at his eyes with the sleeve of his gray tee-shirt.

A gust of wind sprayed pine needles around their feet. The helpers loading the chairs on to a trailer stopped to chase the hats that had blown off their heads. Though the sky was still half-bright and the storm was still out in the gulf, it was reaching out to touch them.

Manning Laird sat with his back against the picnic table, his elbows resting on the table top. He snapped his fingers once softly. The dog jumped up from its shady rest and ambled over to him. It was a big lab with gray around the muzzle. The animal rested his head on the man's knee.

Forte knew it was futile to think he could out-silence his friend. "How's Honey doing?"

Manny ran his palm absently over the dog's head. "She's dying," he said, his smile still genuine. He noted the slight surprise on his friend's face. "We are all dying, aren't we? I just have a better idea when Honey's departure will occur." He blinked. "But you didn't come find me out here to talk about my dog, did you?"

Forte turned from the dog. His friend's piercing blue eyes were trained at him from beneath their bushy ledge of white eyebrows. "No," he said. "I didn't. But I didn't really have a plan for our conversation."

Manny tugged on his right earlobe. "Ok, then."

The truck slowly pulled away from the open air meeting area with the trailer full of folding chairs in tow. The chairs clinked together like metal skeletons.

Both men said nothing as the truck disappeared around the bend.

Forte spoke without meeting his sponsor's eyes. "Rough night last night."

Manny nodded. "Seven years."

"Yes," Forte said.

"Still wipes you out, huh?"

Forte nodded without speaking.

"Be surprised if it didn't. Hard thing seeing your wife die."

"Yes." Forte's voice was very soft and controlled.

"Be a while before the anniversary doesn't get to you. Maybe never."

"Probably."

"Made you want to use?"

"No." Forte avoided his friend's directness and focused furiously on the road even though the truck was gone. "Yes, it did."

"You feel guilty because of that?"

"Yeah."

"You should be tougher than that, huh." It wasn't a question. Manny put his arm around the bigger man's shoulders. "But you aren't, and that's okay."

Forte's swallows were audible as he choked back any response he wanted to make.

"I remember," Manny said, "how ashamed I felt when my drinking problem came out and I was fired from the church. And how surprised I was that a year later I still felt so ashamed that I wanted to drink every time I felt lonely or hurt or tired." His voice was so soft now he could barely be heard. "Then an old-timer at an AA meeting pulled me aside and told me something."

Forte faced him expectantly.

Manny leaned forward. "He said, 'Manny, your problem is you think any of us give a damn if you feel ashamed. You just ain't that important, really.'"

The two men kept a straight face for five seconds. They burst into laughter.

The sound of distant sirens came from the highway.

They came closer. And closer.

Forte focused on the curve of the road that led to the levee.

"Guess they decided to give you a ticket," Manny said.

Two highway patrol cars came tearing around the corner. They headed straight for the pavilion.

They stopped. The sirens went silent but the blue lights kept flashing.

The passenger door on the patrol car closest to the two men opened. Jackie Shaw got out and walked briskly toward them. Her mouth was pressed together in a tight line.

Forte said, "How'd you find me?"

"Cell phones," she said, "are a wonderful thing when they are powered on."

Forte glanced at Manny. He was carefully studying the kite fliers across the lake.

Forte said, "I control the phone, not the other way around."

Jackie matched his anger, her mouth white at the corners.

Forte spoke first. "Are you feeling okay?"

"Yes," she snapped. "Obviously, you haven't seen or heard the news."

He remembered the camper people huddled around the television.

"No," he said. "What's up?"

She turned to walk back to the car. Over her shoulder she called back, "The governor needs to see you. Now."

Forte grinned and put a hand on the old preacher's shoulder. "Guess he heard about me lying about that license tag."

Jackie stopped, her hand on the door handle of her car. "His daughter has been kidnapped."

Chapter 10

"Daddy!" Freddy screamed the word a dozen times before the fat man opened the door of the room, flicked on the light switch, and warned him to shut up. The man's voice was more annoyed than angry. He held a donut in one hand and a paper cup full of coffee in the other. He put the donut in his mouth, clicked the light off, and closed the door. Freddy noticed the man was favoring the leg slightly from the kick he'd gotten earlier.

Somehow the sight of the man's limp calmed him a little.

After they finally pulled him out of the van, Freddy had spent the first two hours of his kidnapping huddled on a mattress in the corner of a cave-black room. The boy had crawled around the room to determine what was here. He had started to run his hands over the walls but jerked them back. What was that? The walls were soft and mushy. Then he realized what it was: Mattresses had been strapped to the walls. Was it for sound-proofing?

He had trailed his fingertips over the wall mats enough to feel the boards nailed over the windows. On the floor was nothing but a mattress and some fabric that, like everything in the room, seemed soaked in stench. He sat balled up so that his body touched very little of the rancid mattress. He wished he could have buried his face in the greasy blankets strewn around him. He was afraid he would throw up.

He began to cry. Then scream for his daddy. Eventually he fell asleep.

He opened his eyes to see fire. The fat man had set fire to mattresses on the wall of the room. Freddy was surrounded by flames. But the window was open. His daddy was outside, calling for him. The boy scrambled. If he could just dive through the window into his daddy's arms... his legs churned as he prepared to leap.

But he was not moving. He could not get any closer to the window. In fact, he was sliding backwards. Over his shoulder he saw the Jersey Man and the fat man holding a huge metal pot. "Time to eat!" they yelled. Freddy scrambled away but his feet wouldn't take him.

"Blam! Blam!" The men rapped a big metal spoon on the pot. "Come on, boy! Time to eat!"

Freddy screamed as they grabbed his arm.

Then he realized he was dreaming.

He was on the dirty mattress in the dark room.

He shook free from the grasp of the Jersey Man who was grinning as he squatted next to the filthy mattress where the boy had slumped. The man gripped a pot in one hand and rapped a spoon on it with the other. From within the pot came the aroma of oatmeal.

"Eat this, boy," the man said. "You won't get anything else anytime soon."

Freddy pressed himself into the corner. "Leave me alone. Where's my daddy?"

Still squatting, still grinning, the man just observed him. Freddy repeated his question, this time pleading. "Where's my daddy? Tell me where he is."

Jersey's eyes were slits now. "You don't need to worry about yo' daddy, boy. He's the one who should be worrying about you."

Freddy felt the fear rising in him again. "What do you want from us? We ain't got any money. Don't you know that?"

The man chuckled. "Oh, we not asking for money. Don't fret, cher." He set the pot down on the floor. "How's that head feeling there? You hit it pretty hard on that curb last night."

Freddy ran his hand over the back of his head. He winced. He could feel the abrasion through his hair.

Jersey beckoned with his fingers. "Come here, let me look at it."

The boy stayed rooted in the corner. "It's fine. It doesn't hurt."

When the man spoke again, his voice was so soft it was barely audible. But it seethed anger. "Don't make me come get you."

Freddy crawled over the mattress to him. When he got closer he noticed the crude tattoo on the mocha skin of the man's forearm. He squinted at it.

"Loch Ness monster," the man said.

"Whaaaa..." Freddy whispered.

"See them loops. That's the back of the monster going in and out of the water," Jersey said. "Yeah, it's a jail tat. Guy in Angola did it for me. He had a thing for monsters." The man's hands roamed over Freddy's head until they found the bump.

"Owwww," he yelled, jerking away.

Jersey Man looked thin from a distance but the boy could see the muscles bunch up on his arms when he grabbed him. "Stay still, boy." Freddy felt like he was wrapped in steel cable.

"Bad bump but you okay. That hard head saved you," the man said. Something that faintly resembled compassion flashed over his face then was gone. He pushed the boy back on the mattress.

While the man had been examining his head, Freddy had whimpered and acted cowed. But he used the opportunity to examine the room while the light was on. At one end of the room was a closet with the door closed. He was sure it was locked. The only other items in the room were the mattress and three frayed blankets. But it was the boards on the windows he examined the most. In the dark, he had imagined the boards were nailed to the window frame.

Now he could see that the thick plywood covering the windows was screwed down.

His mind flashed back to a day the previous summer. His dad and he were helping an old woman cover her windows with boards. "Don't worry about using a hammer and nails, son. That hurricane can pry them right out like a big old crowbar." He had pronounced the word *HURR-eh-ken* as he hefted a portable drill. "We gonna put these screws in. It'll hold them better and then we can just reverse the drill to get them off after the storm."

Freddy's heart sunk. He had no drill. He had nothing resembling a tool at all, for that matter. He was lost.

When the man pushed him toward the mattress, he rolled toward the wall then sprang up, running toward the door.

Jersey's eyes were wide now.

Freddy faked to the left, then dodged right.

The man lunged and stumbled.

Freddy darted around him. He grabbed the doorknob and flung open the door.

And ran into the belly of the fat man.

The boy bounced back into the room.

Right into the grip of the Jersey Man.

"Boy," the man hissed.

His fingers dug into the boy's shoulders.

"Owwwww," Freddy screamed.

Jersey flung him hard back to the corner. The boy tumbled and slammed his ribs against the wall.

The door slammed.

He was alone in the dark again.

Chapter 11

Forte counted seventeen vehicles in the circular driveway around the Governor's mansion. Law enforcement of every variety was represented: city cops, deputy sheriffs, Louisiana capital police, Marine military police. Unmarked cars bristled with antenna that were undoubtedly receiving and transmitting FBI messages.

Jackie was rattling off facts about the disappearance of the governor's daughter as they strode toward the heavily guarded front door of the 25,000 square-foot home of the state's chief executive. "Ashley Barreaux, age 13, last seen this morning at the Riverwalk in New Orleans. She had been at an all-night 'End of Summer' celebration for cheerleaders who had been in town for workshops to learn routines. She and another girl had ditched their chaperone – the other girl's mom – in order to hook up with some boys from another school they had met at the workshop the night before."

Forte stepped on to the front porch and stopped. Two broad patrolmen flanked the front door of the mansion. "So, the girl is making out with some pimple-faced geek. What's the deal?"

Jackie shook her head impatiently. "No. The boys have been questioned. New Orleans PD scared the crap out of them. They said the girls left them behind and were talking to some other guys, older college boys, they thought."

She seemed as if she was in motion even while standing still.

Forte noticed the whiteness around her mouth. "You okay?"

"Just a headache. Let's go in."

The patrolmen's expressions remained blank. Jackie began to speak. One of the guards reached for the door. "Miss Shaw, Mr. Forte. The governor is expecting you," he said.

Just inside the door, a young woman with a leather binder was fidgeting in a brocade-covered chair. She sprang to her feet and was about to usher them through the foyer when she stopped and looked at Forte. "What's that smell?"

"What smell?" Forte said. Jackie did not smile.

The woman blinked twice and said, "Please follow me."

Within ten seconds they were in a long narrow hallway leading to double doors. Another guard stood at that door. When he opened it, the noises of busyness spilled out into the quiet of the hall: Phones rang, TV's clamored for attention, and, above all, human voices engaged in a half-dozen conversations.

A massive table divided the conference room. Three groups of uniformed cops dotted the corners of the rooms, most of them gripping coffee cups, as they spoke in low tones to each other. There were three women in the room: Jackie, the secretary with the leather binder, and a tall woman in black pants and jacket. The other dozen people in the room were men in suits. They were making most of the racket. Some were pointing at maps spread at the table. Some were pointing at the two television sets in the room that were both showing the progress of tropical storm Esther out in the Gulf. Some were scribbling on a whiteboard with markers.

All were talking. Until Forte stepped into the room.

Then the noise level ebbed. He shook hands with the group of cops closest to him, most of whom he knew, then nodded at the other policemen in the room, all of whom noticed when he came in. None of the suits noticed his entrance except for the tall woman. She peered at Forte over the top of her reading glasses while listening to the short man beside her – the governor. She was holding an FBI binder open for the man to read. On the cover in gold stamp lettering was the name "Rosalind Dent."

Jackie Shaw stayed with the group of cops closer to the door while the secretary led Forte to where the governor stood with his back to the room. By the time they reached the tall woman and the governor, the only sounds were the weather forecasters on TV.

The atmosphere in the room seemed denser now, as if the storm from the TV screens were circling in the foyer outside and down the hall.

The governor finally noticed the change. He jerked his head to the side but did not turn completely.

The woman with the binder touched his elbow. "Governor," she said, "Al Forte is here."

Governor Raymond Barreaux was 5'8' and weighed 220 pounds, most of it muscle. He was wearing a gray pinstripe suit with a red tie.

He stepped forward until he was inches away from Forte.

"Where the hell have you been?" he said.

"Just enjoying the summer," Forte said.

The governor's nostrils flared. "You smartass sumbitch, we have been looking for you all over south Louisiana. You better wipe that smirky grin off your face before I wipe it off."

"Governor," said the tall woman.

The short man poked Forte in the chest with a thick finger.

The next five seconds happened as follows:

The first second: With his right hand, Forte brushed away the governor's poking finger. With his left hand he back-handed the governor across the face. That only took three-tenths of the second. During the remainder, he flipped his hand back toward the man's face and slapped him with the palm side. Then he back-handed him again.

The next second: Forte calmly placed his right foot behind the heel of the governor's left wingtip shoe. He short-punched the governor's chest. He stepped back.

Forte observed the faces of three people. The squat governor's expression went from outrage to stunned pain as he stumbled backward. Rosalind Dent rolled her eyes and began to shake her head. The FBI agent had yanked the folder out of the way. The secretary's mouth flopped open and her hands flew up, sending papers flying.

The big patrolman who served as the governor's bodyguard began to charge at Forte. An FBI agent nearby pulled his gun. Agent Dent yelled, "Don't shoot" and flung her binder at the other agent. The governor tumbled backward.

The third second: The bodyguard sank to his knees, gasping for breath after being punched in the solar plexus. Forte followed with a spinning perfect roundhouse kick into the second bodyguard, coming at him from behind. The man's head snapped back and two teeth flew up into the air. The teeth hit the shiny conference table and bounced twice. It reminded Forte of dice being thrown at a casino. The bodyguard fell to the carpet and bounced only once.

The fourth second: Forte whirled to spot any attacks from any other part of the room. Nobody was moving. He noticed that Jackie Shaw was on one knee near the door with her Glock drawn but pointed at the floor.

Jackie holstered her gun quickly. The governor began scrambling to his feet.

The fifth second: Forte tensed and went back into a fighting stance as the governor came toward him.

The governor stopped about seven feet from Forte. All of the suits in the room had gone into a half-crouch. Four of the administrative aides were sprawled under the conference table. The cops had thrown down their coffee and had fanned into a semi-circle. Most of them had quickly wiped the smiles off their faces.

The governor snorted at Forte like a bantam bull, his eyes bloodshot. Both of his cheeks were crimson from the slapping he had received.

Forte expected another charge.

It never came.

Instead, Governor Barreaux continued to huff for a moment. His mouth started twitching. Then he burst into laughter.

All the tension flushed out of the room. A few of the suck-ups added their nervous chuckles.

The governor bent over, grabbed his knees and gasped for breath between the deep belly laughs. Finally he straightened and wiped his eyes.

When he spoke, very little of the country Cajun accent was in his Harvard-educated voice. "Mr. Forte, you dumped me on my rude posterior and I don't blame you a bit." He held out his hand. Forte shook it.

"No problem," he said.

To the rest of the room, Governor Barreaux announced, "I apologize for causing such a ruckus. Now, let's clean up this mess and get on with finding my daughter."

As if they had been cued by some off-stage director, two janitors with cleaning supplies and towels rushed into the room. The quickly swabbed the blood from the table and the floor. All the papers were picked up and re-collated. Chairs were set back in place. Then, as swiftly as they had appeared, the cleaning crew was gone.

The governor motioned to the conference room table for everyone to be seated. He began talking as if nothing had happened.

"Thank you all for coming. You can see that several different law enforcement groups are represented here. Our goal is to find my daughter, who has been missing for several hours. Before I let Agent Dent take charge of our meeting, I want to ask for your help in keeping this incident from the media as long as we can. Hopefully, we can find Ashley quickly." As he spoke his daughter's name, his voice broke slightly. He nodded to Rosalind Dent to continue.

The FBI agent stood and made eye contact with everyone in the room. An attractive woman, she had not overdone her make-up or attire. She was all business at the moment and reinforced the seriousness of the briefing by letting a moment of silence pass before she started talking.

"Most of you have reviewed the incident report. You know the details of Ashley Barreaux's disappearance. The FBI will provide oversight for the case." She caught herself. "For the operation of bringing back the governor's daughter safely, Mr. Forte will be assisting us. I'm sure you all know of his reputation in situations such as this."

She continued for another quarter hour as she efficiently broke down the specific assignments for the cops in the room. She fielded a few questions then wrapped up the meeting quickly. Everyone picked up their paperwork and left without the usual small talk that would occur.

As Forte began to walk away from the table, the agent caught his eye and motioned for him to remain behind.

He glanced toward Jackie Shaw who had remained standing by the double doors leading out of the conference room. She came to the table and sat at the end of the long table.

The FBI agent said, "Jackie" then sat in the chair at the head of the table.

"Agent Dent," Jackie said.

"You know you can call me Rosalind," the tall woman said.

Jackie nodded.

Forte sat on the other side of the table from Jackie. "Isn't this cozy?"

Rosalind Dent said, "You had to hit him?"

"I didn't hit him. I slapped him. A few times."

Jackie spoke up, her voice soft, "You knocked him down."

"I pushed him off balance. He needed to cool down."

Rosalind snorted. "His daughter is missing, for God's sake."

Jackie leaned forward. "Couldn't you cut him a break? He was waiting all day for you to get here."

"A break? Damn bully. He's lucky I didn't knock HIS teeth out."

Rosalind said, "Al. What is this? Junior High?"

"Hey, he apologized. He knew he was out of line."

Rosalind barked the words: "He. Is. The. Governor."

Jackie said, "Didn't you think someone might get hurt?"

Forte held up his hands. "Can I ask you both something?"

The two women said "What?" simultaneously.

"This thing you are doing here. This 'gang up on Forte' thing. You really don't think I'm going to put up with it for more than five more seconds, do you? You've both known me for a while."

Neither women spoke. Both kept their focus on his face for a long beat. Forte maintained eye contact with the FBI agent until she looked away. He switched to Jackie. After another moment, she began flipping through the pages of the brief.

Cool air from the overworked air conditioner whistled through the ceiling vent above. Somewhere outside a helicopter lifted off.

"Can we talk about the case now?" Forte said. "First, why are we searching for a teenage girl just a half-day after her disappearance? Usually we delay 24 hours. Kids cut class and hang out with boys all the time. And, second, what am I doing here? Every cop who could have jurisdiction was represented here today. Rosie, why did you feel the need to bring me in?"

"I didn't," said Rosalind. "The governor wanted you."

"That's not much of a vote of confidence for his state cops and you Fibbies. Both fine organizations with a lot of firepower. Even if you are a laced a little too tight."

The FBI agent's eyes narrowed.

Jackie just rolled her eyes.

"Not you, Rosie. You ain't laced too tight."

"Ok, enough of this bullshit," said the agent. "There is more to this case than what all the cops involved know. The governor wants me to share it with you. Confidentially."

"Tell it, then."

The tall woman's focus shifted to Jackie.

"She can be trusted with it," Forte said.

"It's ok," said Jackie. "I need to get back to the office and take care of paperwork." She stood up quickly and offered her hand to the other woman. They shook. To Forte she said, "I'll see you back at The Refuge." Her voice seemed strained. She turned and walked out of the room.

The FBI agent watched her go. "Is she okay?"

Forte nodded. "Far as I know. We had a little job last night. Maybe she's tired."

"A little job, huh? Nothing I should know about, I'm sure."

"Like you don't know about it already, Rosie. But the NOPD mopped it up nicely, I hear."

The agent said nothing. She flicked the binder shut and leaned back in the leather swivel chair. She unbuttoned her suit jacket and stretched. Under the jacket she wore a white silk tee-shirt. She was obviously more feminine than when she had addressed the room full of men a few moments earlier.

Forte ran a hand over his head. "So what is it that you need to tell me that's so private? Because up to this point, this looks a case of a spoiled rich girl costing the taxpayers a lot of money just because she wanted to play smacky-lip with some boy."

Rosalind Dent's fingers drummed softly on the table top as she gazed out the window. "No, she's been abducted."

Forte sat up straighter. "By who?"

"We don't know."

"Then how much money do they want?"

"No money."

"Political favors then."

"No."

"What then?"

Outside another helicopter elevated above the live oak trees that adorned the nicely-manicured lawn of the governor's mansion. It hovered then slowly flew out of sight. The FBI agent turned and looked Forte right in the eye.

"They want you," she said.

Chapter 12

The western sky was clear, the horizon tinged like blood washing into a gutter. Forte caught the crimson glow in the periphery of his right eye. He rode in the passenger seat of the big FBI car as it cut through the wind coming toward New Orleans on Interstate 10.

"So, whoever they are, they call you and say 'We have the girl, and we'll kill her unless you hand over Forte.' That about cover it?" Forte's realized his mood was better than it had been for two days. *You are one messed-up individual, Forte.*

Rosalind Dent recognized his mood change. "Nothing like a death threat to perk you right up." She had taken off her jacket, revealing toned and tanned arms. She held the steering wheel with her right hand, lightly and expertly nudging it one direction or the other as the long car hurtled along the highway. Her left arm was propped on the door ledge. She reached over and dialed down the volume on the Sinatra CD that had been playing.

"That's basically the story," she said. "They didn't stay on the line long enough for a trace. They didn't give any other instructions. They seem to know that you would get involved as soon as you heard." She glanced at him then focused again on the road ahead. "Of course, they probably assumed the message would have been delivered to you about four hours ago."

The only sound coming from the man in the passenger seat was a soft humming to the tune of "Love and Marriage."

The pair glided along the road with the kind of bump-absorbing comfort afforded by boat-like American-made autos. The FBI agent stayed in the left lane and kept the speedometer at 80. Occasionally, she flashed the blue lights hidden in the front grill of the car to shoo slow drivers to the right.

"So," the woman said, "why did you disappear like that today?"

Forte stayed silent and looked out the side window to his right.

"Jackie was really worried about you." Her voice sounded husky now, less official than when she had commanded the room earlier.

The man with the yellow eyes studied the view through the passenger-side window.

The woman's voice was barely audible now. "Still a hard case. Hiding behind that wall, aren't you?"

Forte focused on the road ahead now. When he spoke, his words seemed as if they would shatter against the windshield. "Rosie, I just needed some time."

The tension inside the cabin of the car dissipated immediately.

Frank crooned a few more lines through the car speakers for a few more miles before Rosalind spoke again. "I'm sorry. I know it's hard for you at this time every year."

He wanted to say "you only think you know." Or "you have no idea how hard it is." He wanted to explain what it was like to feel the blood of the person most dear to you, to have the cardinal essence of that love slip through your fingers no matter how hard you pressed against the hole to keep the life inside them. He wanted to describe how clear it became to him that he could never hold it together, this life he thought was his, because a boy with a gun could blow apart the pieces of his existence with the mere twitch of his finger, so that the fragments of his joy would just float away no matter how much he flailed and plucked at them to keep them in his grasp.

He wanted to say all those things. But he said nothing.

The agent had put both hands on the wheel. The muscles on her forearms bunched as she intermittently squeezed the steering wheel hard. A man in a bright yellow Corvette convertible pulled in front of her and slowed. She pressed a button and gave him a burst of siren, sending him scurrying back to the right lane.

They rode for five more minutes without talking. Finally Forte broke the silence.

"Who did they call first, you or the governor?" he asked.

"Me, why?"

"Did the call come straight to you or through the switchboard?"

"He called my cell." She drummed on the steering wheel with her fingers. "Let me cut to the chase on this line of questioning. Yes, he must've known about our past relationship. Yes, he sounded like a pro. Yes, he gave enough information about the girl to let us know that his group actually had taken her."

Forte glanced at the woman. Her face was grim. *There is more to this.* He had known her for a dozen years. She had dealt with difficult cases with calm proficiency. She had exceeded the expectations of the Bureau many times over; how else would she have been put in charge of the New Orleans office of the Federal Bureau of Investigation?

But now, something had shaken her.

"Rosie," he said, "What exactly did the man say to you?"

Her hands had stopped drumming. She clenched the wheel now. "He said..." She bit her bottom lip and let air hiss through her teeth. "He said that if I didn't get to you about this, he would start killing my family." Her face was ashen. "He named them and started telling personal details about their routines, their clothes sizes, the cars they drive."

Forte felt the sorrow and self-pity he had been enjoying the past few days drain out of him now. He knew why. It was the challenge of doing something that few others could do. *We can't rebuild our broken past, but we can use it to make bricks for our future.* It was a favorite saying of his friend and sponsor Manny Laird.

To the woman driving he said, "I am here for you."

She glanced at him, her eyes shiny. "I'm sorry, Al."

He grinned. "For what? This little problem?" He snorted. "Piece of cake."

She blinked and faced forward again.

"Look, Rosie," he said, "you've handled some tough cases before. And you've done as well as anyone would expect. Better, even, most times. This time, it's personal. But you've got to handle it like it isn't personal. You have to do the impossible: You have to make your decisions based on the facts, not on emotions."

He reached over and squeezed her arm once, then released it.

She swallowed and cleared her throat. "Thanks."

In the rear-view mirror on his side, Forte could see the Baton Rouge policeman who had been selected to drive the Fat Daddy back. The cop was grinning.

When he looked back at Agent Dent, her face was composed.

Her cell phone chirped. They both tensed.

"Agent Dent here," she said into the phone. Her face relaxed, but not pleasantly. "Yes, busy." A pause. "No, not today." Another beat. "We'll see." She hung up.

"So, still going out with that doctor?" he asked.

"Off and on," she said. "Hard to coordinate the hours."

"Dumped him, huh?"

She allowed a tiny smile. "Yeah. He just hasn't let it sink in yet."

"Well, doctors are trained to be diligent."

"So are FBI agents." She glanced at him then back at the road. "He has no idea about diligence."

"So, what is your problem with him? I mean, apart from the fact that he could never measure up to my handsomeness?"

She snorted louder. "You aren't that handsome, sweetcheeks, but the thing is – you couldn't give a rat's ass whether anyone thinks you are nice-looking or not. He does. He's a pretty boy and knows it. He makes sure of it – his looks, the clothes, being cool. He's a nice guy. Gives money to help poor kids. But you get the feeling he does it because someone said it would reflect well on him if he did. Not because he really cares about them. Ugh."

"Okay, first, just because I don't CARE if I'm a hunk doesn't mean I'm not. And, second, if you really dumped Doctor Cutie, why did you 'We'll see' to him when he asked about going out with you? You could've shut him down completely."

She reached forward and ejected the Sinatra CD. The all-news radio station was blaring away with news of the tropical storm. It had been upgraded to a hurricane. Even though it still had to travel another 20 hours before landfall, the storm had pushed dark clouds over the coastal states. The low canopy had crawled almost all the way over the area. Only a thin strip of blue remained on the northwest horizon.

She clicked off the radio. "Don't think I don't know what you are doing here," she said.

"No idea what you are talking about," he said, his face pointed again away from her.

"That yakkity yakking about my love life. Since when did you become King of Small Talk?"

"Just trying to be friendly. No idea what you mean."

"And if you did make small talk, it sure as hell wouldn't be about my boyfriend's fashion habits."

"None. No idea."

She took her right hand, made a fist and punched him lightly on the arm.

"You are a sweetie, trying to take my mind off the threats of the kidnapper." She patted him. Her voice was softer. "Thanks, Al."

"Absolutely no idea what you are talking about," he said.

Chapter 13

The house was old but well-kept. The others on the street, not so much. Forte sat on the Fat Daddy under the Magnolia tree in the tiny front yard. Smoke arose from the one and only Checkers cigarette he allowed himself each day. The hot wind of the impending storm snatched the tendrils of smoke away before they had a chance to drift into the dark sky.

He had never smoked before he went into treatment. Even if his coaches would have overlooked the habit, the rigors of chasing down running backs would have quickly canceled out the smoking habit. Not to mention the five-mile runs in basic training or, worse, the inhuman requirements of Hell Week to qualify as a Navy SEAL.

In treatment, however, cigarettes were the least of the evils the people in the program had endured. "They might kill you," one ex-nurse said, "but you won't overdose on them today." Forte had bummed a smoke from her, one of the vilest, cheapest brands – Checkers. True to his nature, he had stuck with the brand through the program and beyond. In the years since he'd gotten clean, he had steadily decreased the number of cigarettes he allowed himself – down to a pack a day, then 15 a day, then 10, five, four, three, two – until he just carried a single cigarette with him.

The man inside the house had hated the fact Forte smoked. But he had never chided him about it. He had never really chided him about anything, from the day that 13-year-old Al had come to live with him. In his quiet way, Larue Hebert had merely loved him, without being demonstrative about it. He had just been there for him, at every football game, at his graduations from high school, the Navy SEAL initiation ceremony. Being there was what he did best.

And now he was inside the house, dying.

Forte blew out the final drag of the Checkers and let the wind whip it into nothingness. He bent and ground out the embers of the cigarette butt, putting it into his pocket. He walked along the stone path, up to the big covered porch and through the front door.

Once inside the dark wood foyer of the old home, he half-expected the sadness to settle over him. It didn't come. He had known about Larue's diagnosis for the past year. The final days were mere extensions of a life lived well and long. He just wanted the suffering to stop soon.

He walked back to the bedroom through a long hallway. A nurse was bent over the small figure in the bed. She straightened up at the sound of Forte's footsteps. She smiled kindly, stepped over to the stereo on a nearby table, lowered the volume, dimmed the lights, then left the room.

Never a large man, Larue was a shriveled shell of his former self. His eyes were closed, his hands folded neatly over his stomach. An intravenous line ran from his arm to a bag on a pole next to the bed.

Forte stood next to the bed as he tried to determine if he were asleep.

Without opening his eyes, the old man said, "Still smoking them nassy cigarettes, you?"

Forte sat on the edge of the bed. "I figured you were playing possum, Rue."

The man in the bed opened his eyes. "What you up to, cher? I just seen you yesterday."

"I can't come see you two days straight? I had to make sure you weren't chasing Nurse Goodbody around the bed."

Larue released a soft laugh that became a fit of coughing.

Forte picked up the cup of water, held the straw to the old man's mouth. He sipped then lowered his head to the pillow again.

For a full minute, there was no sound in the room except for the strains of a big band song from the stereo. Larue's chest barely expanded as he breathed. Except for the hospital bed, the room looked as it always had. Framed photos covered the walls. There were some family photos of Larue and his wife, long deceased, and some other old yellowed prints showing people in overalls and faded flour-sack dresses on the front porches of cabins perched on stilts above the swamp. There were photos of Larue as a young man in his then-new barber shop on St. Charles, some of his favorite customers, and another of 13-year-old Al Forte with a broom sweeping up hair from the linoleum floor. There were pictures of a young Forte holding a fish in the canoe with Larue and one of him with a rifle in camouflage clothing. Then, the series of photos of him in football uniforms, all the way back when he started playing as a grade school boy before his grandmother passed away. Then there were photos of his grandmother beaming as he held up a trophy, his helmet cocked back on his head, and of his high school days as an all-state linebacker knocking the helmet off an unsuspecting opposing running back. Then there were the Navy photos of Forte in uniform, standing next to a younger Larue with the thinnest of close-mouthed smiles on his face.

Then there were the photos of Forte and Ruth. Their wedding. Laughing together at a cookout. Dancing together at Larue's birthday party.

"That was some purty gal. Inside and out."

The old man's voice startled him.

"Yes," Forte said. "Yes, she was."

The music switched to a more mellow song from the 1940s. A clarinet solo slid across the airwaves, its plaintive cries stoked with more emotion than mere words could have evoked.

"That song, she brought my sweet wife to me. We must've danced to it seven or six times straight. I paid the band extra." Larue was smiling. His eyes sparkled more than they had in months. The three sentences he had uttered could be considered a major speech.

"She gone now, and so is Ruth," Larue said.

Forte realized his adopted father was focusing on him intently now.

"And there ain't nothing we can do about that. 'Cept hear the songs and dance with them in our hearts." Larue cleared his throat. "Better that than to miss the dance at all, eh cher?"

He reached over and put his hand on top of Forte's.

"When I'm gone, just 'member the good times. I'll be in the better place, my boy."

Forte squeezed the man's hand. "You need to rest now, Pappa Rue."

"I'm fine. Tell me about what's going on with you."

Forte told of the rescue of the girl at the biker bar the night before, then about the video interview earlier in the afternoon.

Larue listened, nodding slightly without raising his head from the pillow.

When Forte told of the alligator and the highway cop, the old man erupted into laughter again, followed by another spasm of coughing.

"Hoo boy," he gasped when he had settled down again.

Forte held the water cup to his mouth again.

"That gator thought he had some ready-made dinner, him."

"It kinda put things in perspective real quick," Forte said.

The old man nodded again and closed his eyes. "Guess I need to get me some sleep now." He lifted his hand and let it fall to the sheets. "T'anks for dropping by, Al."

Forte stood at the foot of the bed for a while as the man in the bed seemed to drift off. Just as he turned to leave, he heard the old man's voice again.

"Whatever the other t'ing is that's on your mind, I'm sure you'll work it out."

"Other thing?"

Larue smiled, his eyes still closed. "Don't know what it is, but I know it's something."

Forte shook his head slowly. He walked back to the head of the bed, bent down and kissed the man on the forehead. "Good night, Rue."

He walked straight out to the front porch. From the shadows of some porch not far away came the bouncy chords of a zydeco song. Forte leaned against the brick column to the left of the stairway leading down to the stone sidewalk. He reached into his pocket and pulled out the cigarette stub. A quarter inch remained above the filter. He pulled out a lighter, lit it, and took a long pull as he listened to the music.

The call had not come yet from the kidnappers of the governor's daughter. Until it came, there was no way to know what they were dealing with. Other than they wanted Forte.

He drained the last of the burning tobacco. He bent and extinguished the fire. As he straightened, he saw the shape of a person standing under the tree behind his motorcycle.

He dropped and rolled behind the low brick border on the porch. Somehow, his nine-millimeter Glock had appeared in his hand, the result of hundreds of hours of training.

Down the street, the zydeco music had stopped.

He raised himself enough to see that the figure was still there.

He crawled down to the far end of the porch. He peeked again. The man was still there, unmoving, as if he were a cardboard standup.

Forte's phone rang.

He stood up and pointed his gun at the man under the tree.

"What do you want?" he shouted.

The phone rang again.

The man flinched but stayed where he was. He raised his arms slowly.

"Stay right there. Don't move," Forte said. He moved down the steps of the porch.

The phone rang again.

He answered it, gun still leveled at the man in shadows.

"They called," Rosalind Dent said.

"Tell me," Forte said.

"They wanted to make sure we had located you, that you knew."

"And?"

"Tomorrow afternoon. They will call at 2 to give us the place."

"Okay. Thanks." He hung up.

He stepped closer to his motorcycle. The man hadn't moved from his stance with arms raised. Was he shaking? He didn't seem menacing.

"Come out into the light where I can see you," Forte commanded.

The man slowly stepped out.

He was young and slim in an athletic way, like a basketball player or long distance runner. His hair was closely cropped and his features handsome and intelligent on a caramel colored face. His clothes were well cut but in disarray, as if he'd been in a scuffle, with street grime on the knees.

The most arresting feature was his eyes. They were brown and filled with the kind of despair that few know. Forte had seen it many times on the faces of parents whose children were missing.

He began to lower his gun. Then something began to buzz deep inside him.

No. He took a step backward.

"What are you doing... why are you here?" Forte mumbled.

The man looked more scared than he had that night in the alley seven years earlier. Forte rubbed his fingers together on his left hand. *The blood.* He could feel its slickness on his fingertips. His wife's blood.

"I'm sorry," said Martin Bailey. "You know I never meant to do that."

The look on his face was so crestfallen that Forte felt his shock draining from him. He opened his mouth to ask a question but immediately forgot what he was going to say.

"I don't know what to do," Martin said.

Forte sat on the Fat Daddy and stared at the man who had shot his wife.

"I need... I had to see you," the man said. His voice cracked. A tear trickled down his cheek.

"It's my son, my boy...Freddy." Martin Bailey gulped air then blew it out forcefully.

"They took my son," he said.

Forte blinked. "And...you want me to get him back for you?" He knew his face looked incredulous.

"No," said Martin.

Forte rubbed his eyes. "Martin, what do you want?"

The man slumped to the ground.

"They want you. They will kill Freddy if you don't turn yourself over to them."

Chapter 14

"So," said Nomad, "you knocked Governor Shorty on his ass, huh?" He chuckled.

Rosalind rolled her eyes. Jackie Shaw shook her head. Martin Bailey was slumped in the oversized leather chair in the corner of the den on the third floor of The Refuge. He looked shell-shocked.

"Just kinda happened," said Forte.

"Can we deal with the issues here?" said Rosalind. "It's almost midnight." She looked around the room. "I'll go first.'

She ran through the details of Ashley Barreaux's disappearance. Everyone listened. Martin gasped softly when she got to the part about Forte being traded for the girl.

"Now, for the kidnapping of Freddy Bailey." She looked at Martin. He opened his mouth but no words came out.

She proceeded to tell the story. "Dad and son out for the evening. Boy gets grabbed by unknown men. Dad gets a call later with the message to bring Forte to a meeting tomorrow and the boy will be set free. No time set yet. No indication of who the kidnappers are. No other details."

She glanced at Forte. His face was impassive.

The agent was standing with her back to the bank of windows that overlooked the street outside. Rain from the approaching hurricane was beginning to fall. The windows were fortified with double layers of bulletproof glass. Very little noise seeped in from the street which lay on the edge of the French Quarter. She gazed out the window for a beat. With her back to the room, she resumed talking.

"Two kidnappings. Both high-profile, for different reasons. Both of them connected to Al Forte." She faced the room again. The strain on her face was evident, but her voice remained calm. "What is going on here?"

At that moment, a college-aged boy walked into the room. Under his arm was a laptop computer. "Just got an email from the 'A Group'." He saw the puzzled looks on the others' faces. "The kidnappers who grabbed Ashley. I call them that."

Agent Dent addressed Martin. "This is Fizer Beal. He handles computer work here at Forte Security."

"Dude, sorry about your son," Fizer said.

Martin sank deeper into the chair.

"Anyway, they sent a photo," Fizer said. He pushed some board games out of the way on the big wooden table and set his laptop down. The others gathered around.

On the screen was a photo of a teen girl tied to a chair with a scarf tied over her mouth.

Martin moaned slightly. "Oh no."

Jackie patted his back. "She doesn't seem to be hurt."

Nomad bent closer to the computer. "She isn't tied very tightly. There is a lot of slack in that rope." He stood up. "And who the hell uses rope anymore anyway? Duct tape works better." He looked at the others. "So I've heard, anyway."

Rosalind leaned closer to the computer screen. "She almost looks like she is smiling. Forward that email to my office," said Dent. She gave Fizer the email address.

Fizer clicked and tapped and said, "Done." He got up from the table and closed the laptop. "I'll be down the hall if you need me." He left the room.

Rosalind stepped over to a whiteboard mounted on the wall opposite the windows. With a marker, she divided the board with a vertical line. At the top on one side she wrote "Ashley" and on the other side, "Freddy." She began to scribble everything about the cases that was known.

Martin Bailey had made a teepee of his hands and pressed the fingertips against his lips. He tapped them nervously on his mouth as the agent wrote on the board.

Nomad toyed with a 3-D wood block puzzle on the table. He sat on a rolling desk chair with his legs splayed out in front of him

Jackie Shaw stood behind the chair where Martin sat, her hand resting on the young man's shoulder. She focused on each letter scribbled on the whiteboard as if she were trying to telepathically yank the stories of the kidnappings from those squiggles.

Forte stood with his back to the board, his hands braced against the window frame as he looked out at the darkness. Outside the rain increased as the wind buffeted the building.

"The storm's getting closer," he said.

Rosalind's marker remained poised above her head. Then she resumed her scribbling.

"They think it's going to go west of us," said Nomad.

"It'll throw some wind at us," Forte said.

Katrina had changed the way the people of New Orleans thought about the storms that rolled in off the gulf every summer. Previously, everyone pretty much acted as if they believed the city was protected by a magic spell cast centuries earlier by some Cajun storm god. They had partied in the face of news that a storm was brewing, confident in their alcohol-induced bravery that they would come through it safe and somewhat sound, if not hung-over. Relatively few precautions had been taken.

Now, they might party but only after making sure the levee was fortified and the windows taped and boarded. The entire area had yet to recover physically from the flooding that Katrina had caused when she pushed the river over its banks. Tens of thousands of people had fled the area, never to return. Many were confident that the town would never recover from the psychic wounds of seeing neighbors looting each other in an ugly display of greed and false entitlement.

Outside, the wind pounded against the bulletproof panes.

Forte studied the two columns on the whiteboard where Agent Dent's neat penmanship told two stories of pain and fear in perfunctory style.

Ashley	Freddy
Age 14 – daughter of Gov B	Age 7 – son of M. Bailey
Taken Sat. 10:30 a.m.	Taken Sat. 1 p.m.
Where – River Walk	Where – Quarter
Phoned FBI	Phoned boy's dad
Unidentified perp	Unidentified perp
Kidnappers demand – Forte	Kidnappers demand – Forte

"Anything else we can add here?" said Rosalind.

Everyone studied the board far longer than required to read the few words there. Martin was the first to look away.

The agent took a deep breath and let it out slowly. The sound of her exhaling mixed with the noise of the wind beating against the stucco façade of the building.

"Okay, let me overstate the weirdness of these crimes," she said. She looked at Martin Bailey pointedly, then at the others.

"First, there seems to be only one connection between the two. Different ages, different sexes, different schools, different socio-economics." Again, she glanced at Martin, whose head was bowed now.

"In fact, given the realities of political pressure, the taking of Freddy would not ordinarily be given the same priority as the

Ashley case." She let the sad truth of that statement settle. "Yet, here they are, these two cases tied together by one Al Forte."

The only sound to accompany the wind now was the clicking of the wooden pieces in the puzzle on the table. Nomad was intently studying the formation of the 3-D puzzle while tapping one of the pieces on the table top.

"And the other big connection," Rosalind continued, "is Martin Bailey's accidental shooting of Ruth Forte seven years ago."

A small moan came from Martin. His head was held in his hands now.

"I think I'll go get a soft drink," said Nomad. He walked out.

For almost a full minute, the room was silent except for the sound of the wind outside. Forte had once again braced himself against the window as he faced the darkness. He felt the attention of the women in the room on the back of his head.

Martin Bailey broke the silence.

"Look, I will just go. I'll go to the police. The guy on the phone said not to, but I'll do it." His voice was high-pitched and fragile now. "It's all I got." He got up to leave and spoke directly to Forte's back.

"You think I'm saying this now just because of Freddy, but I'm not: I'm sorry for what happened to your wife. I was a dumb kid doing a dumbass thing but I never meant to see anyone hurt. Much less killed."

He walked out of the room.

Jackie Shaw followed him.

Forte did not turn around.

Rosalind left the room.

Chapter 15

From her position behind the swing set, Ruth waves at her husband on the other side of the playground. The little boy she is pushing in the swing is laughing loudly and pleading with her to go higher, higher, higher.

Forte smiles at the sight, so perfect for a spring afternoon in this crazy city he loves. I'll remember this forever, he thinks to himself.

He leans against the big pecan tree on the edge of the playground. The sunshine has lulled him into the kind of cozy, relaxed state he seldom allowed for himself. Just a few more minutes and then it's my turn to swing the boy.

He doesn't notice the shadow at first. Though relaxed, he has been scanning the horizon in every direction since they came to the park, a habit he had developed after years of battle-trained wariness. No dark clouds have been encroaching on the joy of this day.

Then he looks directly above his position under the tree.

Through the branches he sees it. A swirling mass of gray violence dropping straight down over the park.

He begins to dart out from under the branches as the helicopter drops like a ravenous bird of prey. He is yanked back by a black chain that tethers him to the trunk.

What the... He pulls again and sees the blood running down his hand and dripping off his fingertips.

He screams at his wife and the boy. No one seems to hear him.

The metal claws drop from the belly of the chopper like a vicious arcade game. They are coming straight for the woman and child, who are still smiling and swinging and laughing.

How could he not hear it coming? He had been inside and around helicopters for years. And how could his wife and child not hear him screaming, even with the noise of the chopper blades? How could he fail to protect them after all his training and successful missions? He yanks against the chain again hard. The blood trickles from his fingers in a steady drip now.

Ruth! He screams her name so loudly now that he feels something tearing in his throat. He puts his free hand to his mouth and feels the blood, slick on his lips. He continues to scream her name.

The sunshine has vanished. The wind from the chopper blades kicks up dust, plucks leaves from the trees. Forte is pelted with pecans being hurled at him by the tree itself, it seems.

Then he sees something. A man is running from the other side of the park. He is coming directly for the playground.

The claws are so close to the woman and child now. They are blissfully unaware, despite the noise.

Forte sees the man coming toward them. He can do nothing to stop the attacker on the ground either. He yanks again. The blood is flowing now, spilling from his hand onto the ground.

But the man is not attacking. He is trying to help.

He reaches the playground's edge just as the claw envelopes both mother and child. It begins to retract upward toward the gaping maw of the hovering dragon above.

The man flings himself against the huge claw. It struggles with his weight, but continues to pull the woman and child upward. They are still laughing and singing, unaware of the terror. The man tries to hold on to the claw but his grip slides off the slick metal. He tumbles back to the ground. He springs up and leaps again.

But the claw is too high now.

Forte sees everything but is unable to scream more pain through his tortured throat. He slumps next to the tree, defeated. Above him, the door clangs shut on the helicopter. It begins to ascend again.

Another scream rings out.

Forte raises his head. The man, the would-be hero who failed in his rescue attempt, is on his knees with his arms raised as he howls at the departing metal monster. His face is twisted in horror.

Forte blinks away his tears and realizes something: He and Ruth never had a child. The boy wasn't his.

The boy was the son of the man screaming on his knees.

The man's face is dirty and streaked, a mask of sorrow.

Forte recognizes him. He is Martin Bailey.

The chopper lifts straight up but the velocity of the wind increases. The tree above Forte is shaking. The limbs are cracking and flying through the air. Everything seems as if it will be torn from the earth by the effect of the blades whirling away.

The tree begins to fall.

But not on Forte.

It falls straight on Martin in the center of the playground. The tree seems bigger now and is falling like a hammer on the man. Forte realizes he is free of the tree.

For a hundredth of a second, everything freezes. Except for Forte. He bolts toward the man and dives at him. Both of them tumble out of the way of the killer trunk. It whumps to the ground with such force that the two men feel the tremor.

Yet, the wind keeps blowing harder and harder, tearing at them, lifting them off the ground. They try to cling to the earth but can't. It howls against them, unrelenting.

"Al! It's okay," Martin Bailey yells at him above the noise. "It's okay, Al." The man is smiling.

But it's not his voice. It is the voice of Jackie Shaw.

Forte opened his eyes and rolled over in bed.

Jackie sat in the big leather chair in his bedroom. A black cat was curled up on her lap. Outside, the wind pushed against the walls of his apartment which occupied the eastern side of the block-sized building that was The Refuge. A gray light filtered through the windows. It was morning.

He propped himself on one arm and looked out through the double doors of his bedroom into the den.

Martin Bailey was asleep on the sofa.

Forte sat up and rubbed his eyes.

"I went and brought him back," Jackie said.

Forte rolled his head in every direction, stretching. "It isn't about him."

"I know," she said. "It's about the boy."

"Yes. The boy."

The rain sheeted against the windows. There was no rattling of the panes because they were installed the same as those in The Refuge: double paned and bulletproof. But the wind outside was loud enough to penetrate the secured apartment.

"What's the storm up to?" he asked.

"It's still out in the Gulf. This is just the front edge."

The bedroom was shadowed and would have felt cozy on another day. Jackie was back lit by the meager light coming in from the den. The cat stood and stretched, then sauntered out to the kitchen area of the open space that included everything in the narrow apartment except for his bedroom.

Forte stretched, still sitting with his back against the headboard of the bed. "How long you been here?"

"Not long. Half hour. Came to check on him. He's a basket case, you know."

"Yeah."

"You were yelling out."

Forte pressed the heels of his hands on his forehead. "Yeah, bad dream."

She did not ask to hear about it.

He told her anyway. She sat with her feet folded under her, looking small against the ample chair back. Boo appeared as if by magic and nuzzled Jackie. Her hand ran over the black back of the cat as she listened. Apart from that movement, she did not budge. Her face was shadowed.

"And that was it?" she said. "You saved him even though neither of you could save your wife and his child?"

"That was it."

She gently lowered the cat to the floor and came to Forte. She sat on the edge of the bed and leaned over him and kissed his cheek. "You are a good man to have been so damaged."

He took her hand and placed the palm over his eyes. "I'm not good."

"No, not in yourself, you aren't."

"I just do what comes next, day after day, minute after minute."

"Yes, and people live because of that."

"And some die."

"Yes, some. But more live."

He ran her palm down his nose to his lips and kissed it. His eyes were focused on hers.

She looked at him as if she were studying a phenomenon previously not in her experience. The corners of her mouth upturned slightly. Then she pulled her hand slowly from his face.

"Admit it," she said. "Many more children live."

Forte shrugged.

"In the dream, you didn't realize the boy wasn't yours, at first? You thought of him as your son?"

"Yes."

"You wanted that, to have a son." It was not a question.

Forte looked away from her now, as if the shearing rain outside would wash his memories away. "Yes, we had talked about it. But, that day...."

"The day she was killed?"

Few people could have been so direct with him.

"Yes, that day. We had just found out."

She looked puzzled, then her hand, the one he had kissed, covered her mouth. "Oh, Al."

That day rushed back to him now. The words coming out of the doctor's mouth "You are having a baby" then other words that were lost in the joyful noise of hope found. The hours afterward were a fog of giddiness for both would-be parents as they spoke of pink or blue and nursery wallpaper. They decided to keep it to themselves for a day and enjoy it just between the two of them.

But, within 24 hours, Ruth was gone. Along with their unborn baby.

It hadn't taken long to track down the boy who pulled the trigger. Kids that age are like sieves with information like that. The word had spread and within 12 hours the other boys had scattered to the homes of friends or relatives throughout south Louisiana and Mississippi.

Within 24, Forte was on his way across the bridge to the west bank. It was 1:30 a.m. None of his training in stealth and covert tactics came into play. He skidded the van into the front yard of a clapboard house, crushing a tricycle on the way. He grabbed a shotgun and a sledgehammer from the back of the van and strode through the yard. He tapped a snarling dog across its snout and sent it howling. Blew the cheap doorknob loose, then smashed the door off its hinges. Flicked on lights as he went through the house, firing the shotgun into the cheap ceiling twice more as he walked. Grabbed everyone in the two tiny bedrooms and made them lay on the floor – a haggard woman and two small children. And Martin Bailey.

Dropped the shotgun and put his pistol to the boy's head. Seeing the pain and fear scramble the boy's features. Hearing him scream "No please no" and the others shrieking and his own voice wailing *You killed them you killed them you killed* until his finger constricted on the trigger. His vengeance would be fulfilled in a burst of red.

But it did not come.

He dropped the boy that night into a pile of misery and went out to find another way to blot his own grief.

And now the boy was a man. A man sleeping on his own sofa. A man with a boy of his own who was in danger.

"You will help him, then?" Jackie's voice was barely a question.

Forte listened to the wind howl outside. The fury of the impending storm seemed less threatening than it had a few moments earlier. He remembered Larue standing on his front porch on a dark day years ago with a cup of muscular chicory coffee in his hand. "That storm, she ain't the worse thing to cross you, cher. Look out for the hurricane people in your life."

Forte had never had imagined he would find the storm inside himself.

"Yes," he said, "I'll help the boy."

The man on the sofa began to stir.

Forte studied him for a moment.

"I'll do the best I can."

Chapter 16

As he ran, he let his mind roam over the details, scant as they were, of the two kidnappings. They were totally unconnected but it was improbable that two cases would land so close to Forte with the same demand: Forte in exchange for a kidnapped child.

The storm had swept west of the city during the night. Plenty of rain had been dumped on south Louisiana, but the water had drained just fine. The sun had already burned away much of the wetness from the streets. More minor storms were on their way, the weather guy had said, but for now the city was safe. At least from hurricanes.

Forte's morning run took him north and east away from the Quarter, through neighborhoods that would have been considered dangerous for mere citizens, as Nomad called people who had no special forces training. Even in the bright heat of the New Orleans morning, the area seemed to seethe with leftover anger that had somehow failed to be released in the dangerous night. He passed a car up on jacks, a burned-out school bus half-slumped over the cracked sidewalk in someone's front yard, two houses side by side with police tape across the doorways, and a shriveled brown hooker twitching her way back toward the edge of the Quarter to get a head start on her more comely competition. "Run back this way, white boy," she called after him. "You know mama got what you need!"

He kept going, having settled into that familiar lope that he could still maintain for miles if need be. It was mainly to keep his heart rate up and achieve the cardiovascular effect he desired, but it was comforting to him to know his stamina was intact. His breathing wasn't labored, and a feeling of accomplishment was released into his brain.

It was the time when he felt most in control of his out-of-control life. Most people who observed him felt he was confident and assured about whatever challenge was thrown his way. Little did they know how much he relied on instinct and past training. The realization, years ago, that he was unable to smash every barrier in his path had been nearly as severe an emotional blow as the loss of his wife. He and his SEAL buddies had joked about the wimps and losers who were unable to hold their liquor or, worse, resorted to drugs to make up for the weakness.

And then, he had dropped into the abyss.

Forte felt his skin cooling with the sheen of sweat as he ran through the narrow streets, dodging around potholes and the occasional pile of smashed beer bottles.

It took him a half block to realize something was wrong.

There were no people outside.

This was a neighborhood where people escaped from their apartments and sat outside on their porches and front stoops. Where kids ran up and down the sidewalks or played homemade games with sticks and cans out in the street. This morning, everyone seemed to be behind closed doors.

A head ducked out of sight behind the bent window blinds of a house.

Within two seconds of his realization, he heard the motorcycles behind him. He looked over his shoulder and saw them: two bikers about a hundred yards back.

Immediately he darted to his right, crossed the street. A warped wooden fence spanned the side yard of the house. He grabbed the top and prayed it would hold his weight. He vaulted the fence, hit the ground rolling, and came up running . A snarling pit bull lunged at him but was yanked back by a chain. He hurdled a rusted bicycle, kept running along the narrow side yard of the house.

A strangely pleasant chill ran over him. At least here was some action he could face.

The two bikers roared past the house. Forte assumed they were looking for the next alley connecting to a parallel street.

He heard one of the cycles double back. He kept going, through the back yard. He looked back in time to see a biker crash through the wooden fence. The biker skidded in the grass. He caromed against the side of the house and nearly fell into the path of the dog. He righted himself and came straight toward Forte. The biker's left hand was bringing up a sawed-off shotgun.

Forte leaped over the back fence and rolled right. Immediately the shotgun blasted a hole the size of his head in the fence. Forte yanked his Glock from his back holster.

The biker crashed through a second wooden fence, tumbled off the bike, still holding the shotgun.

As he came up to a kneeling position, Forte shot him twice, once in the shoulder and once in the leg. The man screamed and dropped his gun.

A little girl cracked open the back door of the nearest house and peeked out.

"Get inside!" Forte yelled. The door slammed.

He scrambled back toward the fence, vaulted it and went back toward the original street where he had been jogging.

As he ran, he pulled out his cell and hit a single speed dial button.

He scrambled back out to the street and sprinted back toward the Quarter.

In the distance, he heard two sounds: police sirens and more bikers.

The bikers were closer.

He crossed the street. He was 50 yards away from the next intersection of streets.

He sprinted toward the closest house.

The fence around the house was eight feet high and topped with razor wire: A typical drug dealer hangout.

He headed straight for the front door and lowered his shoulder while praying the deadbolt was unlatched. He smashed the door open and tumbled into a darkened den.

He came up running straight through to the back of the narrow house.

A thin woman stood rubbing her eyes in the doorway of a bedroom, naked except for a pair of boxer shorts.

"Get down," he said as he passed. A shotgun blast came through the front window of the house. She hit the floor.

Forte yanked at the back door, snapped the security chain. He could hear the bikers skidding into the front yard

He jerked the door hard. The chain broke. He went in low.

A shotgun blast shattered the door frame at head level. At the same time came the crunch of a vehicle crashing through the fenced yard.

Forte flung himself out into the back yard and came up firing.

A tall biker went down on his left. Forte spun to his left and put two shots into the wood corner there. Splinters flew as another biker went down, grabbing at his shoulder.

Sirens filled the neighborhood now. The sounds of gunfire came from the front of the house and from down the street. There was the bark of automatic fire mixed with the boom of shotguns. After a moment came the chattering of a machine gun on full auto. The SWAT team of NOPD had arrived.

Within fifteen seconds, all gunfire stopped.

The crackle of police radios answered each other back and forth.

Forte leaped up and ran into the house to check on the woman there. She was still lying on her stomach. She whimpered softly when he came into the room.

In the semi-darkness, he knelt next to her. "Are you hurt?"

She raised her head, her eyes wide with fear. She slowly shook her head.

Forte ran out of the house into the back yard again. He sprinted over to the corner of the house. A battered gray truck had smashed down the fence there. He could see the legs of the first biker he had shot. The man was kicking against the dirt and cursing. The man's shotgun lay about four feet from him. Forte could not make out his face yet.

He stepped around the corner. The biker saw him and tried to roll toward the shotgun.

"Don't," Forte said.

The biker stopped.

He was one of the men from the biker bar two nights earlier. He was clenching his teeth. Blood had soaked his left leg from the thigh down.

Forte knelt next to him. He jerked the sweaty bandana off the man's head. "This is going to hurt," he said. Quickly he wrapped it around the man's thigh above the bullet wound and twisted it tight. The biker's screaming intensified. Then he slumped over, unconscious.

Forte sighed. "Tough guy, huh," he said aloud. He slapped the man twice to wake him up.

The biker came to, moaning.

Forte bent lower. He put his face close to the other man's. "Is this about the other kidnappings?"

The man's face was locked in a grimace of pain and hatred. Through clenched teeth, he said, "What the hell are you talking about?"

Forte slapped him again. "What is this about? Why'd you come after me?"

The man's eyes rolled up in his head. Forte shook him. He came to again.

"It's about you busting up our bar the other night, dumbass." he said, his voice weaker now.

"How'd you find me?"

"Some guy called, said you were jogging out here."

Forte stood up. A cop was peering over the bushes, his gun drawn.

Forte motioned to him. "Need an EMT over here."

The cop scanned the man and his bleeding leg. He called in the request on his radio.

The cop knelt next to the bleeding biker, checked his makeshift tourniquet. Without looking up at Forte, he said, "They seemed a might peeved. Shot up half the neighborhood."

Forte chuckled. "Peeved? Did the Chief crack down on language again?"

"Nah. Wife's taking a college course. It's one of her vocabulary words." He shrugged.

Around in the front of the house, an unmarked car screeched to a stop. Rosalind Dent leapt out of the passenger side and quickly began searching the area. She saw Forte and came toward him. Before she could take two steps, a motorcycle rumbled into the front yard. Three cops drew their weapons before they recognized the biker was Nomad. He wore his combat face: fierce and focused.

When he saw Forte was unharmed, he looked sheepish, then annoyed. "There I was, trying to get some extra beauty sleep, and you gotta go shooting up some pesky biker punks."

"Awww, you know you're cute when you get all protective," said Forte.

Nomad scratched his eye with his middle finger. "I'm just damn handsome, period, son."

Rosalind trained her sunglasses on both of the men. "If you two cavemen are done, maybe we can debrief a little." She nodded toward the side of the house and walked over to the bushes. In the front yard, the bikers were being loaded into cop cars and ambulances.

"So," she said, "tell me about it."

Forte told her exactly how the shootout had unfolded. The FBI agent listened, her arms folded over her chest, eyes still shaded. When he had finished, she said, "And you believed the guy, about it just being payback for the bar incident?"

"Yeah."

She took off her sunglasses. Her eyes looked like she had been up all night worrying. "We are going to set aside the fact that no law enforcement agencies were notified about the little operation you did at the biker bar. We have bigger fish to fry here." She looked back and forth at the two men. "It is just too strange to have this happen this morning in the middle of the two kidnappings."

Forte shrugged. "They were pissed about us messing up their bar. The drug dealer was peeved about losing his ransom money. He thought he could dabble in the kidnapping arena and pick up a little jack to shore up his drug income stream. He didn't appreciate our interference."

Nomad looked at him. "Peeved?"

"Yeah. I'm trying to polish my conversation skills."

Rosalind ignored the banter. "And you are convinced it had nothing to do with the other cases?"

Forte said, "Don't think so. But what does it matter? We don't even know who either of the kidnappers are yet. Let the NOPD cops question the bikers a little more. Maybe they can find some connection. But I doubt it."

The woman agent kept her eyes locked on his for a long beat, then looked away.

People were peeking out from their houses now that the gunfire had ceased. On the back porch of the house next door, a boy took note of the proceedings while casually eating a biscuit. *Sadly, he probably has seen it all before.*

Rosalind spoke again. "The Bureau has uncovered a couple things." Both men stepped closer to her. "The photo analysts think there's a good chance the girl, the governor's daughter, isn't really feeling threatened in that picture. They say it may be a hoax, the whole kidnapping."

"Why did they want Al to come there?" Nomad asked.

The woman shook her head, her mouth set tight. "We don't know. We've found no connection between him and the governor. We think maybe it's all just a diversionary tactic away from the other kidnapping."

"Why?" Forte asked.

Rosalind shrugged. "We don't know why, exactly. But we have gotten a possible lead on the Freddy Bailey kidnapping."

A TV news helicopter arrived on the scene about 200 feet above them. It began to make a slow sweeping half circle of the neighborhood. Rosalind stepped back under the eave of the house.

In an instant Forte's mind replayed his dream of the night before. The monster blades slicing the air above the park. The mammoth metal claw descending. The screams of two men as the ones they loved were plucked upward.

He blinked and was surprised the sun was shining.

"A lead?" he said. "What lead?"

The boy on the back porch had finished eating his greasy breakfast. Unsmiling, he wiped his fingers on his shorts. A voice called out to him from inside the house. Reluctantly he went back inside.

Rosalind kept staring at the back door as if she wished she were inside, too.

"Rosie, what is the lead?" Forte said softly.

A thin vertical line had formed between her eyebrows as she squinted in the light.

"It's not good," she said. "At all."

Chapter 17

Freddy plucked at the splinter in his finger. "Ow," he said aloud, though alone in the room.

A tiny hole in one of the plywood window coverings allowed a sliver of sunlight into the dark room. It was the only way he knew it was daytime.

Storms had never bothered him much. Of course, his dad had always been nearby when the wind howled. The previous night had been different.

He had huddled in the hot darkness with his arms wrapped tightly around himself, listening to the wind shake the small house. For a moment, he had thought the whole house was going to be snatched up like that Wizard of Oz movie. Eventually, he had fallen asleep from sheer exhaustion.

Jersey Man had awakened him with sack of greasy fast food from the breakfast menu. The man was more wary with him now, but he seemed nervous about something else. "Won't be long now."

Freddy swallowed a bite of hash-browns, then took a slug of orange juice. He wiped his mouth with the back of his hand. "What do you want with my daddy?"

Jersey leaned against the wall next to the door. "It ain't just him. It's bigger than your pop. He's almost nothing in all this, really."

Freddy felt his face go hot. He caught himself before screaming *My daddy is not a nothing!* He swallowed more juice before speaking again. "Why you want him then? Just let me go. I won't say nothing."

Jersey made a noise that Freddy realized was supposed to be a laugh. "I said *almost* nothing." He threw a quick sneer at the boy, then left the room. The noise of a newscast sprinkled into the room. Freddy could catch the sounds of gunfire and the words "amateur video footage of the shootout shows the motorcycle gang and Al Forte..."

Then the door closed. Nothing on the news about a boy being stolen. The name "Forte" sounded familiar to him but it meant nothing to him in the midst of his troubles.

Freddy swallowed his fear and went back to picking at the splinter embedded in his hand. He had been tugging at the edges of the plywood particleboard from the time his eyes opened that morning. He had no idea if the windows would open even if he could pull off a piece of the board. But it was all he had. The splinter had slowed him down but once he got it out he could resume his only escape plan.

He pressed hard against his finger where the splinter had entered. He bit down on his lower lip to keep from crying out against the pain. Taking a deep breath, he pinched the splinter between his fingernails and pulled. It came out. The boy put his hand to his mouth and sucked the blood away from the puncture in his finger.

A cabinet door slammed out in the kitchen. Freddy froze.

He could hear the fat man yelling something about "No coffee." Other words were exchanged. Then the front door to the house opened and slammed shut.

Freddy walked over to the door of the room and pressed his ear to it. He could hear the faint sounds of a vehicle starting up.

He spun and began plucking at the plywood over the window again. With the television up louder, his work was masked better. He kept tugging at the edge of the board. "Owww," he cried out when he scraped his hurt finger over the wood. He immediately stopped and kissed his hand then blew on it as he listened for the Jersey Man. If only he had something sharp or hard enough to pry against the board. For the twentieth time he walked the room and drug his feet across the filthy shag carpet for anything he could use. He bent and picked up the orange juice container. As he sipped it, he studied the pinhole of light coming through the board. He absently scratched his tummy. His fingers grazed over his belt buckle. *Belt buckle.*

Quickly he whipped his belt out from the loops. His pants felt looser but they stayed up fine. He took the edge of the square metal buckle and began chipping away at the board. Pieces of splinters started coming off. He increased his effort.

Down the hall, the TV droned on. Freddy could hear nothing apart from the usual noises.

Though his fingers ached from the effort, he continued making a small opening at one side of the board next to the window frame. Pieces of the wood flew away from the covering. *Got to get out and warn Daddy.* In a few minutes, he had made enough of a hole to insert one hand under the board. He tugged. He could feel a slight give in the board but not enough. He needed room for both hands.

He stopped and listened for a moment. Still no sign of the Jersey Man. The fat man was still gone for more coffee. Freddy renewed his effort. More splinters flew. One hit the boy in the eyelid. He whimpered and rubbed his eye to determine if it had done any damage. He blinked until his vision cleared up. *Just a little more.* His fingers and hands were cramped and scraped but he kept going.

Almost there. He tried to slip both hands under the edge of the board. *Just a little more.* He chipped some more, gasping with the weariness of the effort. He tried again. He could get both hands under the board. He smoothed the edges of the board as best he could, then put his hands into the crevice of the board again. He put one foot against the wall and leaned backward. The board creaked. The wood began to separate from the screw closest to his handhold.

Outside, the van pulled up. Freddy heard the door of the vehicle slam. "Oh no," he whispered to himself. He kept pulling. The board began to crack. *Please don't let them hear it.* He could hear the men arguing down the hall. He pulled the board again. It split even more. Then, with a popping noise a quarter of the board came loose. Freddy fell backward.

He could see the lock on the window now. He reached for it, stretching, his fingers almost touching it. His arm pressed against the jagged edge of the board. When he pulled back, little dots of blood appeared on his skin. He ignored it, his adrenaline pumping into his system now.

He reached again, pushing for the latch. "Oww," he said, slapping his hand over his mouth. Blood from a small gash on his arm trickled down to his wrist and dripped off his fingertips. He took his shirt and dabbed at the cut on his arm. He remembered his daddy's words. *If it ain't flowing, you ain't really hurt. Suck it up.*

"Suck it up," he whispered to himself.

He needed to have the window unlatched before he tried to yank the board more. He needed more of a hole through which to get out of the window. The sound of the wood ripping off the window would almost certainly bring the men who had kidnapped him.

Got to go warn my Daddy. Got to warn him.

He wrapped his shirt around his arm to stop the blood and to protect it. He slowly snaked his arm under the board, straining toward the latch.

They will kill him. Got to warn him.

Three blocks away, a man strolled toward the house. If the summer heat of New Orleans bothered him, it didn't show. He was 6' 3" and weighed 247 pounds, his body chiseled into the kind of ripped physique rarely seen outside of celebrity gyms.

Or prison yards.

He was whistling as a he walked. Hmm, what was that tune? It had been playing on the $2,000 stereo system of the BMW he had left parked at a house a half mile away, a luxury car in rough section of town made safe by two bodyguards who made him look puny. The song was something about an umbrella. He hit the notes perfectly, something he had been able to do since he was kid. He chuckled as he thought of how he'd been slapped around for whistling. But did he stop? "Hell no," he said aloud.

A boy on a bicycle stopped about 20 feet from him when he said it. The man kept his pace, staring down the boy from behind his Ray-Bans. The kid pedaled quickly off the sidewalk and cut across the burnt grass of the scrabbly yard.

The man felt nothing for the kid. Punk should stay out of sight. He had learned to do it, to disappear in plain view, when he was little. That boy should learn it, too.

Then there came a time when he didn't have to worry about hiding. He reached his full height by age 13 and the muscles followed quickly. It only took his old man one trip to the hospital to learn his lesson. No more angry demands of his son. No more insults. No more slapping him around to show who's boss. He had passed his temper down to the boy and had watched it multiply as crime after crime pulled the boy out into the hood. The boy had spent plenty of time in the backs of squad cars before his 18th birthday. And one nice, instructive stint behind bars after he had reached the age to be tried as an adult.

It is true he had learned many lessons about survival as a boy.

Now the boy was a man. A smarter man. A man with a plan.

He unzipped his wind-suit to his waist. On a gold chain around his neck hung an ebony pendant in the shape of a panther skull. Quarter-carat rubies formed the eyes of the panther. He touched the skull as he moved along the cracked sidewalk in the sunshine like a big black cat himself. The piece of jewelry was one of the first things he had bought for himself after his release 18 months earlier. That had been his nickname in prison. *Panther.*

He had read up on the animal. He discovered quickly that the Choctaws considered the black panther a symbol of death. Deadly and soulless, the big cat was stealthy when needed and attacked with lightning speed. One bad cat.

He released the pendant and let it tap against his chest as he kept moving forward. His head swiveled back and forth, scanning the street and the nearby houses in the lower-class neighborhood. There was no reason for anyone to take notice of him. Even if they knew about the kidnapping, they wouldn't connect him to the crime. Who would care about the punk boy anyway?

The plan had been in the works for a while, even before he had left prison. It wasn't his idea, but when he got the first letter requesting a meeting, he was interested. He had a personal stake in it, but when they started talking money, he definitely paid attention. It had made his release much smoother than most ex-cons.

And now here he was, about to the clinch the deal.

The house was 75 yards away. The man slowed down a bit and scrutinized not just the safe house but everything around the house. The home to the left was vacant and overgrown. The one to the right was occupied but its resident was gone for the day. Everything seemed to be in order.

He tapped on the side door on the carport. Inside a television blared then abruptly went silent. To his left, the blinds over a window parted slightly.

The door opened. The fat man stepped back. The newcomer stepped inside.

The room was dark compared to the sunshine outside. The man took off his sunglasses, let his eyes adjust. He took in the scattered junk food wrappers on the kitchen table and the worn sofa in the corner of the den to his left. The aroma of sweat and stale food hung in the air. He wanted to be back outside five seconds after he had come inside.

He had no desire for small talk. No fist bumps. No gangster signs. "Where's the boy?"

The other men, hardened criminals themselves, almost winced at the casual menace in the man's eyes. It was like looking into two gun barrels.

The Jersey Man recovered his cool. He jerked his chin toward the hallway. "Down here." He walked ahead and clicked open the dead bolt on the bedroom door where they kept the boy.

He swung the door open and stepped inside carefully.

He gasped. Then cursed.

The new man pushed him out of the way.

The board was half torn off the window, which was open.

He cursed even louder.

Then he yanked a pistol out of his waistband.

He shot the Jersey Man.

When he spun around, the fat man had already pulled out a gun.

The newcomer put a bullet in his chest.

He ran back out through the house, out into the yard. He whirled in a circle, searching for any quick movement.

None.

Seething, he took several deep breaths.

Then he began walking casually back in the direction of the car.

In the house, the silence of death reigned. The blood of the two dead men seeped out into the carpet, adding yet another permanent stain.

A quarter hour passed.

A bird flew in through the open window, perched on the window sill. Alert for signs of a predator, it hopped down on to the floor. It stopped for a long moment and kept very still as if it expected the two men to move. Finally, it hopped over to the crumpled fast food bag. It picked at the bag until it came open. Its head twitched back and forth between the two corpses on the floor. It poked its head back into the sack and pulled out a piece of biscuit.

The bird put the morsel on the carpet. It jabbed at it a few times with its beak.

It froze, its beak pointed at the pile of blankets lying among the shadows in the corner of the room.

One of the blankets twitched.

The bird streaked out through the now-open window.

The edge of the blanket lifted two inches. An eye peeked out.

Nothing changed for another sixty seconds.

Finally, Freddy pulled the blanket off his head.

His face was wet with tears and sweat.

Chapter 18

Forte glared at the image of a man's face on the flat-panel monitor. He had not seen the man's face for years, but the malevolence came off the screen as if he were there in person. In seven years the sneer had matured into a brutal leer.

A title under the photo read: Maurice "Chug" Johnson.

Forte's fists rested on the table of the conference room at the New Orleans offices of the Federal Bureau of Investigation. He willed himself to unclench them.

"So, how did you find out it was him behind the boy's kidnapping?" he said.

Rosalind Dent tapped the TV remote control lightly on the table top as she also studied the man's face on the screen. Jackie Shaw sat in the leather rolling chair next to the FBI agent. She was focused on Forte's face instead of the screen. Nomad sipped coffee as he tipped a straight chair against the wall, his cowboy boots propped on the table. Since it was Saturday, the open office space outside the room was almost empty. A couple of people tapped on computer keyboards. The phones were idle.

"We've been tracking him since he was released from the state prison last year," said Rosalind. "We had buzz that he was up to something with the help of someone with money." She exhaled audibly. "Then we lost him about three months ago. This morning, we got a call that he was connected to the boy's disappearance."

"Who called you?" Forte asked.

Rosalind shook her head. "Confidential informant. One of our snitches."

"Who was the C.I. Tell me."

She stood up, her hands splayed on the table in front of her. "Al, you know I can't."

He pounded the table hard and cursed loudly. Two agents looked up from their desks in the open office space outside the windowed wall of the conference room.

Forte closed his eyes and saw red. Then he saw blood. His wife's blood. After he had tracked down young Martin Bailey that night and realized he could not exact revenge on him, he had discovered the truth. That the other one, Chug, had been responsible for it. He had lied to Martin about the bullets in the gun and had known they were real. He had wanted to see someone die that night. Forte had searched everywhere for him.

Chug, 21 at that time, had already made enough contacts among the New Orleans underworld to go into hiding safely for a few months. By the time Forte had discovered his whereabouts, the former SEAL had become distracted by the black hole of drugs and alcohol into which he had slipped. The cops had caught up with Chug, and he had gone to trial on a charge of accessory to murder. At the trial, Forte had drifted up to the witness stand in a cocaine-hyped frenzy and had almost gotten thrown out of the courtroom. As it was, Chug was sentenced to 10 years in the state prison.

He served six years, but by that time Forte had moved on with his life.

Until now.

He inspected the polished wood of the conference table. He could see his reflection, his forehead streaked with dirt from the back yard where he had rolled and come up shooting at the bikers. He could see fury in his eyes.

"He killed my wife." The words were bitten off. "And now he wants me." He looked up at the others. "Let me go to him." The words were soaked with vengeful yearning.

Everyone remained still in the disinfected silence of the room.

No one met his eye except for Jackie.

"Rosie," Forte said. "Just let me have him."

Still leaning on the table, the agent kept her head down as she spoke. "You know we can't do that. The boy. We have to try to get the boy back."

The man with the yellow eyes groaned, his mouth clenched tightly closed. The flood of darkness was smothering him as it had in the weeks and months after her death. So strong and tough he had been for all those years, all those missions, all those accomplishments, all of the drugs and the abandonment of anyone close to him who could have helped if he'd only let them, all the pain and sorrow and hate that had no place to go but down deep inside the hole his life had become. *Ruth, the blood, no, can't stop it, seeping through my fingers. Don't leave me, no, can't keep you from dying. And their baby, inside her, only a few weeks growing inside her womb.* All of it gone, his life, his wife, his baby — gone. Because of Martin Bailey and the man on the screen, his life, the life he would have known, had died.

Forte put his head down on his fists, clenched again. The others said nothing.

It's not all about you. It's not all about you. The phrase had been repeated dozens, probably hundreds, of times during rehab and in the thousands of meetings he had attended in the years since he began his healing. Even when he had realized he was powerless to transform his life all alone, he had held on to the belief that, deep down, he could take care of himself once he was freed from his addiction.

That notion had been beaten out of him, figuratively, in the months and years since then. *It's not all about you.* All his life, since the deaths of his parents and the passing of his grandmother, he had been a fixer. He had been the strong one, the one people looked to when they needed rescuing, the one who made the tackle at the goal line to save a victory, the one to go in and rescue the American consulate held hostage by rebels, the one to save a child taken by drug dealers. He had been the problem-solver.

But he couldn't solve himself.

"You might as well go on back out that door and score the first crack you come to," a wiry bald old-timer had drawled at rehab so many years earlier, "if you think you got the power to beat this by yourself. You don't. Nobody does, I don't care how tough or how much a badass they have been about so many things in their lives. All you got is today, Mr. Forte, and you are wasting it by waiting it out until you are on your feet again." The old man had given a smile that Forte barely resisted slapping off his face. "Because you ain't never gonna be on your feet again, with that attitude. So, get out of here and stop wasting our time. We are busy living this day here."

That had been the start of the truth for him. He had begun to realize that a Higher Power existed who knew more than he did. Forte didn't understand exactly how it worked that God could allow his wife and unborn child to leave him. But he had been reminded many times of the dying women and children he had seen in war-torn places across the world. What about them? Why was his loss any different than those peasants living just a notch above stone-age conditions?

But this man, this monster who killed his wife and child, this man was right in his face, taunting him.

Forte kept his palms pressed hard against the waxed wood of the conference table. His head was still bent almost to the surface of the table top. His breath exploded from behind clenched teeth. In. *Whoosh*. Out. *Whoosh*. He would not allow himself to look up at the image of Chug Johnson on the screen. His breath hissed in a ragged wrenching stream.

Calm. Calm down. Next step. The next step is all you have. In his mind he could hear the words of his sponsors and hundreds of others who had been down roads as bad as or worse than the path his life had taken. He had spoken the same words to others many times. *Next step.*

They are gone. Nothing you can do will bring them back. But others can be rescued. The memories of the first missions to rescue stolen children came back to him: the feelings of rightness about saving those kids; the realization that his great loss fueled a resolve that had prevented that great sadness from visiting hundreds of other parents. *The memories of Ruth, of the unborn child.* He would always have that.

His breath had eased now. The monitor still displayed Chug's face. Forte slowly looked around the room at the other three people.

"Okay," he said, "What is the plan?"

Rosalind sat back on her chair, the tension almost visibly uncoiling itself from around her shoulders. "We are expecting a call from Chug or whoever he hired to take Freddy. We can't plan any specifics until we know what he wants and where he is." She took a deep breath and let it out as she checked her watch. "But we have heard from the other group, the ones who took the governor's daughter."

Both Forte and Jackie leaned forward in their chairs. Nomad remained in the same position, his boots still crossed atop the table. He took another sip of coffee and casually faced the others. "What time is the scoop?"

"In a half hour. A warehouse on the west bank in Harvey," said Agent Dent. "The Hostage Rescue Team is already set up there. Snipers are in position. I'll review the details on the way." She stood up. "Any questions?"

"And we'll just wait on the call from Chug?"

She nodded. "It's all we can do." She folded her binder and walked out of the room.

Nomad put his feet on the floor, yawned and stretched. "Shoot up a neighborhood at 9. Rescue the girl at noon. Save the boy later in the afternoon. Sounds like a productive Saturday." He crumpled his paper coffee cup and sank it in a metal wastebasket in the corner. "Maybe we can go out for a dinner and a movie later, just to cap things off." He sauntered out of the room.

Jackie arose from her chair. "You coming? You are the featured guest of the next kidnap rescue."

Forte studied her face for a moment. "You feeling okay?"

Jackie shrugged. "Yeah. Sinus headache. The usual."

"You look a little green around the gills, that's all."

"Guess I need a new makeup artist instead of the $500-an-hour expert I currently use."

"Yeah, maybe they can do something about that white streak, too."

"Yeah, yeah." She walked out the door.

Forte rotated toward the image on the monitor again. He studied the face of the man responsible for the death of his wife. "Chug," he said aloud, "I hope to see you later, old pal."

He got up and followed the others down the hall.

Chapter 19

By the time Chug got back to his BMW, he was drenched in sweat. A block away, his two bodyguards dutifully stood guard.

"Pea, this ain't good," said Troll, the smaller of the men. Troll was 6' 4" 295 pounds of bad intentions. His partner, 30 pounds heavier and two inches taller, merely grunted from behind his shades. They had a clear view of the hideout house several blocks away. They had not seen the other two men come out with the boy. They noticed that the van had not moved from in front of the house. Sweat dripped from their faces but they stood, unmoving, spaced about 15 feet apart on each side of the black Hummer. They shifted their weight slightly, a pair of rhinos letting a jaguar walk between them.

Chug walked past his own car and approached them.

"Boy got away from the idiots," he said softly.

The monsters Pea and Troll said nothing. They had not been chosen for their jobs because they chattered away to the boss. They knew he despised small talk from yes-men. They knew now the men in the house were dead. They knew they could crush the boss, strong as he might be, if it came down to a hand fight. They also knew he was a different type of killer than them. They called him Vamp behind his back – he loved the blood.

They just nodded silently to him, while scanning the neighborhood around them. The boom of a rap song thudded from a house nearby. A lawnmower ripped into action somewhere on the next street over.

Chug examined his image in the smoked glass windows of the Humvee. "All they had to do was tend a little boy 'til I got there," he said to his own reflection. His voice was barely audible above the nearby music and the hum of the mower. He grabbed one of his wrists with the opposite hand and held his arms straight up over his head, stretching. His warm-up jacket rode up enough for the bodyguards to see the handle of the pistol stuck in the holster at their boss's back.

"Y'all take the Hummer and ride around the neighborhood in that direction." He pointed down the street. "I'll go this way and meet you back here in ten minutes." He spun and strode back to his car. The bodyguards were moving toward the SUV before their boss stopped talking. They had both played football, Troll as a defensive tackle and Pea as offensive tackle. They were gargantuan men but not sluggish. Their combined weight caused the truck to sink very little, thanks to reinforced shocks. The Hummer slowly pulled out and moved down the street like a killer whale searching for a lost seal pup to have for dessert.

Without speaking, Pea scanned the right hand side of the road while Troll, behind the wheel, searched the left side. A young woman was bent over, her brown skin shining as she washed the hubcaps of her subcompact car. She glanced up as the Humvee glided past, smiling at the heavy black vehicle going by. The bodyguard in the driver seat did not dwell on the brevity of her shorts. He focused on every area around her where the boy might be hiding. He had known friends of his to be killed after being set up with the visual decoy of a pretty lady. Not him, not today.

People were out cutting their grass, tidying their driveways, loitering in lawn chairs in front of their battered houses. The men continued to look everywhere they could from the dark cool interior of the Hummer. Both knew that a search like this from the safety of the car was useless. But they did it anyway. What was it to them? It was their job. Who knows, the boy might run out in front of them and jump into their truck.

At the end of the street, a group of boys were playing baseball in a vacant lot. The grass has been mowed down neatly enough so the baselines were visible. Only about half the boys had gloves. None wore shirts and all looked to be between ages 7 and 12. But they were out there swapping trash talk in baggy, ragged short pants of every hue in 100-degree heat. Four boys sat on a rusty overturned refrigerator next to a chain link fence that served as the home-run line. A makeshift awning had been fashioned above the group of four as they rested in the shade before taking their turn at bat.

The Hummer slowed as the men studied the faces of the boys. Pea reached up and took down the photo of Freddy from the visor. He looked at it for a few seconds as he checked out the baseball players. He handed it to his partner. None of the boys matched up. A few of the boys glanced over at the truck but they had more important things to do than scope out a pair of drug dealers staking out the neighborhood. In their 'hood, they had seen it all.

The men kept looking as the truck inched alongside the lot. They were not focused on the faces of the boys now. They were carefully checking out any possible movement that signaled nervousness or fear, anything that would telegraph they were hiding Freddy Bailey – any glances toward the bushes or the houses on either side of the vacant lot. They were looking for what *wasn't* there, anything that didn't fit in with the usual weekend game among boys in a poverty-smashed area where joy was squeezed out of the smallest of events.

Satisfied that everything was as it should be, they sped up slightly and moved down the street. Still searching the yards and carports of houses, they turned the corner about 100 yards away and moved out of sight of the baseball game.

For a half minute after the Humvee disappeared around the corner, the boys kept tossing the ball and swinging their bats and flinging insults. Then the boy on the mound nodded to another wiry kid wearing green basketball shorts standing close to the street. The green-shorted boy sprinted all the way to the corner and peered in the direction the two men had driven. He about-faced and waved at the boys back at the makeshift ball field.

The bigger boy on the mound nodded to one of the boys sitting atop the dead refrigerator. The other boys jogged over and surrounded the area with the awning. Back at the corner, the boy in the green shorts maintained his position, glancing back and forth from the baseball field to the street.

The other boys in the crowd kept poking their head up from the huddle like prairie dogs. One of them stepped over and lifted the edge of the awning.

Freddy was huddled there, his eyes wide.

"They gone," said another of the older boys, "but they looked like some bad mofos..."

"Shut up, man," said the biggest boy there, the pitcher who had sent the sentry to the corner. "No need to scare him no more." He bent down closer to Freddy. "So, dude just came in and killed them men, huh?"

Freddy stretched his legs out, then got into a squatted position still inside the wall of boys. "Yes, he shot 'em dead. Quick." The group of boys gasped as one. A couple of *dayum's* were sprinkled on the fringes of the group.

A scrawny kid with one of the newest baseball gloves piped up. "I thought I heard that. POP POP." He squinted and pointed his finger like a pistol.

The big pitcher scowled at him. "Sh'up, Smitty. You ain't heard crap. You live three blocks from there." Smitty bowed his head and mumbled something unintelligible.

The bigger boy poked his head above the huddle and scanned for signs of the searchers. Satisfied, he knelt next to Freddy. "Here's what you do. Climb this fence and go through the ditch 'til you get to the next neighborhood. It don't link directly to our 'hood 'cept by that ditch. From there, you can see the barbershop on the corner. My uncle Remmy will be there. Tell him what happened. Tell him you talked to me." He fist-bumped Freddy. "I'm Timbo. Now go."

The boys held the sheet awning so that it hid Freddy as he crawled over the fence. He scurried low down to the water-filled ditch that ran along the back fences of houses accustomed to ignoring incriminating sights.

When he looked back, the baseball game had resumed as if they had never stopped playing.

* * *

Chug slumped low in the leather seat of the BMW, waiting for the Hummer to circle the neighborhood. The windows were shut tight, sealing off the sounds and smells of people living their stinkin' little lives. He had lived a life like that once, long ago. Now he could shut it all out.

And he wasn't going back to that life, no matter what. Not for no little punk kid. Not for his rat daddy, Martin Bailey. And sure as hell not for no yellow-eyed bodyguard.

He wasn't particularly worried about getting Freddy back. He knew the boy would call his father. And he knew his father would get everything back on track.

The boy would come to him.

Chapter 20

In a port city like New Orleans, warehouses abound. Along the Mississippi, especially, the ships unload cargo and store it to be trucked or shipped elsewhere. Cranes and forklifts are busy night and day, moving the goods. The activity easily masks the movement of SWAT team members into place, when necessary.

In one of the warehouses, the daughter of the governor of the state of Louisiana was tied to a chair.

The workers milled about the waterfront, a group that included several cops in their undercover outfits. A man in a hard hat read from a clipboard as a crane swung out over the deck of a ship stacked with trailer-sized metal containers. Another worker was unloading tools from the back of a beat-up red pickup truck. The third man was perched on scaffolding as he spray-painted cover-up for graffiti on the side of a metal building. A pile of scrap cleanup cloths were piled next to him, enough to easily hide a rifle.

The fishy smell of the river wafted through the open window of the van door. A boom box on the tailgate of someone's truck released the chainsaw noises of heavy metal music throughout the area. Forte and Rosalind sat in a dusty van in the shadow of a tottering pile of tires stacked twenty feet high.

"Let's run through it again," he said.

Rosalind spoke in soft but confident tones about the nearby warehouse that Forte was about to enter. "They said for you to come through the blue door on this side of the warehouse. There are metal exposed stairs leading to a second level. When you reach the top of the stairs, they will release Ashley Barreaux through that metal door on the front of the warehouse." She pointed to an unpainted and rust-rimmed door. "At that point, when she is safe, we storm the building." Her eyes bore into him. "For twenty to thirty seconds, you'll be on your own. Got it?"

Forte shrugged. He wore gray coveralls streaked with grease. On his head was a striped cap with "Nawlins" on it. A dented metal lunchbox rested on his lap. Inside the box were his Glock 17 and two flashbang grenades.

"You got the Kevlar vest," she said.

He nodded.

"And your Glock."

He made no movement, still staring at the warehouse.

"Nervous?"

"Nope."

She looked at her watch. She knew he would not admit it if he were anxious. She continued briefing him. "We've got two minutes. We immediately dispatched undercover people to this area soon as we got the call. We couldn't risk putting someone inside the building but we are pretty sure there are no getaway vehicles parked anywhere close to the warehouse. So, they will be parked inside. They will come through the rollup doors on the far side of the building. In addition to six undercover cops scattered around the outside of the building, we have three snipers stationed out of sight on top of nearby buildings. They have scoped out the inside of the building as best they can through the high windows there and there." She pointed. "But they have detected no movement."

A tugboat honked out on the river. The deep tone of the boat's horn temporarily drowned out all other sounds except for the heavy metal.

"The governor and his wife are secure in a bulletproof car about a quarter mile from here. Nomad is with them."

Forte focused on her as if he were hearing her for the first time. "And Jackie?"

Rosalind kept her voice neutral. "She said she would see you back at The Refuge."

Forte studied her face hard, trying to penetrate the blackness of the shades. Her eyes were hidden.

An alarm buzzed softly on the agent's cell phone. "It's time."

He opened the door.

She put a hand on his arm. "We will come in fast. Stay low if you can."

For the first time, he smiled. "Yes ma'am," he said. Then he was out of the van, strolling casually toward the blue door.

None of the undercover people paid any attention to him. He saw two others as he approached the building: They were unloading boxes from the opened doors of an 18-wheeler two buildings past the warehouse. The barrel of an assault rifle poked from beneath a canvas tarp on the floor of the trailer just a few feet from the men.

From the corner of his eye, he could see that one of the undercover SWAT team members in the back of the truck bent to tie his shoe. As he did, he covered the gun barrel with the edge of the canvas. The action was so subtle as to be unnoticeable.

Forte kept walking toward the blue door, the metal lunch box dangling from his hand. The picture of a dock worker in no hurry to start a late afternoon shift, he reached for the doorknob.

As he did, the heavy metal music suddenly stopped.

He glanced to his right. A worker on the other side of the narrow street separating the warehouses was laughing at another man who had accidentally tipped over the boom box. The man switched on the music again and the screeching resumed.

Forte twisted the doorknob on the blue door and went inside.

The inside of the building was lit only by the windows lining the very top of the thirty-foot walls. The windows were open. The muted sounds of machinery and the heavy metal boom box drifted down. Shafts of light sliced downward through the dust particles floating in the stifling heat of the building. The only sound inside came from an unbalanced ceiling fan above the stairway to Forte's left. The metal stairs went up to a storage loft encased in chain link. A half-wall blocked the view of anything in the upper level.

Five seconds passed as Forte stood to the left of the door and allowed his eyes to adjust to the light.

There was no movement anywhere inside the building.

He moved straight toward the stairs. Without hesitation he walked up the stairs. He flipped the latch on the lunchbox. Before he had reached the midpoint of the stairs, he had dropped the two grenades in one pocket of the coveralls and the Glock in the other.

When he had reached the final two stairs, he could see the top of a girl's head above the half wall.

He continued rising to the top and stepped into the enclosure.

Fifteen seconds had passed since he had entered the building.

The Barreaux girl was tied to a metal folding chair in the center of the space. Her arms were behind her now, instead of in her lap as they had been in the photo the kidnappers had emailed. Her legs were duct-taped together at the ankles. A red bandana was tied around her head, covering her mouth.

Above the gag in her mouth, her eyes showed some nervousness but little fear.

Forte held her gaze for a beat as he circled slowly to his left.

There was no movement behind the metal shelves along one side of the storage area. No sound except for the squeaking of the fan.

Is this a trap? Forte quickly circled the girl. No tripwires.

He bent close to her and whispered, "Shhhh." He pulled the bandana over her head. "Where are the people who kidnapped you?"

Ashley looked directly into his eyes. "They left."

Forte knew the agents on the SWAT team would be crashing through the doors any second. He grabbed the girl's arm. "Let's go. Quick."

She began to follow him, then stumbled. "My legs are asleep," she said, her voice trembling. Forte scooped her up and went down the stairs.

Where are the kidnappers? Still no movement anywhere in the warehouse.

Forte flung open the blue door and called out, "All clear!" as he stepped out into the sunshine with the girl.

The scene outside was different than when he had gone inside. All the legitimate workers had been moved away from the vicinity of the warehouse. The undercover SWAT team people were poised outside both the side door and the front door of the building. Their guns were drawn.

As Forte came out, the team members moved in. No sounds of their movement could be detected outside the building.

Forte handed the girl to a nearby Emergency Medical Technician. The EMT whisked her to a portable gurney and another medical worker joined him as they sped toward an ambulance parked around the edge of the building.

Forte walked toward the van where Rosalind Dent stood, a cell phone to her ear. He heard her say the words, "We have the girl."

At that precise moment, they felt the explosion more than heard it.

Everyone instinctively ducked low behind the open doors of vehicles or behind heavy boxes. Then they realized the explosion came from a distance.

About a quarter mile away. The thought popped into Forte's head. He knew it was probably accurate. His training and experience in the SEALs had taught him to differentiate the types of bomb sounds and their distances.

This one sounded like a car bomb.

Forte felt his gut lurch. The governor and his wife were about a quarter mile away, waiting for their daughter. In their car.

With Nomad.

Before that thought had fully settled in his mind, Forte was sprinting toward the sound of the explosion.

Chapter 21

Freddy rocked back and forth behind the bush on the bank of the ditch, muddy water squishing between his toes in the sodden sneakers. His legs were mud-spattered from his dash from the fence back at the ball field to where he now stood.

He could see the barber shop through the leaves of the bush.

He remembered the words of the boy. *Ask for Uncle Remmy. Tell him Timbo sent you.* Freddy felt the tears burning his eyes. He shook his head. *Don't get weird now.* He had survived the kidnapping and the murders without crying much at all. *Almost to safety now. Almost there.*

There was no sign of the Humvee the boys had seen moving past the baseball game on the vacant lot. He saw nothing moving anywhere in the neighborhood. The heat pressed him down like one of the blankets back in the room where the kidnappers had kept him. He had lain under those coverings in the room for a while, smelling the stench of the dead men's loosened bowels.

He raised his face to the sun. At least he was outside now.

Eager as he was to cross the street to the barber shop, he still delayed. He once more scoured the area. No traffic was moving. No one was outside in the yards that backed up to the drainage ditch he had just walked in. The passing storm the day before had dumped enough water in the ditch that it was knee high as he waded along. The fences of the yards backed up to the muddy water. The banks of the ditch were not treacherous. They were just steep, making the waterway a mere gash in the earth.

But he was here now.

He took a deep breath, inhaling his own stench. *Almost over now.*

He burst out from behind the bush. Without slowing down, he sprinted toward the door of the barber shop. His shoes *slap-slapped* on the pavement, the mud from the ditch oozing between his toes.

His toe caught on a crack in the asphalt. Down he went, tumbling in the middle of the street. The hard surface scraped him, snatching the thinnest surface of skin from his hands, his elbows, his knees.

He tumbled twice and came up running. *So close, so close.*

Bang. He hit the door and snatched it open. An old-fashioned bell clanged as the door swung open.

He slammed it shut and whirled to look through the heavy glass door.

No men with hateful leers were chasing him. No cars were screeching around the corner.

No one out on the street had noticed him at all.

He realized he was holding his breath. He put a hand on the glass of the door and bowed his head. Suddenly, he was exhausted. When he pulled his hand away, a smudged hand print was left on the door. He scanned the street and sidewalk through the glass once more before turning around.

The barber shop was one long room with mirrors along one wall and three barber chairs in a row. Old leather chairs and a sofa lined the opposite wall. At the far end of the room was a door with "Bathroom" painted neatly on it. Another door was beneath an exit sign.

The barber was a man of about 40. His hands were poised above the head of an older man whose hair had been half removed. In his right hand, an electric razor buzzed like a big bee trying to harmonize with the Duke Ellington tune coming from a stereo at the far end of the room. The clean smell of aftershave filled Freddy's nostrils. He suddenly felt dirty. Another man, white-haired, was sprawled on a cracked leather loveseat facing the three barber chairs that occupied the center of the small room.

All three men were staring at him as if he were an alien.

The barber spoke. "Boy, what's wrong?" His voice was gentle.

Freddy opened his mouth to explain. Instead of words, a mewling noise spilled from him. He collapsed on the floor in anguish and relief.

The barber and the man on the loveseat hurried toward him.

They pulled the sobbing boy over to the loveseat. The customer in the chair brought a wet towel over to him. The barber took it and wiped the dirt off Freddy's face as his crying subsided.

"Who are you, son?" the barber asked.

The boy tried to focus on the man's face, his eyes still blurred from tears. Then he remembered.

"Are you Mr. Remmy? Timbo sent me," he said.

The three men looked at each other.

"Yes," said the barber. "That's me. Tell me what happened to you."

Freddy glanced at the men then looked back at the door. He wiped his eyes, looked down at his hands. *Why are they shaking now?* "They are after me. I need to call my daddy!"

"You can, son. Who's after you?" He put his hand on the boy's shoulder.

Freddy screamed and jumped back. "Call my daddy!"

Remmy spread his hands and stepped back to the counter under the big mirror. He picked up the cordless phone and handed it silently to the boy.

Freddy gripped the phone tightly to still his shaking fingers. He carefully punched in his dad's cell number.

While the phone rang, he noticed the white-haired man walk casually over to the front door of the shop. He opened the door about six inches and peered down the street.

A voice came over the phone.

Freddy nearly dropped the barber's phone when he heard his father.

"Daddy!" he began, then broke down sobbing.

The men gathered around the boy could hear crying on the other end.

Freddy tried to tell Martin Bailey where he was but failed. His voice cracked with emotion.

Remmy the barber gently pried the phone from the boy's hands. He put it to his ear and spoke softly to Martin Bailey on the other end.

"No, I don't know what happened to him. Yes, he seems to be okay. Just dirty and tired and scared. Okay, we will be here." He listened for a few moments. His face furrowed in slight disbelief. "Okay, we won't call the police if that's what you want. But they could help.... No, I won't call them. The boy will here waiting for you."

He set the phone on the counter and considered Freddy.

"Your daddy will be here in a few minutes. You'll be safe here." He motioned to the white-haired man. "Bring the boy a Coke, Jimmy. And a bag of them peanuts in the back."

He pulled a fresh face towel from the cabinet beneath the big mirror. He handed it to Freddy then directed the boy over to the sofa and sat next to him. "Tell us what happened, son."

The customer with his half-cut hair perched on the arm of the sofa. He settled himself, then remained motionless.

Freddy swabbed the tears from his face. He looked back and forth between the barber and his customer. The old man came shuffling from the back closet. He handed the boy a chilled soft drink and a bag of peanuts. Then he took several steps back, giving the boy space.

Freddy crunched the nuts and gulped down the Coke while the peanuts were still salty in his mouth. The tastes almost made him smile. But the terror of the past two days still hovered over him. After another mouthful of peanuts and several more swigs, he wiped his mouth with the back of his hand. He began to tell the story.

It came out painfully, slowly, at first. How the men snatched him off the street, then recaptured him. The nights in the suffocating stench of that room. The horror of the men's murders just inches away from him as he huddled beneath the pile of blankets.

The words rushed out of him now, even as his tears began to flow again.

But now, he was safe.

Remmy the barber leaned forward and patted him on the shoulder. "You're okay, now, son. Your daddy should be here any second."

Freddy leaned back on the worn soft leather of the sofa. He closed his eyes and sighed from deep inside. His daddy would make everything okay. *If I can just see him.*

The front door opened.

The boy was blocked from viewing who was coming through the door by the arm of the sofa.

But he could see the face of the barber.

His expression was one of surprise.

Then, one of anger.

"You ain't this boy's daddy," the barber said.

Freddy was rising from the sofa when he heard the response.

"You got that right," said the man who had come through the front door.

It was the voice of the man who had shot the men in the house.

Everything exploded at that moment.

The barber reached for a razor on the cabinet behind his chair.

Three shots barked from the gun in the intruder's hand.

Remmy clutched his chest with his hand. Red seeped through his fingers.

But Freddy was already past him before the barber slumped to the floor. He was darting to the back door. He expected to feel a bullet slam into his back any second.

His legs churned as he flung himself toward the exit.

Three more gunshots tore through the slender sweet-smelling room.

A magazine rack crashed to the ground as the white-haired man grabbed it on his way down.

The customer with his half-shaved head fell backward over the footrest of the barber chair.

Freddy heard screaming and realized it was him.

He grabbed the doorknob of the exit. As he yanked it open, he looked back at the killer.

A man in an expensive wind-suit and shades was standing back lit by the front door. His arm was extended. A pistol was pointed at the boy.

Almost out. Help me. Help me.

Freddy spun and went through the door.

And slammed into a wall.

Except the wall was breathing.

A huge hand clamped his upper arm. It yanked him up as easily as a giant metallic claw picks up a stuffed toy in an arcade.

He looked up into a pair of black lenses on a mammoth brown face.

Chapter 22

Forte sprinted in the direction of the bomb blast. Members of the SWAT team were slowly coming out of a crouch after hearing the explosion. Behind him the voice of Rosalind barked a staccato warning he could not hear.

Black smoke above the warehouses beckoned him.

Workers peeked from behind trucks and through the windows of the metal buildings lining the service road.

Forte churned past all of them, his thighs burning with the sudden effort. He realized his pistol was in his hand.

Nomad. Unbidden, his friend's name flashed to the top of his concern. Before the governor or Mrs. Barreaux's.

Forte kept running.

The flames came into sight ahead.

This is bad. For a split second, the sight of the explosion shocked his system like an energy vacuum.

In that sliver of time, memories of Nomad flashed through the yellow-eyed man's mind: Hell Week at the beach during the SEALs' training, when Nomad winked in the face of a screaming instructor; running into a bar with Nomad in the clutches of three angry Marines, as his friend shouted, "I got 'em where I want 'em now!"; limping through the Nicaraguan jungle, each with a bullet in them, as Nomad mumbled, "Sure, join the Navy. See the blankedy world."

Forte stumbled then righted himself.

Panic later. The training from his SEAL days kicked in. *Nothing's personal in a firefight.*

Fifty yards away, the flames and twisted metal of the bombed car told the tale instantly: nobody in that car survived.

Forte clenched his teeth, slowed to a jog. He forced himself to look beyond the bombed car and scanned the area. No one had begun to approach the wreckage yet. Sirens shrieked in the distance, but nothing was moving in the immediate area.

Except for the door of a storage building twenty yards from the car. It swung open three inches, as if someone had left it ajar by accident.

Forte took two more seconds to scan the area again. Then he darted around a building to the other side of the storage shed.

He stopped and listened. No sounds. He scurried low to another building on the far corner of the shed. He ducked and again studied the area for any sign of movement. Nothing.

Whoever bombed the car might be still be here. Forte wanted to spy the watchers, if they were there.

He took a deep breath, let it out, then darted to the corner of the shed. He crouched and listened.

On the other side of the wreck, two police cars and an ambulance screeched to a stop simultaneously. The sirens stopped, bathing the area in eerie silence now.

From inside came the sound of something shifting slightly.

Forte brought his Glock up to ready position. He edged over to another corner of the shed.

He eased up to the closest window on the warehouse. Just as he was positioned to peek inside, something creaked. He jerked his head down.

A bullet shattered the corner of the window. Forte dropped to the concrete and rolled to safety behind some scrap metal.

The shot came from outside the warehouse.

Forte crawled a few more feet. He jerked a long piece of scrap metal from the pile. He raised just the tip of it above the heap, about five feet away from where he lay.

A bullet tore it from his grasp. *Sniper.*

Immediately, he jumped up, his gun extended.

He saw the shooter on top of a taller warehouse, three buildings away.

As he ducked back, three more shots sent metal flying where his head had been.

Then, other shots barked, closer.

They were coming from inside the warehouse Forte had been approaching.

And they were directed toward the sniper atop the building.

From the other side of the warehouse came shots from the cops on the scene.

Sirens started up again.

Forte crawled away from the firefight, the scrap pile hiding him. He got to his feet and sprinted to the far corner. No gunfire followed him. The sniper was busy returning fire from the police now.

Forte ran full-speed around the corner of the warehouse and doubled back. Without slowing, he sprinted across the service road separating the rows of warehouses. He glanced up to see the sniper as he bobbed up and back, firing steadily, keeping the police low.

As he reached the far side of the road, a voice shouted, "Forte! Stop!" It was Agent Dent. The FBI had reached the scene. Forte kept going.

He churned down the narrow alley next to the metal building two down from the sniper's. Then he cut around the back. When he reached the building with the sniper, he flung open the back door and ducked inside.

The outside shots were muffled. The gunman was still firing. In the dusty dimness of the building, he could see a metal staircase at the far side of the huge room. He ran for it. He tested the first step, then the second. Snipers sometimes booby-trapped their escape routes.

There were no tricks here. *Maybe the man knew he wouldn't be escaping.*

He went up the metal steps slowly. The sharp crack of the high-power rifle became louder. The door at the top of the stairs was open.

Forte examined the doorway.

Two strands of fishing line spanned the opening – one a foot from the bottom, the other at chest level.

Forte was sure they were attached to grenades or explosive charges.

He peeked around the edge of the door. He could see the grenades, duct-taped to the outside door frame, the filaments tied to their triggers.

He pulled a multi-tool from his pocket and carefully cut the lines.

Moving deliberately, he put the corner of his eye to the opening again to study the gunman.

The sniper was 15 yards away from the stairs. He wore a gray work shirt and pants mottled with paint. On his head was a hat of the same color. Perfect camouflage for the warehouse district. A stack of magazines for his rifle lay at his feet. His cap was backward on his head, a typical look for snipers. Wraparound sunglasses shielded his eyes from the fierce summer sun. He braced the rifle against his left shoulder, making him either left-handed or ambidextrous with a stronger left eye than right. The rifle was pointed away from Forte.

Need him alive. Need to know what he knows. Forte crouched, and advanced. *Need to find out why they are after me. Need to know who "they" are.*

The shooter pulled his rifle back from the ledge of the building. He crouched and pulled out a cell phone. He spoke into it, then listened. He put away the phone. He rolled his head around to loosen up his neck muscles. He resumed his position: One knee on a small cushion on the metal flooring of the building's roof, the butt of the rife snug against his shoulder, his cheek against the stock as he sighted down the barrel.

He began shooting again.

Forte focused on the thigh of the shooter. He imagined a four-inch round target right there. As he concentrated, he could almost see it – the red and yellow and blue concentric circles. And the dime-sized black dot, right in the center..

The gunfire faded. In some part of his mind, he knew the volume of the weapons firing was just as loud. He knew that as his adrenaline spiked, his senses so sharply tuned to his mission that his brain shut down other sensory perceptions it deemed useless or distracting to the task at hand.

Forte's eyesight sharpened within two seconds of this dulling of the cacophony of guns exploding. He could see that the man was wiry with strong, veined forearms. The hands were wider than one would expect. Not stubby. Just strong. As he squeezed the trigger, the sniper's flexor muscles of his left forearm bulged slightly then smoothed out again.

Forte leaned out of the doorway a few more inches. His pistol sights were trained on the imaginary target on the man's leg.

The gun battle paused, allowing a sliver of silence in the chatter-boom of bullets. As Forte leaned out, the door creaked.

The sniper whirled.

The action was lightning fast.

But Forte's laser focus was so acute that every movement of the gunman was broken into distinct high-resolution photos.

The raised eyebrows. The pushing up from his knee. The barrel of the rifle cutting through the brilliant light like a black knife.

Forte shot him in the leg.

The man's hands and arms jerked upward. His gun erupted, sending a high-powered slug into the metal doorway six inches above Forte's head.

The man's head whipped backward, exposing it to the shooters below.

No. NO! The shout was only in Forte's mind.

The snipers below were too good to let the brief opportunity pass. They shot the rifleman on the roof.

Forte slumped to the metal flooring of the warehouse roof. He leaned back on the door jamb of the stair exit. The gunman lay face down, a pool of red spreading out around him.

More sirens were advancing on the warehouse district. Radio static crackled in the cop cars jammed into every available space in the narrow lanes surrounding the warehouse rooftop where Forte sat.

Forte pulled his cell phone from his pocket. He hit speed-dial button number 2. The phone rang. Then rang again.

The man with the yellow eyes wiped the stinging sweat from his eyes. *Answer, dammit.*

It rang again. Forte felt the heat bearing down on him with more wet weight than he remembered in all the hot places he had endured.

Someone answered. But not with the usual hello.

The voice on the other line said: "Are we having fun yet?"

Forte felt his breath catch.

"Nomad, are the governor and his wife safe?"

"Yeah. They are a little shook up. And First Lady Shorty broke one of her heels. A real fashion tragedy. But that's the worst of it."

Forte nodded, then realized the other man couldn't see him. "Good," he said.

"Shooter's down, right?"

"Yeah."

"Dead?"

"Yeah."

Forte heard the other man curse. "Well, hell, there goes that info."

"I'll be right down. Tell the SWAT guys not to shoot me."

"Al," said Nomad, "One more thing."

"Yeah?"

"Next time, you ride out the bomb and I'll play hero."

"Deal."

Chapter 23

The girl on the opposite side of the streetcar was a people watcher. She took notice of everyone getting off and on the car as it rumbled along St. Charles away from downtown.

The big houses of the Garden District lumbered past the windows of the trolley. Then Loyola University. Then Audubon Zoo. Shops and restaurants and renovated storefronts glided past as the car rolled along with its cargo of tourists who wanted to ride the streetcars of New Orleans at least once before leaving town.

The girl, who looked to be eight years old, paid little heed to the sights. She studied the people.

Like the German couple with their maps and cameras and fanny packs. Or the urban scarecrow of a man with his carpentry tools clinking together in a five-gallon bucket. Or the group of three fourth-grade boys with their backward caps and fake toughness. Or the other large man in the back of the car with his Hawaiian shirt and knife tattoos.

But as much as she kept tracking all the other riders on the car, her attention kept returning to the man across from her.

He was dressed in black: Black chinos, a black tee-shirt, black leather high-top shoes. His black hair was cut short and finger-combed. He was not huge but when he reached up to flick the sweat off his earlobe, his biceps flexed enough to stretch his sleeve. When he took off his sunshades, he revealed unusual eyes. It was a color she had not seen before. They were an amber color, with violet highlights close to the pupil.

Arresting as they were, the man's eye color was not what interested the girl. It was something else, something behind the eyes. The girl only saw them for an instant as the yellow-eyed man pushed up the sunshades. But it was enough. Enough to see a sadness unlike any she had seen before in her young life. She wondered if it was always there in the man, this sadness. Or whether it was a one-time thing. Or maybe it came and went for him.

She realized she was staring.

The trolley rattled to a stop in front of an immaculately restored building with freshly painted white columns standing at ease along a wide front porch. The yellow-eyed man got off the streetcar. He stopped on the sidewalk as the car rolled away. The girl was looking out the window at him.

Forte finger-waved at her. She smiled. The trolley moved away.

He glanced to his right. The guy in the Hawaiian shirt had exited at the back of the streetcar. Forte nodded at him, but the man was taking note of all the shrubbery around the white-columned building, the traffic on the street, the bicyclists on the sidewalks, any movement anywhere.

Finally, the man nodded back at Forte, then led the way up the steps to the front door. He opened it for Forte before taking a seat on one of the sturdy rocking chairs.

Forte went through the door and kept walking straight down the dark-wood paneled hallway, past the bar where businessmen were partaking of early afternoon relaxation. The place was an upscale watering hole, far from the French Quarter tourists, where local power brokers or anyone needing a discreet meeting could come. Security cameras were casually disguised throughout the building. The bartenders and wait staff seemed particularly fit to be working in the hospitality industry. But they performed their jobs well here. As Forte passed the bar area, a broad-shouldered man in a starched apron deftly sliced lime into a mixed drink.

It was Nomad's place, an intriguing site beneath a façade of respectability. Nomad liked it that way.

Forte never asked where his SEAL partner procured the money needed to buy the house and renovate it into the kind of establishment it had become. He knew that Nomad had been approached by many in desperate need of his particular skill set. He never asked for details and his friend graciously never shared them.

He trusted that his longtime companero would draw a line against doing anything, even for money, which would hurt people who didn't deserve the pain. It was a belief that had never been controverted. Yet, he still was careful not to question Nomad too closely.

Forte came to a stairway with ornate carved handrails. He went up quickly. At the top of the stairs was a landing that led to a large meeting room. Through the open double doors he could see a heavy antique table about six feet by fifteen feet. The chairs had been pushed back against the wall. Brocade curtains were gathered at the corners of the ceiling-high windows. Sheers over the windows filtered the searing sun.

Forte knew that extensive renovation had been performed on the bar and not just for historic authenticity. Every room was fitted with hidden cameras and microphones. The glass of the windows could stop multiple rounds fired from all weapons but the most powerful. The fine Kevlar screen on the other side of the window glass would slow down most other bullets. In several rooms were secret compartments with weapons stowed for easy retrieval. A high-tech digital system could control everything in the house, from locking down every door and window, to pushing up the spikes on the roof's edge to thwart attackers rappelling from helicopters and extinguishing any fire with the latest flame retardant materials.

Nomad had covered the conference table with felt. A dozen weapons were laid across the felt in various stages of disassembly for cleaning purposes. Nomad sat on a high stool, hunched over an automatic rifle, a headlamp strapped to his head, the light focused on the gun.

"Nice ride on the streetcar?" he asked without looking up.

Forte shrugged. He slumped in a leather chair in the corner of the room.

Nomad kept working on the weapon. "You know I can't hear a shrug."

"Yeah, splendid ride," said Forte.

"Benny wear his big flowery shirt?"

"Yeah."

Nomad chuckled. "He thinks it's perfect for undercover security. Thinks nobody would suspect him of being a bodyguard when he's wearing it. As if he didn't have a 30-inch neck and arms the size of thighs."

Forte said nothing.

Nomad sighed and put down his metal file. He carefully took off the headlamp and set it on the felt. He walked over to another leather chair next to his friend and flopped down into it.

"I know they screwed up, killing that sniper on the roof of the warehouse," he said.

Forte grunted. "Just doing their job."

"True. But they screwed up our chances of finding out what the guy knew."

"You know about him, right?" Forte was looking at him directly now. "He looked familiar to me."

"Yeah, I went over it with Rosie...Agent Dent by phone a few minutes ago."

Like a phantom, a man in black pants and a starched collarless white shirt appeared at the door. "Rum and Coke for me and water with lemon for my friend Mr. Forte." The man disappeared down the hallway.

Nomad continued. "Here's what I know: We have a tentative verification by photo of the shooter. He was Jerry Courson, a retired Army Ranger who mainly worked as a sharpshooter. He mustered out of the Special Forces seven years ago. His whereabouts are a little murky in his official file after that. But it doesn't take much guesswork to assume he has been involved in some shady mercenary stuff."

Forte glanced over at him. "It's not really guesswork for you about that."

Nomad nodded. "No, but it's not useful to share that with the FBI people. Jerry was on a team I led to escort a big shot out of Central America about four years ago. It was one of those blind arrangements: we never knew who we worked for; the money just showed up in our accounts.

"But I remember him being knowledgeable about the region, about the whole setup, more than the other team members, as if he had inside knowledge." He cursed softly under his breath. "If he was alive, we might know something."

The steward arrived with two glasses on a tray. He set them down and left without a word.

Nomad took his drink and took a slug of it. "Ahhh, the pause that refreshes." He set down the drink. "Oh, well, no use crying over spilt brain matter."

Forte looked over the top of his glass at his friend. "So, where are we in all this mess?"

Nomad slumped lower in his overstuffed chair, his drink balanced on his chest. "Here's the rundown: We have two kidnapped kids, one boy and one girl. One is the child of the Governor, the other the child of the man who accidentally killed your wife. The demand from both sets of kidnappers is the same: Al Forte for the hostage. There is no established connection between the two situations. It is suspected that Chug, the ex-con gangbanger, is behind the taking of Freddy Bailey. We think his puppet strings are being plucked by a bigger mover yet to be determined."

He took another pull at his drink, then continued. "The boy is still gone but the girl is recovered easily. In fact, too easily. She seems to be merely a decoy. The bombing occurs and even that seems set up to draw a certain Mr. Forte closer to the area where the sniper is waiting."

Forte interrupted. "You never told me how you suspected the car bomb."

Nomad set his drink aside now. "I didn't suspect much. The place was crawling with the governor's bodyguards and undercover cops. The governor seemed more nervous than scared for his daughter. He steered us to a specific car, one about 30 feet away from his official car that blew up."

Forte abruptly stood. He walked around the table fingering the components of the weapons. "Sounds like he knew something ahead of time."

"Nothing surprises me anymore," said Nomad.

"Sounds like we need to talk to the governor," Forte said.

"Sounds like we do."

Forte stopped fiddling with the guns on the table. He caught his friend's eye. "You didn't happen to mention to the FBI about the governor steering you to a particular car, did you?"

Nomad slapped his forehead. "Lawhavemercy, it completely slipped my mind."

Forte chuckled. He realized it had been a few days since he had laughed.

He came back to the chair and dropped into it again.

Classical music permeated the entire building, as if it came from nowhere and everywhere. Forte closed his eyes and listened to it. It seemed familiar, but he wasn't one to take pride in the names of famous composers and their works. Chopin maybe. He drifted and as he did he replayed the action on the warehouse roof. He could see the man's eyes, the flash of surprise then recognition when he whirled toward Forte. In his mind, he zoomed all the way to the man's eyes. They filled the entire screen on his mind. The surprise only lasted a tenth of a second. Then another emotion replaced it.

What was it? Forte furrowed his brow, his eyes still closed. Maybe it was anger. Hmm, a bit of anger, yes. But that wasn't the main emotion he saw. He replayed it again. The head turning. Eyes widening. Big surprise. Recognition. Then…what was that flash of feeling?

Rewind. The man firing at the officers below as the music trilled, the staccato piano notes keeping time with the automatic weapons. Then, the crash of a cymbal as the bullet hit his thigh. The soaring violins as he spun toward Forte.

Then, the eyes. Wide. And then, recognition. And that emotion.

What was it?

As his mind dug it out, that emotion, he felt the blackness of dread spreading over his consciousness like an oil slick.

Still drifting, he shook his head, trying to free himself from the fear.

Fear. That was the emotion in the sniper's eyes. More than anger, more than surprise. It was fear.

But he had seen that look before when guns were being fired.

At a special place and time.

What was it?

He felt himself sinking. He knew he was drifting into sleep, sliding toward a nightmare.

Where had he seen that look of fear when someone was firing a weapon at another?

He could see it. The darkness only tinged with the yellow of streetlamps. The late night darkness of an alley.

When was it? Where was the man with fear in his eyes while a gun was exploding?

He saw the gun in someone's hand. No, don't shoot.

He saw red. Oh no, please, not her. Can't hold it in, all the blood. All the life oozing out of her, squeezing between my fingers no matter how tightly I hold them together.

The fear, the awful fear that could not be prevented.

He jerked. Martin. Martin Bailey, the gun bucking in his hands. Was the fear in his eyes? Yes, yes, it was. But not like this fear.

This fear was one of understanding. One of going forward because the fear of shooting was trumped by the larger terror of something else.

Whose eyes held that fear?

Forte moaned in his sleep in the chair.

Who? Who!

He bolted upright.

It was Chug. His eyes were both fascinated by the sight of Ruth Forte being killed and so afraid of it at the same time.

Forte turned to see Nomad focusing on him.

His friend said nothing.

What does it mean? Why would Chug be so afraid so long ago in that senseless accident?

His cell phone rang. He put it to his ear. He said "Thanks" and hung up.

"Got a car I can borrow?" he asked.

"Sure," said Nomad. "I'll have Benny bring a car around front."

"I don't need a babysitter for this."

Nomad repeated his statement as if Forte had said nothing. "Good. I'll have Benny bring the car."

The two men stared at each other for a long beat: Forte's face stony and Nomad's a mask of serenity.

Finally, Forte looked away. "Okay, but this little trip is just among us."

Nomad sipped his rum and Coke mixture.

"Ain't that how it always is?"

Chapter 24

Forte leaned on the lamppost out in the median of Canal Street, across from the sign that read "Saratoga Garage" at the Tulane Cancer Center. From where he stood, he could see the line of palm trees the city had spent $13 million replanting after Katrina. He spent little time second-guessing the decisions of politicians. Or anyone, for that matter. He usually just dealt with what was in front of him. It was both his strongest and weakest trait, a counselor had once told him.

Two blocks away down South Liberty he could see Benny's Hawaiian shirt as if it were a vacation billboard. The big bodyguard was leaning against the Jeep that Nomad had let them borrow.

After 10 minutes of baking in the Big Easy sun, Forte saw Jackie Shaw come out of the building on the opposite corner.

Just as she was about to take a left on the sidewalk of Canal, she saw him. She stopped and cocked her head, the sun catching the white streak in her otherwise black hair. Then she grinned at him.

For a full second – a long time in this world sometime – Forte took in the image of her standing there. It seemed as if his mind were embossing this particular scene on his mind.

He pushed off the post and jogged to her. When he got close to her, he removed his sunshades.

Her smile had become impish. She took both his hands in hers and stood on her tiptoes to offer a kiss. He kissed her, his eyes open.

Hers stayed open too, and they viewed the unfocused color of each other's irises as they embraced. The traffic whooshed past. Someone honked a horn.

Jackie closed her eyes. She pressed her lips against his a fraction longer than he expected. Then she pulled away.

Her eyes were shiny. "I'm not even going to ask how you knew I was here."

"Good," he said, "don't ask."

She took his hand and said, "I walked here from The Refuge. Walk me back." She tugged and he easily went with the motion.

Ahead, the Jeep crossed Canal and idled on the street. Benny carefully avoided looking in their direction. He was continually scanning the surrounding streets and buildings.

Jackie squeezed his hand. "So, Nomad sent Benny to look after you. He must be worried."

"Yeah, he's afraid he won't get the twenty bucks I owe him."

She punched his arm lightly. "You know he would die for you. And you for him."

Forte did not reply quickly. When he did, his voice was low. "I know."

"I heard about the car bomb and the shootouts. Both of them. You've had a busy day."

"Yep. Barrels of fun."

"Sorry I missed it."

They made their way to Rampart and turned left.

The Refuge was in the northern part of the French Quarter but still a long stroll from the cancer center. The August heat emanated from the pavement. Forte was mildly amused at himself for being relieved to be alive after the past 24 hours. At this point, the heat was a mere nuisance to him.

He glanced at Jackie. "So, you knew about everything today. And about Benny trailing me today."

"Yes, Nomad told me."

Forte shook his head and mumbled, "That traitor."

Behind them about thirty yards, Benny crawled along in the Jeep. Occasionally, his muscled arm would jut out of the driver's side window and wave other cars around him.

"So, he knew about your visit to the cancer center," Forte said. His voice carried more of an edge than he intended.

"Yep." The woman at his side kept her face forward, her eyes now hidden behind sunglasses. She squeezed his hand and it almost startled him. He had forgotten they had been walking along with hands clasped.

He had been thinking about her. Jackie Shaw had grown up the daughter of widowed Boston cop who taught her how to shoot at an early age. Her dad had done the best he could for his daughter, paying for gymnastic lessons when he saw she had that talent. He told everyone he knew that she would make a great cop. But her heart wasn't in it, at that time. She married young to the wrong kind of man and after he left, she refused to go home to her daddy for comfort. Instead, she became a nun. She gravitated toward helping the poorest of poor children and found herself on the border of Mexico for years. When her priest was found red-handed guilty of impropriety, she drifted along for a while. Until she connected with Forte Security.

A bout with cervical cancer years earlier had left her barren. Forte's commitment to rescuing children resonated with a deep longing within her. She had experienced every facet of The Refuge and the operation of Forte Security: the administrative behind-the-scenes drudgery that Forte never touched; the therapeutic play with children who had been threatened; the tutoring and emotional healing of older children who found themselves sequestered at this secret hideaway in The Quarter; the actual missions to rescue children.

And she had found a place in Forte's heart.

"You are a thousand miles away," Jackie said.

He realized he had been walking with no memory of the actual cracks in the sidewalks or the unique whiskey-garbage-sweat aroma of The Quarter or the sizzling sun on his face.

"In some ways, yes," he said. "But in some ways, I'm closer than I've ever been."

They had reached the back entrance of The Refuge, in the back alley where he had left on his motorcycle.

He pulled her to him and kissed her again. He felt her press into his arms, folding herself into his grasp. They had kissed before, but this was different. She seemed eager to be as close to him as possible, as if his strength was what she needed. He could feel the buzz of a moan on her mouth more than actually hearing it. Her gymnast body seemed more vulnerable than usual against him, her smell sweeter, her skin softer. The kiss built in intensity. He felt the blood rushing through him as they embraced in the heat of the alley. Her hands gripped his back and began to roam over him, differently than she had ever touched him. A desperate sensuality moved back and forth between them.

He picked her up, her legs around his waist now, her back against the batter bricks of The Refuge. He could feel his pulse in his temple as she broke the kiss and began rapidly kissing him all over his face, his neck. The hot puffs of breath from her mouth warmed his skin. A groaning passed back and forth between them, and it was building.

He wanted her as much as he ever had.

"Oh, Al," she murmured.

Then she put her face against his shoulder.

And began to cry.

"Oh, baby," he whispered. "I'm here."

And he held her.

After a moment, their breathing subsided to near normal.

He gently lowered her.

She tiptoed and kissed his cheek.

He pulled her hand up to his lips and kissed the palm.

Out of the corner of his eye, Forte saw the red Jeep. Benny was studiously looking in every direction except toward the couple in the alley. Even from this distance, however, a smile was evident on his face.

Forte looked back toward Jackie.

Her face held an expression unlike any he had seen before. A serenity was there, a peace not of this earth. And there was something else. What was it?

He studied her eyes, those beautiful eyes.

And he saw it. The acceptance of it.

His cell phone rang. He answered and listened briefly. He clicked it off.

Her eyes had changed now. They mirrored the look he must have had when he answered the phone. He saw a sadness in them, not for herself but for him.

"Larue?" she asked.

Somehow she knew, of all the phone calls with news he could have received at that moment, that it was about the man who had assumed the role of father after his grandmother had passed away.

In that instant, an image flashed in his mind: Larue, standing behind his barber's chair in the shop as a 13-year-old Al Forte came through the front door, bell clanging. The old Creole's cracked-leather face rarely let a smile wander across its worn features. But that day, the slightest of grins touched the corners of his mouth.

"I am quitting," the young Al said, letting his football helmet drop to the floor of the barber shop. He slumped on the ancient leather sofa.

"Bad game, eh, cher," the barber said. He took a broom and began herding clipped hair on the floor in his meticulous strokes.

"We lost," the boy said. His jersey was streaked with mud and spotted with blood. His hair was spiked with dried sweat. A bruise was forming on his cheek bone. "And coach didn't put me in at the right time."

"Ah." Larue continued making neat piles of hair around the three barber chairs.

The boy hit his thigh band hard with his fist. "I could've stopped them. I could've tackled that guy." Already Al Forte was becoming a formidable defensive player at the linebacker position.

"So, you want to quit then?"

"Yes."

Larue slowly lifted the broom and hung it on a nail in the corner of the shop. "Go on, then. Do it."

Al sat up and searched the man's face. "It is okay with you?"

"Sure. It's your game."

"Just like that?"

"Yes, cher. Just like that." The words came out: Jes Lack Dat.

The boy jumped up from the sofa and paced. He continued talking as if Larue had argued with him. "The coach doesn't know what he's doing. I could've helped him." He ran his hand over his bruised face.

"Quit then, baby boy." Larue pointed at the clunky black rotary dial phone on the counter. "Just call your teammates and tell them."

"My teammates? Why? It's the coach who screwed up."

"Maybe true, but the team is the one be sufferin' when you quit. You owe it to them to tell them like a man, don't you?"

The boy stood. He took a single step toward the phone. He stared into the middle distance for a long beat.

"Then what did he say?" Jackie asked.

Forte snapped back to the present, back to the alley where they were standing behind The Refuge.

"It was the doctor. Larue's gone."

She wrapped him in her arms again, this time to comfort him.

Chapter 25

Freddy looked out over the garden from the balcony of the guest house. It was something like he had seen in a magazine at school. A path meandered through lilies and orchids. Palm trees towered above Elephant Leaf plants and ferns with various stripes and hues of green. A stucco wall, twice his height, provided the boundary for the garden.

He had no idea where he was. He just knew he was still a captive.

The walls and locked doors and security alarms had nothing to do with it.

The boy had been standing on the balcony thinking about his situation for the past half hour. It was the longest he could remember being still for that long while he was awake. The breeze blew the fronds of the tropical plants and the parrots danced on the limbs of the magnolia trees. On another day, the scene would have been interesting to him.

He was thinking about what the new man had said. The man who owned the big house.

The others – a man called Chug and his two giant friends – had thrown him into the back seat of a Hummer after they caught him at the barber shop. He had tried to scream but the one named Pea had gently clamped a hand the size of a baseball mitt over his face. It had covered his entire face, blotting out any sights along the drive to the mansion where he was now. But he remembered the look on Chug's face before the hand covered him.

It was a look of seething disgust, one devoid of compassion. As much as the pair of muscled bodyguards frightened him, they were practically comforting compared to the chill he felt under the leader's gaze. It reminded Freddy of being a few feet away from the cobra at the zoo, separated from death by a pane of thick glass. Something was restraining Chug from destroying the boy. Freddy was pretty sure the thing that kept Chug at bay was not the man's conscience.

When the big SUV had stopped rolling and the hand was removed, he was in paradise. But one without joy, like the way a beautiful sunshiny day seems sapped of its beauty on the day a loved one dies. The two giants had walked him between the columns and through the massive front doors of the house. Chug led the way.

Freddy watched the leader advance ahead of them. He had the dangerous athletic walk of a man who would deliver pain without flinching. His smooth movements were not exaggerated, like so many of the street punks and gang bangers Freddy had seen in and around his neighborhood. An odd thought crossed the boy's mind: what a great athlete Chug might have been in another world. If not for the fear, Freddy would have pitied the man.

Now was not the time for pity. It was the time for paying attention.

The men led him through a large room with fancy paintings on the walls but very little furniture. Their steps echoed against the polished marble floors. They kept going until they passed through a sunroom that was larger than the apartment he and his dad lived in.

Dad. The mere thought of his father nearly stunned him with sadness. If he could only see him again, Freddy thought, he would always be a good boy, never give him a second's worth of trouble again. It wasn't just for himself he mourned, however. It nearly crushed him to think how much his dad missed him and was hurt by his absence. He had heard rumors of the trouble Martin Bailey had brought on himself as a boy. But he knew this: his father loved him more dearly than anything else in this world.

Freddy had been careful to notice as much as he could about the big house as they walked through it, trying to memorize every door and window. If he got a chance, if the scary men ever left him alone, he was gone.

The sun room was filled with plants and small trees, so much so that the man at the rattan table in the corner was hidden from the group until they were right on him.

The man was dressed in riding clothes, the kind that Freddy had seen on TV at a polo match. He was seated facing away from the group at the table with a tall drink at this right hand. Next to the glass was a riding crop. His reddish hair was thinning but the neck muscles from the back showed him to be strong for a man of 50 or so.

Freddy felt the hand of Troll, the other giant, on his shoulder, stopping him about 10 feet from the table. The hand wrapped over his shoulder until the big fingers gripped him all the way down to his collar bone.

The man called Chug went ahead. He bent and whispered in the seated man's ear. The man nodded once. Chug stepped back.

Freddy felt the hand on his shoulder push him forward.

He walked forward until he was facing the new man.

"Have a seat, please, Freddy," the man said.

The voice was gentle but something about it scared Freddy as much as anything else in this nightmare weekend of his life. His fight-or-flight impulse flared so much that if not for the grip of the huge man to his right, he would have darted away through the simulated jungle of the sun room His stomach lurched.

He sat down.

"I know you have had a miserable couple of days," the man said. "I'm sorry that it was necessary, all things considered."

Freddy swallowed hard, fighting the urge to throw up. Something about this new situation unsettled him. *What am I afraid of?*

"Have a drink. It is your favorite," the man said, his voice still calm.

The boy noticed for the first time the soft drink in front of him. A trickle of condensation ran down the outside of the glass. He hesitated.

"Go ahead. Nothing to fear from that drink."

Freddy wanted to say something, but nothing would come out. He picked up the mug and sipped it. Then, as if he couldn't refrain, he drained the mug.

"Good boy," said the man with the red hair. "Now, I have another gift for you." He nodded to one of the huge bodyguards who spoke into his cell phone.

From a distance came the sound of an animal running through the mansion. Through the big empty room next door the boy could hear galloping noises of a small dog's paws against the tiles.

Freddy sat up straight. He knew that sound.

The running stopped when the dog reached the sun room. Was it smelling the air?

The boy called out. "Callie?"

The dog, still out of sight, spun its feet against the floor, furiously seeking traction now. Then, it was running again, faster.

Through the path between the flowers came a honey-colored bullet of fur. The dog leaped into Freddy's arms and began licking his face.

The boy pressed his beloved mutt to his chest. He burst into tears of joy.

"Oh, Callie," he whispered. He had worried so much about her when he was first taken by the men. Then he had forgotten about her briefly after the men were murdered at the other house. Now, just seeing that she was alive and safe filled him with relief.

The man in the polo clothes picked up the riding crop from the table. With moves both smooth and efficient, he reached over the tabletop and ran the end of the whip over the dog's head and shoulders.

Callie flinched but did not whine. Freddy froze, the terror of his situation hitting him hard again.

"She is your sweet dog, isn't she, Freddy?" the man asked, his voice so mellow and low now it was like he was whispering a lullaby.

Freddy nodded, unable to say a word.

"You love her," the man said.

Again, Freddy nodded.

"You love your father."

Freddy made eye contact now with the man. He was sorry he did.

Though the man's voice was soft, his eyes were dead. Freddy flinched at the evil in those eyes.

"Give Callie to the man," the voice commanded.

Freddy hugged his puppy to himself again, then handed her over.

The man walked away. The click of his heels faded. But the whining of the dog could be heard until a door closed in some distant room in the big house.

Freddy felt the darkness descend on him again, even though the room was filled with light.

"Now is the time for you to understand something, Freddy." The man at the table stood. He tapped the riding crop against his leg as he spoke.

"You will have no locks on your door here. No one will treat you badly. You can leave whenever you like."

Freddy lifted his head, incredulous.

"But if you do," the man said. "Your precious Callie won't be safe. And neither will your father."

Freddy's eyes filled with tears again. He opened his mouth to speak but could only nod.

"Very good," said the red-haired man. "And now I must attend the wake of a dear man who has passed away. Enjoy your stay here, Freddy Bailey."

Chapter 26

Spanish moss hung like tassels from the shoulders of the gnarled oaks standing guard around the church. The building itself was nothing special compared to the modern cathedrals of the cities throughout the South. It was made of white clapboard with a roof patched with newer tiles. The stained-glass windows had surrendered a few panes to the storms over the years. It wasn't a place included on any scenic tours. In fact, Larue had quietly joked that the church wasn't on the way to anyplace else.

It was tucked into the wooded piece of relative high ground surrounded by swamps. It was where the Cajuns in the area gathered to worship.

It was a place Larue frequented far more often than Forte had realized.

He stood in the shadows of one of the smaller oaks on the perimeter of the church grounds. His one and only Checkers of the day hung from his fingertips. He raised it to his lips and took a draw. The expelled haze formed a gauze through which to view the vehicles and people scattered throughout the grounds, the crowd having spilled out of the church building itself.

The sun had settled beyond the horizon but the heat had only begun to diminish a few degrees. His lightweight silk jacket hung from a low-lying branch. He wore a black silk tee and silk pants.

"You know why you pull off this black on black look all the time?" asked Fizer Beal, the resident computer geek at The Refuge.

Forte took another puff from the Checkers. "What do you mean 'pull off' this look?"

"You know. You make it look...cool. It works because you don't really care about it. The whole 'cool look' thing."

Forte glanced at him. "You figured all that out, huh."

Fizer had been rescued by Forte from some very bad men who had also murdered the boy's father. He had been awarded to Forte in a guardianship agreement by the courts. Basically, The Refuge had been his home for the past five years. For the first year, the young Beal had been in awe of Forte for what he had done for him. Forte had done nothing to rush the relationship, allowing Fizer to gain the security he needed. He had come out of his shell as he had discovered his particular skills for computer science.

Since becoming a college student, he had revealed a ponderous curiosity about most everything associated with Forte and The Refuge.

Forte had made the rounds inside the church earlier, hugging and receiving hugs from the dozens of cousins and aunts and nieces and nephews of Larue.

His face was tired from smiling. He had escaped to this hiding place after a half-hour inside. Fizer had been the only one to find him. So far. Now the young man was making small talk to break up the solemnity of the day.

From where they stood, they could see the entire area but couldn't be seen easily.

Everyone from his life, it seemed, was present at the wake of Larue.

Archie and Verna Griffey, his longtime friends and fellow workers at The Refuge, had already organized all of Larue's affairs during his long illness. The old barber had shared simple and straightforward directions about his affairs. The Griffeys had relayed them to Forte, who had done what he had always done about details: he nodded and thanked the Griffeys and others close to him who were gifted in that area. The Griffeys had coordinated everything perfectly with Larue's family for the wake.

His high school teammate, Mack Quadrie and his wife, Renee had brought boxes of favorite dishes from their restaurant in The Quarter. Larue had not been there much but they knew the dishes he liked most: Crawfish Etoufee and Jambalaya, with the occasional Oyster Po-Boy. Mack, who still looked like he could flatten an NFL running back – a feat he had accomplished regularly during his professional career at defensive tackle– set up the church kitchen for the wake and had sung along in Cajun French during the hymns.

Another old high school friend, Jonathan Brach, remained in the corner of the sanctuary where Larue's casket was on open display in the front. He briefly chatted with Nomad, who never stayed in one place for long. Brach was without the reporter's notebook that seem glued to his hand as a journalist for the state's largest newspaper. But Forte knew he was soaking up the flavor of the event. He couldn't help it; he was a writer.

Interspersed with the crowd of relatives and friends of the ancient barber were undercover cops, most from the FBI, some of whom Forte recognized, some not. He knew they were there. And, out around the edges of the church grounds were a few more people with guns. Some were employees of Forte Security, some were former cops, a few were ex-military. Nobody expected trouble tonight, but considering the attacks on Forte recently, everybody was taking precautions.

Two women came out of the church and stood talking on to the front landing of the church. Jackie Shaw and Rosalind Dent both wore black and looked lovely to Forte, even considering the occasion.

Rosie, usually conscious of her position as a leading female agent in a male-dominated agency, wore a dress that couldn't hide her long-legged model looks. She looked more feminine than Forte remembered. Her face was only slightly made up, but it was enough to show her beauty. Even at a funeral service she drew admiring glances from men of all ages.

Jackie seemed bigger than she actually was. Something about her presence projected a persona that made people surprised at her actual size – if they ever heard the specifications. It wasn't as if she tried to seem different than she was. There was no bravado about her, no loudness except in emergencies, nothing that seemed pushy or over the top. It was her assurance in who she was and what she was doing on this planet. That confidence produced a type of energy that seemed to buzz around her even when she was still.

Yet, for all of her strength, Jackie was unafraid to show her feminine side with a man – if she admired and respected that man. And that was the rub. She had met few who fit the bill. Certainly her ex-husband had not. And since then she had not actually extended her emotional antenna in the direction of any man.

With Forte, it caught her by surprise, by her own admission. She had known of his past before she came to work for Forte Security – the death of his wife, the addiction and his slide into hell, then the slow recovery. He had been rescuing children for a few years before meeting her. It was all he did, that and go to AA meetings with his friend and sponsor, Manning Laird.

A spiritual person, Jackie had connected with Manny and, even though the two never formally conspired against Forte, their prayers and influence had been used to soften his heart to God. And to Jackie.

He had never been an open person. His parents had not been warm, and he realized later in life that he had built a tough guy persona to protect himself emotionally. When his parents died in a car accident on the Mississippi Gulf Coast, the seven-year-old Al

Forte went to live with his father's mother in New Orleans. She worked at a liquor store on St. Charles right around the corner from Larue's barber shop. A few years later, she died. Forte was 13. By that time, he was big enough and athletic enough to assume the physical role of tough guy. He excelled in every sport he entered.

His temper, however, came close to ruining any aspirations he had for a clean life. Expulsion from school loomed more than once. His fists were fast and dangerous. Larue patiently walked him through the shaky times without browbeating him or threatening.

His entry into the Navy, and eventually the SEALS, was a perfect fit for his skills and temperament. He quickly impressed every trainer he encountered and, when sent with SEAL teams on actual missions, excelled to the point when he was recognized as the best of the best, a Team Six member. He did it, however, without much navel gazing. He was a natural. Only with his brother-in-arms Nomad would he even joke about his ability.

By the time he met Ruth, he was almost ready to become a human being, Nomad had claimed jokingly many times. She drew him out more. Yet, he knew there was still part of himself buried, some component of his heart he could not uncover. Even with her.

When she was killed, his heart was avalanched again. The alcohol, then the drugs, piled on until he was nearly lost to anyone who ever knew or cared about him.

Forte came back to the present, shaking free from his reverie. He took another long drag from the cigarette and held it as he idly noted the people milling in and out of the church.

"My condolences, Mr. Forte," said a man's voice to his left.

Forte could see the man's shape in the semidarkness beneath the tree. Automatically he took a step back, though the voice was low and nonthreatening.

"It's been a while," said Brock Randall.

Forte recognized the man now. It had been a while. He had crossed paths with Randall a few times since the reception a decade

176

earlier where he had met Ruth. Mostly their conversations had occurred at social gatherings where Randall made the rounds glad-handing politicians and other purveyors of power and influence. Forte could usually be found leaning against a wall, merely making an appearance when requested.

Randall was a tall man with a military bearing, but most rumors pegged him as a former spy in one of the sneaky departments of government. His red hair was trimmed close to his head. He wore an immaculate beige suit, an odd choice for a funeral service. Forte wondered if it was intentional.

He forced himself to maintain a polite tone.

"Yes it has, Mr. Randall. Thank you for coming," Forte said. He extended a handshake. The older man took it.

From inside the church came the sound of the piano launching into another hymn. Voices lifted a song without prompting.

"I didn't know that you knew Larue."

"I didn't, really," Randall said. "I knew he was close to you."

"I appreciate that."

"We are, after all, a close-knit community."

"A community?"

"Yes. Ex-military, law enforcement, security. People who do the things we do."

"The things we do."

Forte filled his lungs with another long pull from the Checkers and exhaled slowly, thankful for the break from talking that the cigarette had given him.

On more than one occasion, Brock Randall had tried to lure him away from the SEALs to work for his international security company. A fog of suspicion had always floated around the company, however. Nothing specific, just the kind of rumors that usually turned out to have some basis of truth eventually.

"Still have a job for you, Al." The man's voice was closer now, and softer.

"I appreciate that, Mr. Randall. I believe I'll just mourn for my friend here tonight."

Manny Laird came out on the steps of the church now. His white hair was as unruly as ever and even from a distance of 50 yards his blue eyes shone. He was wearing a black suit and tie and a white starched shirt. Forte couldn't remember the last time he had seen his mentor and friend in a suit.

When he faced Randall again, the man was standing with his hands folded in front of him. He pointed at the old preacher on the porch. "You have many friends, Mr. Forte. I'm sure you could help them more with ten times the money you make chasing those kids around at The Refuge."

Forte frowned in the dim light. "You have no idea how much money we bring in."

"You would be astonished what I know, Al."

The man's tone was still civil, yet a chilly edge had crept in.

Forte faced the man now. He could see a pair of bodyguards flanking the businessman now under the outer edge of the tree line.

"Do tell, Mr. Randall. What do you know? What do you think is important to share on this night when we are gathered to remember my friend?"

He didn't realize the strength in his voice until the bodyguards had stepped to each side of the man in the tan suit. Forte automatically sized them up and evaluated their combat readiness.

The one on the right had bodybuilder arms and a ponytail but his movements had more strut than skill. He would go down quickly in a real fight.

The man on the left, however, was deceptive. He wore a crew cut and seemed thicker around the middle but when he stepped out a bit further, he showed he would be dangerous. He would be the one to take out first.

Forte saw a flicker in the man's eyes.

A movement to Forte's left caught his eye. When he glanced, he saw that Nomad had appeared out of the darkness without a sound.

"Howdy, boys," said Nomad.

Randall's face had not changed an iota. It still displayed the pleasant fake smile he had worn since he encountered Forte under the tree.

"Well, it seems we've made you uncomfortable, Mr. Forte. Many pardons, friend. We will blend away into the gray now." With that he walked away. The wide man with the crew cut followed. Ponytail stayed behind.

"Shoo, boy. Before you get your ass whipped," Nomad said softly.

The bodyguard took one step forward. Instantly, he was on the ground, holding his throat. The noises coming from him sounded like he was strangling. He was clutching his throat, his mouth wide open in an expression of both horror and pain.

Nomad knelt next to him, slapped his hands away, and gingerly felt around the man's Adam's apple. Satisfied, he stood.

"I didn't think I hit him hard enough to dislodge it. He'll live. He may talk funny for the rest of his life but he'll live." He tapped the man with his boot. "Told you to shoo. Now, git."

Ponytail man struggled to his feet. He scampered away into the darkness.

Forte said nothing for a long beat. "Guess you couldn't help yourself, huh."

"Hey, you got to slap around Governor Shorty." He looked down at his right hand and flexed his fingers. "Beside, his ponytail was too stylish. He needed a little frazzling around the edges."

"You frazzled him alright."

Nomad grinned. "Indeed I did."

The pair stood in silence for a moment.

"Speaking of the governor, you saw him here earlier, right?" Nomad asked

Forte nodded.

"We need to go talk to him."

Again, Forte nodded.

"There's something hinky about his daughter's kidnapping," Nomad said.

Forte regarded his friend for a beat.

Nomad shrugged. "I know nobody ever really says 'hinky' 'cept on TV. I just thought I'd try it out."

"And how did you like it?"

"Sounded goofy, huh."

"A tad."

Chapter 27

Forte stood on the balcony of his apartment, which occupied part of the third floor of The Refuge. His black cat tightroped its way along the wrought-iron railing.

"Boo, you are part monkey," he said.

The cat stopped and peered at his so-called master. He continued on his way. When he came to the end of the balcony rail he simply leapt over the edge out of sight. To someone who didn't know the ledge below, it appeared the animal had jumped to his death thirty feet below. Forte knew that Boo was circling the perimeter of the building, seeking an unsuspecting pigeon to maul.

Forte stood for a moment longer looking out over the railing, seeing nothing. In the distance a band blared from inside a club in The Quarter as someone must have opened the door, then closed it quickly to keep the cool air inside. The night was stifling except for a slight breeze that blew across the upper floor where Forte rested.

The day had started with surprises and had ended with sadness. He had been shot at twice: First by an angry group of bikers, second by a sniper trained in assassination tactics. He understood the first attack; the second mystified him. He had rescued one child who didn't seem to actually be in danger; another child, the son of the man who had killed his wife, was still in the hands of kidnappers who had yet to identify themselves fully. He had seen his adopted father succumb to disease. He suspected that Larue had suffered a good deal more than he let on. "You tough old bird," he said aloud.

His eyes misted. *I'll miss you, friend.* But he wasn't crushed by the news of Larue's demise. He had been around death enough to know there was time to go that was right and a time to go that was wrong. The old barber had lived life in his low-key way and seemed to have enjoyed it exactly the way he wanted.

Forte was thankful the man was suffering no longer.

And he was comforted by the fact that Larue had seen him come out of the dark hole of his addiction and establish an organization that saved kids.

Forte had come back to the apartment to sleep for a while before the next morning's briefing about the kidnappings and their aftermath. But he was still too wired. He changed clothes from the wake. He still wore black, but this outfit was more comfortable. And built for speed. And action. Black cotton tee, black SWAT pants tucked into lightweight high-top rubber-soled boots. Black holster at the small of his back that held his Glock. It was the basic "on alert" uniform he would rest in during the night until the call came from the kidnappers.

He walked back through his apartment. In the back wall of his walk-in closet was a button. He pushed it and the wall slid open. He walked through it into the top floor of The Refuge. He had outfitted the secret entrance before any of the other renovations to the building. He had yet to use the sliding closet wall entrance for anything other than convenience.

But that didn't mean it wouldn't save someone's life one day.

He strolled along the running track that overlooked the play area in the courtyard below. At this hour, no children were present. It was the area where he had been interviewed by the video crew. Was that just two days ago? It seemed like a month ago, so much had happened.

He took a spiral staircase down to the first floor. Usually, two guards were on duty. One manned the security desk surrounded by a bank of small video monitors. The other guard was a roamer – he periodically walked the entire building. Halfway through their shift, the men switched.

Tonight there were four men on duty – desk man, two inside roamers, and one outside roamer.

Forte could have easily let his pride dictate the loosening of the protective details this night. He had spent too much time in dangerous duty, however, not to value the importance of extra trained men when there were clear threats against him.

He nodded to the desk man as he passed.

He continued meandering around the building thinking he would eventually end up in the den where he had seen Fizer earlier.

On the bottom floor were administrative offices where Verna Griffey, Jackie Shaw and various support staff handled the never-ending paperwork of both Forte Security and The Refuge. Because of its ongoing relations with the courts and various government agencies, The Refuge continually updated its records to show it was compliant with childcare regulations of the city of New Orleans, the state of Louisiana, and the United States government.

Every administrative detail was carefully kept current. Forte, though he abhorred the keeping of these details, insisted on it from the start. He had learned during his life in the armed services that a missed decimal on some report by some clerk could cost the life of a man on the battlefield.

The Refuge had been funded originally from the estate of Ruth Forte after her death. Her life had been all about giving hope to children. Her family had been fairly well off, enough so that she actually never had to work. But she had felt a calling to do the work she did with kids. She had left everything to her husband with Verna Griffey as the administrator of a huge trust fund.

It was as if she knew Forte would tumble into a place where availability of resources would have fueled his destruction. Because of the way the trust fund was set up, he couldn't touch any of the money without Verna's approval. Not that Al had shown any interest in the fortune that could have been his during that time. He had his Navy pension and plenty of savings to squander for a while.

By the time he had spent it all on drugs, he had nearly destroyed himself. He surfaced from his self-built prison to find himself in rehab, a move engineered by Verna and her husband, Ozzie, with physical assistance from Nomad in between one of his mercenary missions.

Forte shut down his mental ramblings and realized he was on the second floor of The Refuge. This was the location of the quarters for the children who were being temporarily protected. The feel of this floor was entirely different from other areas of the building. Forte stopped and ran his hand over the crudely drawn poster boards on the wall. Only two children were asleep in one of the large bedrooms on this floor. They had apparently occupied part of their day in art therapy.

The drawing that held Forte's attention was alive with color. In the dim hallway he bent closer to make out the shapes. He could see lopsided trees and a swing set and a couple of shapes he assumed were bicycles. Ah, a park. Two children, one brown and the other orange, were flying kites in a lavender sky. On the edge of the page was a bigger figure, a man in black.

The man in the picture had yellow eyes.

Forte smiled. He continued his nocturnal rambling.

As he passed the small kitchen area off the hallway, he stopped and reversed his steps.

Verna Griffey was seated at one of the small white round tables in the kitchen.

Her large frame obliterated the view of the chair. She was not fat, exactly, just large. She was tall and wide and capable of emotions ranging from serious anger to tender compassion – often in the space of a heartbeat.

A coffee mug rested in her thick hands. Her head was bowed. Her brown face looked as peaceful as he had seen it for days. He realized she was dozing.

Forte tapped lightly on the door.

The only thing that moved on the woman was a single eyelid over her left eye. It fluttered open. The eye focused on him. She smiled.

"Baby," Verna said, "You caught me napping." She leaned back and stretched, still seated in the chair.

Forte patted her on the shoulder as he walked over to the coffee pot. "Decaf?" he asked. She nodded. He poured himself a cup and sat at the table.

He took a swallow of the coffee and made an "ahhh" sound. Over the rim of the mug he could see Verna smiling sleepily.

"What?" he said.

"Oh, nothing. You just been making that same noise after you drink coffee ever since I've known you." She took a sip of her brew. "The big, bad Al Forte. I think it's cute."

"I live to amuse you."

"Least you living. I wasn't so sure for a while about you."

He regarded her for a moment. It was true. All his friends had wondered if he would make it. He had disappeared for weeks at a time. Only Nomad had been able to find him at the very end of his collapse. Forte had awakened with an IV in his arm in the psych ward of Tulane Medical Center. Nomad had hauled him in and practically held a gun on the ER doctor to get quick service. Fortunately, Verna and Ozzie had shown up minutes later before the hospital security officers incurred the anger of Nomad.

"Yeah," Forte said. "I wasn't so sure myself."

Verna reached over and took his hand in hers. "And now here we are."

Forte smiled. "Yes."

"You doing okay, baby?"

"About like I expected to feel. I miss him. But glad he isn't hurting anymore."

Verna nodded. "He was a fine man."

"The finest."

"I know you'll miss him."

"Not sure. He told me not to miss him. That he'd be haunting me."

Verna chuckled and the sound of it was like deep running water.

She began to sing softly. Widely-honored as a soloist in churches throughout the city, Verna filled the kitchen with her rich tones and sent them out into the hallways.

Oh, they tell me of a home far beyond the skies,
Oh they tell me of a home far away.
Oh they tell me of a home where no storm clouds rise.
Oh they tell me of an uncloudy day.

As she sang, the music of her voice and her love flowed over him. A tear made its way down her creased brown cheek and dropped on to the table top.

He felt wetness on his own cheek.

Chapter 28

The governor's secretary kept sneaking glances at the pair of men. They were sitting in the waiting area, seemingly relaxed. Neither of them spoke, apart from the occasional mumbled remark that only the two of them could hear. Both men were dressed like SWAT officers, but without the bullet-proof jackets. So far, it had been 45 minutes.

Forte caught her eye. She looked to be in her mid-forties, stylishly dressed with an efficient yet attractive short hairdo. He smiled. She blushed. Then smiled back. She continued with her tap-tapping on the computer keyboard in front of her.

Nomad elbowed him. "No fraternizing, numb nuts."

Forte whispered a slur in his direction. He picked up the golfing magazine from the marble coffee table and skimmed it for the sixth time. "Why would anyone want to play such a stupid game." It wasn't a question as much as an insult.

"I've played it before."

Forte glanced at his friend. "Liar."

"No, really. I was doing security for this bigwig. Three-week gig. Had to play in a foursome with him." Nomad stretched. "Beat him the third time we played. He got pissed."

Forte had slept a full eight hours, in his clothes. He felt fairly rested. Nomad had called the governor's office for an appointment. "Who's calling?" the operator had asked.

Nomad had answered, "The guys who saved the governor and his family yesterday."

The woman had gushed for a few moments, put him on hold, then gushed more. "The governor wants you to come visit him as soon as possible."

There was much less foot traffic than expected throughout the various offices that comprise a state executive officer's headquarters. Security, however, had been beefed. Fortunately, the X-ray station had been briefed that the two men visiting the governor this morning would be carrying weapons for which they had licenses to carry. The guards seemed wary. Forte wondered what else they had been told. *Just because you are paranoid doesn't mean they aren't out to get you.*

A burly highway patrolman blocked the door of the governor's private office. He wore an expression somewhere between annoyance and boredom.

The door opened and a group of four men came out, none of them looking particularly happy. Except for Governor Ray Barreaux. He was smiling broadly and slapping the others on their backs.

"Not a bad idea, boys," he said. "Go back and do some more ciphering on the problem." Before they had cleared the lobby, he spoke to the men in black.

"I can't express my gratitude enough for what you did yesterday, gentlemen." His voice was showy and loud and deeply seasoned with down-home south Louisiana flavor. "Day after tomorrow we want to have a public ceremony acknowledging your bravery in the face of..."

Nomad interrupted him. "Governor, we need to speak to you privately for a few moments."

A flash of annoyance passed over Barreaux's face. His voice lowered but he regained his smile. "Why, certainly, boys. Step right into my office."

They walked past the patrolmen. "At ease, sonny boy," said Nomad.

The man made a barely audible puffing noise but didn't respond.

He led them to an informal seating arrangement of stuffed chairs and a sofa away from his desk.

He dropped into one of the chairs and waved them to the sofa. "How can I help you?" His face was the epitome of sincerity and warm openness. He held up a hand as if he were stopping traffic. "Before you say anything, I want to tell you again how grateful I am to you, Mr. Forte, for rescuing my Ashley. We are out of the public arena now. This is a father talking to you. I could never repay you." He turned to Nomad. "And you, Mr. Jones, if not for your quick thinking my wife and I surely would have died." He held out his hands, palms up. "If there's ever anything I can do to repay you... maybe extra funding for your Refuge there, or an extra security assignment for your company... just say the word."

Neither of the men in black said anything for a moment. They both studied the governor's face. Forte decided the man was too practiced a politician to reveal anything obvious in his expression.

"We had some questions," Forte said.

"And some observations," said Nomad.

The governor let his eyes travel back and forth between them just once. "About what?"

"About the kidnapping and recovery of your daughter," Forte said. "And the car bomb near your vehicle."

The Governor leaned forward slightly, eager to help. "Talk to me. I still want to catch the people behind this."

As Forte spoke, he forced himself to keep his voice passive and level. "First of all, we never actually got any specific demands from the kidnappers. Which is highly unusual unless..."

The governor interrupted. "Unless what?"

"Well, when the intention is actually to murder the victim, there are no demands. In Ashley's case, she obviously was not killed. And never seemed in danger."

The governor's eyebrows lowered. "Never in danger? Those men took my child, sir."

"Yes," said Forte. "But their whole demeanor was never threatening. In fact, we never heard their voices. There was only email communication. And when the FBI analyzed the photo of Ashley, their experts determined that her expression and body language indicated no real fear or concern."

Governor Barreaux cocked his head. "She was in shock, you idiot. Of course, her expression was interpreted that way." He blew out his breath and sat back in his chair. "I'm sorry. This has been stressful."

"I'm sure it has," said Nomad. His voice seemed soft but Forte recognized a tone he had heard before. His mind flashed back to dank rooms with water dripping down the walls and the babbling fear of a man with information that could save hundreds of lives.

Forte continued. "Then, there was the actual recovery of your daughter." He sighed. "Governor, there was nobody there. Nobody had even been there, the forensics people said. And the preliminary report from the FBI medical people indicated that Ashley was remarkably shock free."

The governor's jaw had tightened. "I'm not real sure what you are getting at, Mr. Forte. My daughter was taken from me. You brought her back. End of story."

"No," said Nomad, "that ain't the end of the story."

"Look, Mr. Jones, I'm grateful to you but…"

"You knew that car was going to blow up."

"What do you mean…?"

"I mean that I've been in dozens, maybe hundreds of situations like that. You were the one who led us to the other vehicle."

Barreaux shook his head as if he were correcting a small child. "Not true. We had more than one car there; my wife was driven there separately."

Nomad had not moved from his position next to Forte. His arm was slung along the back of the sofa. His face wore the same pseudo-bored look he had since the conversation started. And, to the unfamiliar ear, his voice was easygoing, as if he were discussing dinner plans with old friends.

Forte knew different.

"Your wife was trying to pull you back to your car, the one that blew up," said Nomad.

The governor's eyes narrowed. Forte was peering at him closely. There was a flash of something else there. Something that didn't fit in with a man whose life had been saved by the men in the room, whose daughter had been rescued by them. Forte couldn't identify it, but it confirmed to him that something was off kilter.

The governor sat back again, relaxed. "You don't get to be governor of the fine state of Louisiana without rubbing a few people the wrong way. I frequently switch up my vehicles in midstream, as it were." He pulled a carved wooden cigar box off the table next to his chair. "Forgive my manners, gentleman. Can I offer you a cigar?"

Forte shook his head.

Nomad got up and stepped close to Barreaux, still seated. He stood there looking down at the cigar box, then took one, unwrapped it. He picked up the clipper and lopped off the end of the cigar. He put it in his mouth and leaned down to the lighter in Barreaux's hand.

The men's eyes were locked on each other's.

Nomad straightened and puffed. "Ahhh, sweet. I thought all government buildings were smoke-free these days." He blew a cloud across the room.

The governor unwrapped a cigar for himself. "I suppose rank has its privileges, sometimes." He smelled the cigar. "Surely you boys know that, what with your experience in the military. We all have a chain of command, but the buck has to stop somewhere. And the rewards for stopping that buck are different when you are at the top."

The governor stood up. He took a big pull from the cigar. He blew smoke in Nomad's face.

Nomad grinned. "You ain't foolin' me, Governor Shorty."

He puffed smoke back in Barreaux's face.

Forte stepped up and put his hand on his friend's shoulder. "Let's go."

As they were leaving he glanced back.

The governor's smile had vanished.

The two men walked out past the secretary's desk. She kept her head down, her expression completely neutral now.

As they rode the elevator, Nomad put his finger to his lips to signify "no talking." Forte nodded.

They retraced their steps back through security. The guards seemed a bit more tense this time. When either Forte or Nomad made eye contact, the security people gave flat stares now.

Outside, the Baton Rouge sun already scorched the streets at 10 a.m.

As the men walked toward the sidewalk, a black Lincoln pulled to the curb. The window was down on the driver's side.

A woman's hand rested on the door panel there, her unpolished nails tapping slightly on the car's paint job.

FBI agent Rosalind Dent gazed at them directly from behind her sunshades. She crooked a finger at them.

Forte said, "I guess she heard about our little meeting this morning."

He turned to look at his friend.

Nomad was gone.

Forte sighed.

Chapter 29

Agent Dent said nothing as she drove the streets of the capitol city of Louisiana. She kept the windows rolled down and the air-conditioning unit switched off. The air came into the car like warm cane syrup. Her lips were a thin line. Every ten seconds or so, her jaw muscles clenched. Her hands were white-knuckled as she gripped the steering wheel.

Her attire was a striking contrast to her attitude. Instead of the usual severe suit, she wore a blue sundress. Her shoulders and arms were more tanned that Forte expected.

"Your family is safe, right?" Forte asked.

Rosalind Dent merely nodded without taking her eyes off the road ahead. She glanced in the rear view mirror several times. The car meandered through the downtown area. Occasionally she took a quick corner without signaling.

They drove through the sounds of morning traffic – a jackhammer breaking concrete, a bus pulling away from the curb, the honking of a cab.

Dent kept driving – and searching for anyone trailing them – until she reached a park a few miles from downtown Baton Rouge.

She stopped, got out, and motioned Forte to follow her.

A pavilion sat on the edge of the park, which was mostly deserted except for some teenagers performing skateboard stunts at the other end of the park.

"Sit, please," the agent said.

Forte sat.

Rosalind, however, did not. She stood and surveilled the entire park for signs of anything out of place. Finally, when she was satisfied that nobody was paying any particular attention, she sat on a bench next to Forte.

She put her arm on his shoulder and smiled at him.

At first, it confused him. Until he realized her actions and expressions were merely to give the appearance of a couple meeting for a romantic rendezvous in the park. They both knew that people were less likely to walk close to people in that particular type of situation.

Forte whispered, "Is this the part where you crawl my ass about visiting the governor?"

Dent maintained her fake devoted expression. "No, this is the part where you once again discover you aren't as smart as you think you are."

Forte felt his eyebrows twitch upward. *Ahhh.*

"Enlighten me, darling," he said.

"Even as we speak, the FBI office in New Orleans is drafting an apology to the governor."

"An apology for what?"

"For allowing you and your caveman friend to barge into the governor's office and insult him with an interrogation during his...time of stress after yesterday's threats."

Forte snorted. "Stress. Right. He was glad-handing lobbyists. We didn't barge anywhere."

Dent grinned genuinely now. "True. I've seen the two of you barge before. It involves broken furniture and bruises. And blood, occasionally."

"We knew he was up to something. We didn't want to wait for the government machine of the FBI to get rolling on this."

"Honey," she said, leaning forward to whisper in his ear, "we've been rolling on this. We knew about your trip to see Governor Sh...the governor as soon as Nomad picked you up this morning. We thought it would be better to let you go ahead." He felt her lips brushing over his earlobe.

"Mmm. You are doing well with the 'lovers in the park' charade."

"This is more dangerous than you think," she whispered.

He faked a small moan deep in his throat. "Don't I know it. You are about to make me bugle like a stallion."

"I'm talking about the situation with the governor, Neanderthal."

His eyes snapped open. "Of course. I knew that."

She pulled back, still smiling. She winked at him. "But it is nice to know I could affect you."

He shrugged. "I'm a man. If it were difficult to get to me, I'd be worried."

She rolled her eyes. "So sensitive."

She put a hand against his cheek. "Now, listen to me and just keep smiling."

He nodded. And winked.

She leaned forward and kissed him on the cheek, her eyes twinkling. "Some of us in the office knew something was wrong with the whole kidnapping scenario surrounding the governor's daughter – from the start. Little things didn't add up. There was a whole disregard for her security that seemed out of place and inconsistent with how it was previously handled. The governor had been a stickler for security, concerning her. She always had a bodyguard close, in the past, even on group dates with her school buddies."

He ran his hand through her hair. "So, he set it up."

"Yes. We just don't know why. It's what we are investigating now."

"But you can't let the governor's office know you are investigating him."

She scooted closer to him on the bench. She kissed his neck. "You can't imagine how tricky it is."

He felt goosebumps form on his skin. "Oh, I can imagine lots of things."

She giggled. "The investigation, nimrod."

He twisted slightly, his mouth against her neck now. He kissed her skin there. "That's what I meant, Miz Government Agent."

She pulled back. Her face was flushed slightly.

He smiled. "Two can play that tease game."

"Touché, bad boy," she whispered. "Jackie Shaw is a lucky woman. Just keep grinning and listen to me."

In low tones, she spoke quickly, all the while continuing to touch his face, hold his hands, fake-laugh at some imagined funny he had made.

"The Department of Homeland Security has been surveilling Barreaux for the past three years. They know that he is up to something, and they know it has involved the redistribution of money allocated by that department for its intended purpose. Barreaux, however, is extremely practiced at covering his tracks. His network protects him better than anyone I've ever seen. There is suspicion he has been accepting money under the table for allowing illegal armament into the country through the port of New Orleans."

"Ugh. Like that is unusual."

Dent pinched him on his stomach. "We know it happens. We've just not investigated a governor for it. And we've reason to believe that the activity is about to involve big bombs."

"Mass destruction?"

"Yes."

Forte lost his lovey-dovey smile for a second before recovering.

196

Rosalind Dent leaned forward again and took his face in her hands. She kissed him lightly on the lips.

Mischief played behind her eyes, even though the words she had been speaking were deadly serious.

Forte whispered to her. "What I want to know is — what does the kidnapping of his daughter and my involvement have to do with any of that? I've had nothing to do with tracking down gunrunners for years."

Across the park, the boys on their skateboards hooted loudly over a wipeout by one of their group. Someone clicked on a jam box. The one who crashed leapt up and began to dance to a hip-hop tune.

The FBI agent glanced at the boys for a moment. Then she took Forte's hand between both of hers. "There is something else connected to it."

"Okay."

"We aren't sure what it has to do with the gun smuggling..."

"Spill it."

He could see a dash of sorrow in her eyes.

"Somehow, there is human trafficking involved." She took a breath. "Kids. They are using children somehow in this."

Forte tensed. She could feel it in her hands. She held him.

"How many?" he asked. His voice sounded deadly.

She had stopped smiling. "Could be dozens."

"So they knew I would focus on that."

"Yes, obviously."

"That's why the fake kidnapping of the governor's daughter was set up. To get me there."

"It seems so."

"What about the other kidnapping? The Bailey boy."

Dent shook her head. "We don't know how it is connected yet. But it has to be. It's too coincidental."

Forte made a huge effort to resume the boyfriend act. He now understood the need for the role playing.

"Not everyone in your office knows of all this, do they?"

She lowered her eyes. "No."

He sighed. "So basically the FBI office will handle the kidnappings by the book. The governor's kid is safe, so they will close that file. And, the Bailey kid ..."

"Oh we will still pursue that."

"I know that will be the official line, but we both know it's a nothing case compared to the governor."

Her face darkened for a moment. She seemed on the verge of striking out at him. "That's unfair. You know we do what we can."

"Where is Martin Bailey right now?"

She hesitated. "We aren't quite sure."

"What does that mean?"

"We knew he left The Refuge, but we weren't exactly tracking him. He isn't suspected of anything in the case of his own son's kidnapping."

"So you have no idea where he is."

"We called his cell. We called his work. He has called in sick there."

Forte sat very still amid the activities of the park around them. The skateboard boys were still doing their tricks. Another couple was seated on a bench on the exact opposite side of the park. A young mother texted on her phone while tending to her toddler at play in the fountain in the center of the expanse of well-kept grass.

"Is there anything else about anything I should know?" he asked. His voice was cool now.

Anyone noticing them would not mistake them for a romantic couple now.

Rosalind said nothing.

Forte looked into her eyes. They were clouded now. He tried to read the emotions behind them. Embarrassment? Frustration?

"I'll do the best I can for you, Al," she said. "I hope you know that."

"I believe you would, Rosie. I just think you define the rules differently than I do, sometimes."

She did not reply. She let go of his hands.

Forte pulled his cell out of his pocket and hit a speed dial button.

Thirty yards away, in the shrubbery behind the pavilion, a phone rang.

"You can come out now," Forte said into the phone.

The bushes parted. Nomad walked over to where they were seated.

"Y'all almost embarrassed me, all that hugging and such."

The agent stood. "I knew he was around somewhere." She walked away toward the side of the park where her car was parked.

The two men admired her departure.

"Nice little sundress," Nomad said.

"Guess she was working undercover," replied Forte.

Nomad stretched his arms above his head. He bent at the waist and swayed side to side for moment. "Undercover. Right."

"The call of duty."

"Yeah, I think you forgot I was listening for a minute there."

Forte stood up. "I think we've learned about everything we are going to know from the official sources."

On the far side of the park, the skater boys broke into raucous laughter for a moment. *Summertime and the living is easy.*

"Let's go look under the rock now and see what the dark side knows," he said.

Chapter 30

The house boat meandered its way across Lake Pontchartrain in no particular hurry and with no seeming direction. The sun, almost directly overhead, tipped the waves with sparkles.

"Ol' Poochie is really feeling the recession, huh?" said Nomad.

"He probably repossessed the boat from some poor mortgage company executive," Forte said.

They approached the floating mansion as passengers on a ski boat driven by shirtless man with dreadlocks and a dragon tattoo spanning his pale, scarred back. A thin brown man dressed in white sat across from them on a padded bench. He wore orange sunshades and a black straw hat. A compact machine gun rested casually over his lap.

Nomad said, "Cool shades."

Black Hat nodded almost imperceptibly. He left hand moved maybe an eighth of an inch on the barrel of the gun.

Forte felt naked without a weapon. The men on the boat had frisked them before pushing off from the dock. He knew it was just a power play on the part of the man they were visiting. He had lived most of his life with the pressure of a gun in a holster somewhere on his body.

The ski boat spun around the other side of the bigger craft. The driver cut the motor.

"Up the ladder," said Black Hat.

As they came up over the edge of the railing, a pair of woman leaned over the top rail of the upper level above them. One was blonde with a deep tan. The other was African American. Neither seemed to be wearing anything.

Nomad finger-waved at them. "See, Poochie can't even afford clothes for the hired help. Damn recession."

The guard led them along the side of the boat and down a staircase. He stopped and tapped on a door. When it opened, he said, "They here." He stepped aside for the men to enter the room. His look was one of barely contained contempt.

"Thanks, pal," said Nomad. "Keep the motor running for us. Oh, and Bob Marley called. He wants his dreads back."

As he spoke, another woman walked out of the room. Her skin was mocha and unencumbered with fabric except for a leopard bikini bottom. She smiled at them as she slid past in the narrow hallway.

Nomad growled low in his throat.

"Focus," said Forte to his friend.

They entered the stateroom, which seemed to occupy the entire length of the boat. A pool table sat in the center of the room. A 50-inch plasma screen showed an NFL preseason game in full swing.

On a massive chaise lounge reclined a slight man with octaroon features.

"Damn Saints," he mumbled. "Throw that ball on fourth and long, I don't give a…" He muttered a creative string of curse words.

A round custom bed rested beneath a mirrored ceiling at the other end of the room. Blue Dog paintings were lined up along every wall. A bar that would rival most clubs in the Quarter showed a selection of bottles in the usual colors.

The man on the chaise lounge yelled another extensive string of curses. He clicked off the TV. Immediately, jazz music replaced the noise of the football game.

"Poochie," Forte said.

The man walked past them to the bar. He held up one finger. He took out ice, tossed some cubes into a glass, splashed liquor into it, then drained it.

"Damn, Saints," he said. "They just cost me ten G's." Then he grinned. "But, hell, I loves 'em. What can I do?"

He fell back onto the overstuffed lounge chair. "I know when the great For-tay comes to visit, there be some deep doo-doo happenin' somewhere." He waved to the chairs flanking him. "Have a seat, gentlemens. You want a drink or two or 'leven?"

Forte had never known the man's name to be anything but "Poochie" but he also never saw what the connection was between the man and a dog. He marked it up to ghetto slang. Only after Poochie had become a big-time drug dealer in New Orleans did he begin buying the Blue Dog paintings. Poochie's kingdom had grown from standing on street corners in the warehouse district to this.

"I need some information," Forte said.

The octaroon man popped an ice cube into his mouth and sucked it noisily as he regarded the men. "Well, Al, I didn't think you wanted anything else. You lost your taste for candy a while back, I reckon. Or did you?" He picked up a delicately scrolled box from the table in front of him. He tapped it lightly and held it up for the men to see. "You change your mind, it's right here."

He held it for a moment, then chuckled and set it down. "No? Alrighty then."

Nomad had been sitting on the edge of his seat. "Let's cut the bullshit," he said.

Poochie's position didn't change. A man only slightly smaller than the door stepped into the room. He had Hawaiian features with none of the island friendliness. In his hands rested a shotgun that seemed like a toy.

"Al, you need to keep your puppy on a leash, boy," said the gangster. He put his hands behind his head and continued talking.

"Let me guess why you do-gooders have decided to go slumming with me on my little boat this afternoon. What could it be?" He closed his eyes as if he were in deep thought. "Let's see now, what are the choices. Could it be the bikers who are all upset about you tearing up their favorite bar? Which, by the way, I thank you for. I always enjoy it when the good guys eliminate my competition a little. No, that's not it."

Forte remained perfectly still, allowing the small man to have his fun.

Poochie continued. "Maybe it's the fact that bad boy Chug is after you and thinks he can get you to go save that boy?" He dragged out a curse to sound like "sheee-eeeet" and shook his head slowly. "You kill me, Al. The man caused you pain, son. Why would you do that for him?" He let his eyes rest on Forte's face a moment. For a second or two, genuine fascination flickered in the man's eyes.

"Or could it be door number three?"

The drug dealer's emerald-hued eyes shone now. From somewhere in the boat came the smell of ribs barbecuing. The jazz music transitioned to a Dave Brubek tune.

"Door three contains the secrets to what our sweet governor is up to," said Poochie. "You probably want to know why he had his little daughter kidnapped, and what kind of wicked friends he is associating with, don't you, Mr. For-tayyyy."

Forte had partied in boats like this one plenty of times after Ruth's death. He knew exactly what it felt like to spend days afloat – on the water and in his mind – as if he were suspended from reality for a while. He despised those memories yet remembered them as distinctly as any he had ever lived.

"Tell me what you know, Poochie. Don't make me spell it out. Please."

The criminal regarded him through half-closed eyes, the way a python might study an alligator sunning on a rock near its tree. "I haven't forgot what you did, Al." A few years earlier, Poochie's niece had been protected at The Refuge from killers she had agreed to testify against. "This will clear it between us, though."

Forte nodded.

Poochie sat up now, all his laid-back cool slouch gone. "Well, you know we don't mess with gun-running in our operation. But we know people who do. The word is that Governor Barreaux has gotten some undercover cash for looking the other way on some shipments. I don't know exactly who is behind it, but for some reason they are scared of you." Poochie smiled. "I must admit, you do get a little crazy when you go all pitbull on somebody's ass." He chuckled. "Hey Woo," he said to the mountainous bodyguard across the room. "Remember that time old Forte put you on the floor?"

Woo sneered.

"Anyway, there is that other thing – about the children. I'm sure you heard about it." His face lost all humor now. "They use the kids as decoys at the delivery points in other countries. Then they sell them into the sex slave industry. Probably out east. That's some bad, crazy-ass folks out there in them Asian countries." He sipped again. "Perverted bastards. They can't be satisfied with regular hot woman sex?"

Forte felt a desperate hopelessness tug at the edges of his consciousness. He had always known of the child sex-trafficking business. It had seemed far away from his back yard.

"And you don't know who is behind it?"

The jazz notes bounced back and forth between instruments, the piano taking the theme and bowing out to the clarinet as the bass and drums kept the piece moving along. No one said anything for a long moment.

"I'm not sure," said the drug dealer. "But I'll try to narrow it down. I will tell you one thing, though. This ain't no small thing going down. I've been moving some people around slowly once I heard a little about it."

The man's voice conveyed no fear. A shadow of concern passed over his eyes like a summer shower. Then it was gone.

"I think it's gonna happen soon, whatever it is," Poochie said.

Forte stood up. "Will you let me know?"

"Sure, Al. You know you're my boy," said the gangster. He spoke to Nomad. "And I know it chaps your ass to have to come ask me for a favor, don't it?"

Nomad looked down on the small man who remained on the lounge chair. His upper body leaned forward slightly, the way a tiger tenses at a quarry even when caged. Menace emanated from him. The big bodyguard stirred slightly, enough for everyone to be reminded of his presence.

Poochie chuckled. "My man Woo here will take you back to the putter boat."

They followed the bodyguard out. The man had to turn his body sideways to maneuver in the narrow hallways.

After the subdued cabin lounge, the deck was brilliant with light.

Three men with machine guns stood guard. Forte figured that more men were out of sight somewhere. In the distance, a sailboat silently sliced through the blue of the lake. On the upper deck of the houseboat, a man in a chef's hat used tongs to flip the ribs on the grill.

"Just a little outing on the water," said Nomad.

He stood with his hand on the ladder leading down to the ski boat. The dreadlocked man was there.

"We didn't find out much," Forte said.

Above them stood the woman who had come out of the stateroom earlier. A sheer shawl was wrapped around her shoulders. Because it did little to hide her ample assets, the effect was even more erotic than sans shawl. She smiled at the two men.

Nomad smiled back.

"But the view was spiffy," he said.

Chapter 31

The canoe slipped through the swamp without a sound. Though the sun was still high in the sky, only a few spots of light penetrated the canopy of trees and vines and moss above this area. The sounds of car engines and highway noises faded in the distance as the slim boat glided along.

Forte paddled steadily, dipping the paddle on either side of the canoe alternately to keep the boat away from the gnarled cedar roots.

After another ten minutes of steady paddling, he could hear only the sounds of this hidden world. The birds kept up a steady patter in the limbs above. Bullfrogs plopped into the water as he passed while the tree frogs chorused. An alligator thrashed the murky water as it escaped the invasion of the canoe.

Who do you think you are?

The ski boat had dropped them off at the north shore of Lake Pontchartrain. Nomad had then taken him back into the swamp after carefully backtracking several times to catch anyone who might be trailing them.

Nomad had not spoken much during the short ride. He merely asked if his cell phone was charged and to phone him when he wanted to be picked up.

The old dented canoe had Larue's name on it. Forte had spent many a summer afternoon in it with the old barber.

Now, he felt the need to be alone. And there was no place he could go besides this place to achieve the kind of solitude he needed.

Who do you think you are?

When he had first pushed the canoe into the water, he had thrashed the water hard, making the boat jump ahead at a furious pace. Within a few moments, sweat poured down his face. His shirt was soaked.

He was furious and the anger continued to rise inside him instead of ebbing with the exertion. He knew he had to be away from anyone he might hurt if he lashed out.

Why? Why all this trouble, right now? Why?

Another part of his mind spoke, a disgusted tone in its voice. *Oh SHUT THE HELL UP, YOU WHINER. You expect everything to go your way now, is that it? You thought that just because you stopped putting powder in your noise or fire in your veins that everything would just fall neatly into your hands?*

He felt the burn in his muscles as he knifed the swamp with the paddle. He was flying through the water.

Why? He felt the jagged rush of images of the past few days snatching at his mind now. The bikers in the bar, the crash of broken glass, the drugged slack-jawed expression on the teen girl's face they had saved. The governor's proud smirk in his office. The shock of seeing Martin Bailey's grief-stricken face in the shadows outside Larue's house. The surprise on the sniper's face as he whirled to face Forte atop the warehouse, a millisecond before the cop's bullet burst through. The unflappable smugness on Brock Randall's face in the church yard at Larue's wake.

Who do you think you are? He heard his mother's voice, shrill and vicious, in his ear in the aftermath of some disobedience, some rebellious act that had taken on more meaning that the act itself in her mind, transforming her from the caretaker she wanted to be into the accusing ego-crushing monster that nobody else knew about.

Forte realized his fingers were aching from the extreme force with which he was gripping the paddle.

His mother's face morphed into another person, someone shrouded in shadow.

Everyone thinks you are so tough, so good just because you rescue a few kids. You know the truth though, don't you? You know the weakness at the pit of your soul, you know you are worthless, admit it.

He had felt himself sinking when he realized Poochie really didn't have a solid lead for him. The kind of hopelessness he had known in the past had begun to pluck away at the edges of his peace. *No. No!* The blackness of his despair had encroached on his confidence before, even since he had gone through recovery and left the drugs behind.

He was not so naïve to believe, however, that it could not overtake him again, that it could not take over his life as it had done in the past.

You want it, don't you? You deserve it. Nobody needs to endure this kind of misery, this kind of disappointment. You will let everyone down if you don't get on an even keel. You know you can change this, don't you? Just call Poochie. Nobody will know.

He raised the paddle high over his head. He slammed it down on the surface of the water. The sound was like a rifle shot. A pair of cranes flew from behind a nearby tree, their huge wings flapping slowly as the big birds put the treetops of the swamp behind them.

Nobody will know.

He began to paddle more deliberately now. *Just reach the cabin. Just get there.*

Images flooded his mind. Ruth lying in the spreading pool of blood. The leering face of Chug then the faces of a dozen other criminals he had confronted over the years, all lined up, laughing at him. He saw the faces of all the children he had never saved, all the kids slaughtered in countries where his mission had meant something else. He heard their crying, their shrieking, then the cackling laughter of people hanging all over him, spilling their drinks, whispering in his ear, pulling him back to the back rooms or the beautiful vistas that morphed into the dingy back alleys and moldy slimy crack houses.

The terror of his own humanity swarmed over him. He looked at his phone. *Put it away, Al. You know you can't do that. It's not just all the people who will be crushed by it – all your friends and all those children who may never have a chance if you go down. It's not just them – it's you. You can't let yourself down about this.*

He could see it now, the tiny shack on stilts ahead. The safe place, the haven where Larue had so patiently undone the hurt he had known, mostly without saying a word but just being with him, and showing him he was worth something.

So close. A yearning for that safe place sparked inside him.

In an instant, a savage wave of pain slammed him, as if the swamp reared up in a massive tsunami, blotting out the view of the cabin. The face of little Freddy Bailey, twisted in fear and anguish, his voice hoarse from crying and yelling out his father's name as the figure of Chug emerged from the swamp with blood running down his face, his teeth glistening red from his meal of cruelty.

Forte screamed, a primal roar ripping through the swamp noises like a dull chainsaw. He felt as if he couldn't stop the sound of it, his lungs expelling the animal sound as if he were wounded.

The canoe lunged the last ten yards toward the cabin. The boat rammed the front porch and Forte launched himself forward. He stumbled up the weathered steps, slammed against the front door, clawed it open and flung himself into the shadows of the inside of the shack.

A mewling sound of an animal insinuated itself throughout the one-room cabin. Forte realized the noise was coming from inside him.

Nobody will know.

"Please, no," he said aloud. His voice sounded pitiful to his own ears.

Just call him. The pain will go away.

He moaned.

He looked down at his hand. His cell phone was grasped tightly in his fist. How had it gotten there?

Do it. Just this once. It will be okay.

"Help me, God," he whispered.

The phone buzzed. He fell to his knees and dropped it on the wooden floor of the old cabin.

Through the cracks between the boards he could heard the water sloshing.

He picked up the phone and pushed a button.

He held it to his ear without saying hello.

A voice began chuckling on the other end.

"Forget to call me?" said Manny Laird.

Forte slumped to the floor. He rolled over on his back.

He had forgotten to call. He cleared his throat.

On the other end of the line, Manny was humming a song softly. Forte recognized it as "You Are My Sunshine."

Forte swallowed hard. "Yeah, it slipped my mind."

He could almost see the crooked smile on the white-haired preacher's face on the other end. "Been working out? You sound winded." Manny's voice was gravelly from years of drinking and speaking to large crowds.

"Yeah, something like that." He took a deep breath and let it out. Thank you, Lord. "Got a minute?"

"All the time in the world, knucklehead. Just made some tea. Honey's by my side. I'm set."

Just the word picture of it in Forte's mind calmed him.

"Just doing a little canoeing in the bayou," he said.

Then he told his friend and sponsor everything: The visit to Poochie's, the conversations, the shootout at the warehouse, and the worst of it – his overwhelming desire to medicate himself again.

They were words that nobody on the planet would ever hear him say. They were safe with Manny.

When he was finished, he found his breathing had returned to near normal.

"So, you called out to God and your phone rang, huh," said Manny.

"Sounds goofy, huh."

"Does it? Stranger things have happened than for God to prompt a call like this. There's a reason he is called sovereign."

"I know. I still wonder why He would care about me. I mean, enough to rescue me."

"You rescue people. It's what you do," said the raspy voice on the other end. "Why do you do it?"

Forte thought for a moment. "Because I can."

"There's more to it than that. You have a choice, you always have a choice in the matter."

Forte lay still, flat against the slats of the floor. He let his eyes wander over the unfinished ceiling of the cabin, over the kerosene lantern hanging from a nail in a rafter, over the trotlines and traps and fishing poles secured above his head.

"I do it because it is what I was made for." The words surprised him. He had never spoken them before. He felt light-headed, pleasantly free.

"And you don't do it alone." Manny's smile permeated the words.

"No, I don't."

"It is our biggest challenge, any of us, to ask for help, to know that we can't go it alone, that a solitary life is the path to destruction."

Forte nodded, then realized he was not seen by his friend on the phone. "Yes."

"Life will always be hard, my brother," Manny said, "but it doesn't have to be lonely."

"I feel weak."

"There's a reason for that. You are weak. We all are."

"You seem strong."

"And so do you, to everyone with whom you associate. But nobody is strong like God is strong. A plain and simple fact."

The sound of Manny's voice, the warm breeze blowing through the front door of the cabin, the conversation of the birds outside – all lulled him back to a sense of peace.

"Thank you, Manny."

Through the phone came the sound of the old preacher sipping his tea. "Anytime. Now get back to work."

Chapter 32

Brock Randall ran a towel over his damp head as he stood at the window of his bedroom. He felt calmer after his late afternoon workout.

But not calm enough.

The boy had come out on the balcony of the guest house across the courtyard. With the sun low in the sky, the yard was mostly in shadow now. A slight breeze ruffled the exotic plants that Randall had gathered from every tropical corner of the world. A pair of palms flanked the guest house and bowed their heads over the balcony there as if listening to a private conversation.

The boy wore the same lost-puppy expression he had adopted since first arrived. He gazed at the far corner of the lush garden that covered the entire walled yard. One of Randall's thugs occasionally strolled past the guest house on one of the maze-like paths that snaked through the trees and bushes. Apart from that, nothing moved in the area. Electrified razor wire topped the wall encircling the yard.

Most people would have felt some sympathy for the kidnapped boy. Brock Randall felt nothing except satisfaction. The boy was a means to an end.

Randall always seemed calm to everyone around him. He made a point of it. He had presented nothing but a serene impression to Al Forte in the church yard.

He cursed under his breath. The very thought of the yellow-eyed man made his blood pressure rise.

A flurry of wings interrupted his annoyance. A parrot flew through the room from one of his manmade tree sculptures to another. The brilliance of the bird always managed to divert the man from his rages. "Hello, handsome," Randall said. "How are you today?"

The parrot cocked his head. "How are you today?"

Randall listened to the bird echo his greeting. He decided his mood would not be improved by anything except pain.

Randall picked up the 35-pound dumbbell he had set on the floor. He continued his workout as he waited for an encoded message on the computer.

"One!" He curled the weight up and his bicep bulged. He was the CEO of a multimillion dollar enterprise. The men he commanded were the ones whose conditioning ensured his financial success. But he enjoyed leading by example. More than one of his underlings had cringed in surprise at the cruelty of his grip.

"Two!" For thirty years he had befriended those in power, starting back in his college days. He had always had a knack for seeing a person's potential and, more important, how that potential could benefit him and his security company. His company was filled with the best at every position. Even the artwork in his workout lair included the work of the masters. He prided himself on acquiring the very best.

"Three!" He felt the pleasant burn in his muscles. Pain was something he had come to embrace. He had known it as a child and had always associated it with superiority in athletics – the winner was almost always the person who could endure the most pain. His upper arms, chest and back were laced with scars. He had traveled to cultures where the test of a man included blood and suffering. At beaches, he enjoyed the envious glances of those who had chosen safer paths in life.

"Four!" He smiled as he felt the pain of his discipline. Challenges had come and gone for him over the decades, each one more extreme than the last. For him, it had become boring if he were not allowed to add extra layers of difficulty. It wasn't enough to merely smuggle weapons in small lots, as he had in the early days. His mind was always working at bigger schemes, more intricate outcomes.

"Five!" The sweat dripped from his brow again as he strained. When his new client wanted biological weapons smuggled into the country, there had been no mention of using humans as the actual carriers. It had been Randall's idea. And the idea had festered into a beautiful creative storm in his mind. *Children. Use kids for the carriers.* He remembered the look of surprised shock on his client's face – this from a man who had murdered thousands in his campaigns of terror. Then the look had dissolved into a smile. Yes, he had said. Yes, it is perfect.

"Six!" Only two more. The pain was already intense. Randall gasped. From childhood he had known that pain resulted in wisdom – if one had the right perspective. A skinny bookworm, his mother's boyfriends had called him. And they had not limited themselves to mere words to hurt him and please themselves. But they underestimated the power of education. The last of his mother's partners to abuse him received a brief and painful education. Randall remembered with pleasure the startled look on the man's face as he clutched his throat at the kitchen table. The idiot had not even questioned the large square piece of plastic wrapping on the floor beneath his chair.

"Seven!" The last agonizing curl of the dumbbell would finish his regimen for the day. The weight seemed as if it could go no higher, his arm quivering. *Weakling, give up.* He clenched his teeth. *Push, don't let it defeat you.* The veins on his arm stood out, pencil thick. The dumbbell inched closer. He groaned and bent his head down, the sweat dripping down his chest. *Will you win? Are you weak as they said, girlygirl?*

Forte's face appeared before him. Not the man in the church yard, shadowed. But a younger Forte, years earlier, in the bright lights of the ballroom. The foolish Forte who had so lightly dismissed his offer. Randall had heard the name mentioned by more than one higher up in both military and espionage circles. The first time, he had wondered who this man was who had caught the attention of people so far removed from the operational realities of war. The second and third times, he listened more closely. "The perfect SEAL," an admiral had said. "If I had to pick one, Forte would be it," said another. "Never seen such intense focus on a goal, regardless of the cost to him personally," an evaluation report had stated.

Randall had planned the reception ten years ago for the sole purpose of recruiting Forte to join his organization. Nobody else realized it at the time, and still didn't. When he followed the young SEAL out into the sunroom that evening, he expected the conversation to go back and forth a little until he got his way. Most men were smart enough to see the opportunity – and riches – of being part of the Randall team when presented with it.

Forte's refusal was perfunctory. And it wasn't just his words. Randall had seen the eyes of many men in many situations. He could read them instantly – their fears and wants and courage, if any, inside their hearts – just from a glance. In Forte's eyes, he saw finality – and ridicule. That night he had almost stepped back from the sheer simple force of the man's aura. He had opened his mouth to continue the conversation, then had heard himself babbling a weak reply, like a school boy being turned down for a prom date.

Forte had kept his voice from showing his disdain for the older man, that night long ago. But his eyes told the tale.

Randall felt a tear of shame on his cheek.

He thought that when Forte's wife had been murdered, the shame might go away. Randall at first did feel a sense of relief, that the man had been made to pay for his disrespect.

It hadn't been enough. He had realized that it would never be enough until Forte was destroyed.

There had been opportunities. Randall himself had personally zeroed in on his quarry through the scope of a sniper rifle more than once. He had studied him, noting the smallest movement of his face, his hands, his behavior. But he had never planned to pull the trigger so easily.

He wanted him to suffer.

So he stayed patient, his anger captured and contained in that secret place inside him like a caged animal, pacing without a noise, silently padding back and forth. Waiting. Waiting for the perfect pieces of a puzzle to fall into place.

He had perfected the art of waiting. He had waited for his body to catch up with his mind, until puberty made him big enough that he would never resort to sissy measures of killing a man by poison or by disabling his brakes on a mountain road. No, his muscles developed until, in addition to being the smart one, he became the strong one, the fast one, the fearless one. And he had begun to dredge from his memory those men who had hurt him. Those he couldn't remember, he simply forced his worthless mother to tell him about every sordid detail of their lives together.

Then, during his splendid award-winning track-star high school years, he had found them. Each of them: A group of five men who had used him for their own pleasure, men who preyed on a weak boy before his prime, before he became able to defend himself mentally or physically. And he had given them the reward for their cruelty. Never a quick death. Always a look of surprise on their weak faces. Always the simpering pleas for mercy, much as he had done as a boy.

He had recorded their girlish screams and listened to them over and over after making them hear their own crying. Before their ears were rendered useless by death.

He had not spared them.

He would not spare Forte.

Randall screamed and finished the last curl, pushed the weight up, then lowered it, dropped it on the Oriental rug.

He grabbed his towel and wiped down his face and neck again.

He flexed his arms.

On the computer screen, an icon was flashing.

His client was ready to talk.

Chapter 33

The old man shuffled past the group of boys leaning against the rusted car. He kept his head low, careful to avoid eye contact. His knee-length coat was splotched with green stains and looked stifling in the night heat.

"Get yo' stinkin' ass outta here," said one of the tough boys. The others sent half-hearted curses in his direction. None of the crowd made a move toward him.

He shambled over to the opposite side of the street. Everything about him seemed beat down. Head down, he kept moving along the sidewalk, shuffling over the cracks and the crabgrass and the discarded beer cans. The neighborhood was one of those New Orleans areas that had lost its self-respect long before Katrina; the storm had broken its back. Debris still lay in dismal piles here and there, having been picked through enough to ensure the remains were not even worthy of being thrown in the back of a garbage truck.

The old man kept his aimless amble at a pace robbed of hope. Hanging from the fingers of his left hand was a five-gallon bucket, the Samsonite of the homeless. Rags and plastic grocery bags showed at the top of the bucket. A torn Saints cap topped his dirty gray-streaked hair. His painter pants were once white; now the color was urban camouflage.

Every 100 feet or so, the old bum stopped, set down the bucket, and wiped his face with a torn piece of terry cloth towel.

Nothing about the man drew a second glance from anyone. The first glance was enough – disgust was the response.

Only the most careful of observers would have noticed anything about the man that seemed out of character for a decrepit soul who had long ago lost all ambition of another life. But most of the streetlamps had been shot out long ago – who would notice his shoes in this discarded part of the poorest area of the city?

Mostly hidden by dirt and the baggy frazzled pants legs, the shoes were black and scuffed. But knock off the mud and one would discover footwear perfectly suited for a cop. Or a soldier. Instead of flapping soles and no laces, the shoes had sturdy Neoprene bottoms and over-the-ankle leather uppers. Perfect for an undercover mission.

Which is exactly what Al Forte was conducting in the neighborhood where Martin Bailey grew up.

Forte, as the bum, once again stopped and swiped his face as he glanced at the clapboard house on the corner. Someone close to him would have heard that he was mumbling. Or they would have assumed it was the babbling of a man too long on the streets, whose spirit had dwindled to insanity a while back.

Forte was actually speaking into a tiny microphone clipped to the lapel of the stained coat. "Lights are on at the house. No traffic around it. I'll move to the other side," he said.

On the other end, Jackie Shaw said, "Copy that. Nomad, you copy?"

The radio crackled. "Copy," said Nomad from his position in a van a block away.

After talking to Rosalind Dent earlier in the day, Forte had made his own calls to locate Martin Bailey. The man had neither made nor received any calls on a cell phone that could be tracked. He seemed to have disappeared. It was suspicious to everyone involved in the case. Why would a man in his position ask for help, so sincerely, then suddenly vanish?

Forte had emerged from his near-crash-and-burn experience at the swamp cabin with a renewed focus. There was more at stake than the recovery of Freddy Bailey. There were so few leads on the case, however, Forte had decided to start pulling at strings and see what might unravel. Poochie might come up with a specific lead to follow up soon.

After Nomad had picked him up at the swamp, Forte had started making calls for leads on Martin Bailey. "Might as well keep busy," Forte had told Nomad as they rode back to the French Quarter.

By the time they reached The Refuge, Forte had the distinct impression that Martin was avoiding him and the FBI for a reason. He intended to find out what secrets the man had to hide.

Forte, Nomad and Jackie had already discovered that Martin's mother's house was dark. A quick check had shown that it had been empty for several days.

Now they were checking out the aunt's house on the West Bank. The residence had been confirmed by two of the people Forte had phoned. Forte the Bum kept walking around the corner to scope out the other side of the aunt's house.

It was 11:45 p.m. Inside the house, a single light revealed the frazzled lace on once-proud curtains. From another window came the blue-flicker of a television.

It took Forte five minutes to walk 100 feet from one side of the house to the other. A car passed. An unintelligible insult was hurled out the car window at Forte. Crash! A beer bottle shattered at his feet. He stopped and gingerly walked around the broken glass, glancing at the aunt's house.

No change there.

Forte was about to inform the others that nothing seemed suspicious at the house.

A tiny light flickered in the bushes with an electronic glow. Someone on a cell phone.

Forte kept walking until he was past the house and blocked by another.

"It's a go. We need to check it out," he said into the microphone.

"Standing by," said Jackie.

"Check," said Nomad.

"On my signal. Stand by," said Forte.

He continued his bum-style walking until he reached a spot on the block that was almost completely hidden from view at the Bailey home. Then he transformed. He darted into the yard and into bushes next to another house. There, he shrugged off the stinky coat and flung the wig and cap from his head. He pulled out the Uzi machine gun strapped to his back. From the bucket he retrieved his Glock, a silencer, and a pair of flashbang grenades. He knelt, screwed the silencer on to the pistol, and did a quick sweep of the area. Nobody had emerged from their homes to see where the old bum had gone.

He took a deep breath. His black tee-shirt was soaked with sweat. He had no idea if Martin Bailey was even at his aunt's home. But he had seen enough to be confident of approaching it. He was relieved to be moving.

He darted along the side yard between two houses, then went left along a trash-strewn alley that led back to the road where he had strolled past the house.

Forte stopped between the houses. From his position, he could see the shrubbery on the front corner where someone had been using a cell phone. He raised an infra-red scope to his eye. The man was still there. He was leaning against the post on the front porch, still hidden by the overgrown bush. The man's head nodded. *Obviously sleepy.* He clicked on the mic and spoke softly. "I'm taking the guy in the front of the house. Nomad, you take the back. And remember, we do this quietly." Silence on the other end. "Nomad? Remember, no noise."

A sigh came through the cell phone. "Okay, okay. Nobody will know I'm there."

"In thirty seconds, I launch…from three…two…one…now."

He took a deep breath and let it out. Then he moved out, running low over the yard and across the street. He stopped behind a cluster of garbage cans. Still no movement.

He felt his leg muscles bunch, then launched himself. He closed the distance of thirty feet between them. Just before he burst through the branches of the bush, the guard saw him. His hand darted toward a shoulder holster.

Forte kicked him hard in the solar plexus. The guard went down without a sound. He lay in the dirt, writhing and moaning. Forte knelt next to him, wrapped nylon ties around his wrists and ankles. He pulled a roll of duct tape out of his rucksack, wrapped it around the man's mouth.

He listened for any sounds.

No movement came from inside the house.

"Secure here," he said into the mic.

Nomad answered, "Here, too."

"Any sign of more security?"

"I'm not seeing anyone through a crack in the blinds back here."

"Two guards was overkill anyway. Stand by. I'll drive him to you, if he's here."

"I'll be waiting for the punk."

Forte took one step to span the front porch. He tapped on the front door.

Immediately, the sound of the TV was muted.

The blinds at the window parted.

Forte waved.

From inside came the sound of running. Then, the back door being yanked open.

Forte held his position on the front porch, just in case.

Nomad's voice came through the ear piece. "Got him."

Forte scurried around to the back of the house.

In the dim light, sprawled on the ground, lay Martin Bailey.

He was fully dressed. His mouth was bleeding. In his eyes was the kind of terror Forte had seen before many times.

It was the look of a man with a death sentence.

Forte knelt next to him.

"I don't know exactly what you are up to," he said, "but we are about to find out."

Chapter 34

Forte stood at the window of the cabin in the swamp, a heavy porcelain mug in his fist. Sunrise made rose-hued lace of the moss and branches to the east. He took another slug of the harsh chicory blend. Without turning away from the window, he spoke.

"Tell me what you know."

Martin Bailey cowered on the floor in the corner. He said nothing.

A hundred feet outside the cabin, a gray heron arose from behind a mangrove plant. It levitated above the water on its impossibly slow beat of wings, reached a height above the treetops before it banked and disappeared behind another group of trees.

Jackie sat at the table next to the rusty oven. Her face was impassive. And tired looking, Forte thought.

Nomad was standing outside on the front porch, swiveling his head in a 180-degree fan of the area. Something was moving through the water twenty yards out, something big.

They had gagged Bailey and thrown him in the back of the van. The trip back out to Larue's cabin took a couple hours – twice as long as usual. Nomad had twisted throughout the city and surrounding area in an effort to make sure they weren't being followed. They had used a fishing boat with a trolling motor to take the man to the cabin. In the moonlight ride across the swamp, Martin's eyes shone more with sadness than with fear. The men had slept the four hours until dawn. Jackie joined them soon after the darkness lifted.

Bailey had yet to say a word.

The door of the cabin creaked as Nomad stepped inside. "We are running out of time. Whoever is behind this will be checking on those guards we put down last night. If they haven't already."

He walked over to the table and stabbed a hunting knife into it.

Forte glanced around at him. He made no move away from the window.

"It would not be my first choice to let my friend Nomad get the information out of you," he said. "But I will if I must."

Martin sat with his back against the bare wood walls of the cabin. His hands and feet were free, the duct tape gone from his mouth.

"Martin," Jackie said. Her voice was very soft. Martin looked away. She continued. "You came to us because the kidnappers of your son specifically said they wanted Forte to make the exchange." She looked at him intently. "You know who they are, don't you?"

Their captive kept his eyes down for a moment. He looked out the front door past Nomad.

Nomad followed his glance. "Ah, there he is. Hey, Al, you think that's the same killer gator who ate that pervert a couple years ago? He looks as big as the boss gator, doesn't he?"

Forte finally forced himself away from the window. "Could be."

Jackie set her coffee mug on the table. The dented percolator on the stovetop sighed. The swamp lapped gently at the bottom of the cabin.

For a full minute, nobody spoke nor looked at one another.

Except for Martin Bailey. He looked at the three others, expecting more questions.

Nomad cracked his knuckles. "Here's the fun part. I cut your fingertip and let the blood trickle into the swamp." He stepped to the table, pulled his knife free. He stood over Martin. "Get up."

The man looked up him, his eyes wider now.

Jackie got up from the table. "I can't be part of this." She walked out to the porch, stepped into the small boat, started the motor, and left.

The three men listened to the sound of the boat fade in the distance.

Nomad stepped back from Martin. "Stand up. We can do this while you are conscious or not. Makes me no never mind."

Martin said, "Me neither."

It was the first thing the man had said since they took him from his aunt's house.

"You want to die then," said Forte.

"I'm dead one way or the other." He looked up at Forte. "And now you've killed Freddy too."

Forte came closer and knelt next to the man. "Tell me what is going on. We can help you."

Martin looked back and forth between the two men. His face remained passive, his eyes drooping with hopelessness. "When they find out I'm gone, they will kill him."

"Who will kill them?"

The man on the floor stared at him hard now. He put his face in hands and shook his head.

"Martin, tell me. We need to act quickly if we are going to help you."

Nomad walked over to the table and sat down. "Let's just leave him here. He's not going to help us or help himself."

Forte kept his eyes locked on that man next to him. "Martin, I don't want to do that, to leave you here. I want to help you."

Martin put his head back against the wall and closed his eyes. "I'm sorry for that night."

"What night?"

He opened his eyes. "The night…" He blinked. "The night your wife died."

Forte clenched his jaw. *The pool of blood. The peaceful look on her face. The light in her eyes fading, fading, going away to nothingness.* He looked hard into the man's face in front of him. He saw nothing but deep sorrow and regret.

In the space of three seconds, dozens of images flashed through his mind. The funeral of his wife with the faces of Manny and Larue and Verna and Archie and dozens more of his friends encircling, all close, all so distant from his pain, kept there by his inability to let them near. The gray faces of Ruth's family members, none of them looking at him, none meeting his eye. Not that he tried to talk to them. The sight of Nomad in a black leather jacket on a hilltop away from the others, his arms folded, dark shades hiding his eyes.

The deep sadness hovered above him now, that gray blanket he had known so long, so familiar to him, only held at bay but never completely out of sight.

Let it go.

Forte blinked. Where did that come from? He wanted to look away from Martin Bailey's tear-streaked face but he couldn't.

You aren't the only one who has experienced pain.

He wanted to scream invective at the thought that had invaded his head. I know, I know I'm not the only one…but…

But…but what? But you just think your pain is worse, right?

Forte glanced at Nomad. His friend was impassive.

He spoke to Martin, his voice low. "I know you are sorry. I forgive you."

The younger man's entire body sagged.

And the gray blanket over Forte's mind disappeared. In its place was something totally unfamiliar, a garment made of fabric in which he had never wrapped himself. *Don't worry about it. Just put it around you. It is from Me.*

He smiled.

Nomad said, "Al, are you okay?"

Forte ignored him. He reached a hand out to Martin. "Sit at the table. We'll work this out. Don't worry."

Martin hesitated, then took his hand. He struggled to his feet. "You don't know it all. You may hate me worse when I tell you everything I know."

Forte shrugged. "All we can do is deal with what we know." He poured another mug of coffee and pushed it across the table. "But we have to know it in order to deal with it."

Martin took a sip of the coffee, frowned, then took another. He stretched. "At first, I just did what they told me. They said they were going to let Freddy go."

"Who are 'they' and what did they want you to do?"

Martin set the mug down with a click. "Chug and his men. He's working for someone, but I don't know who's above him." He gazed out at the swamp. "You will help me get him back, won't you?"

"Son," Nomad said, "just tell us what they wanted you to do."

Martin ignored everything else now. He searched Forte's face for an answer.

Forte said, "Yes, there's nobody better at this than we are. If he can be found, we'll do it. It's the best I can tell you. But I'll say this." He leaned closer. "If my child was lost, I'd want us to go find him."

Martin looked into his eyes for a long moment. He nodded. "Thank you." He squared his shoulders, as if a weight had been lifted.

"They wanted me to get your attention. And they wanted me to change some paperwork on a shipment."

"We know it has something to do with smuggling children," Forte said.

Martin nodded. "Yes, they are bringing in two dozen kids, in a quarantined cargo tank. All I'm supposed to do is be there tonight and…"

Forte interrupted. "You said they are smuggling kids *into* the country?" Forte and Nomad traded glances.

Martin again nodded. "Yes." He looked down at the table. "I'm sorry. They had Freddy."

"I don't get it. Why would they be bringing children in? I thought they have been planning on making a trade. Arms for kids," Nomad said.

Forte searched Martin's face. "What about the weapons? What are they bringing into the port with the children?"

Martin looked bewildered now. "I don't know anything about guns. I thought it was bad enough they were kidnapping kids."

Forte remembered Poochie's words on the house boat. *This ain't no small thing going down.* No small thing. To Forte, it meant something big was to be bombed, killing thousands. The World Trade Center attacks had shown everyone in the world that anything could happen – if the right people looked the wrong way at the right instant. *I've been moving some people around slowly once I heard a little about it.*

"And you don't have any idea who's behind this?"

Martin shook his head.

"He's telling the truth," said Nomad.

A sliver of red appeared through a crack in the swamp foliage to the east. Forte walked back to the window and considered the black water again. The low angle of the sun cast long shadows over the wild grass and lily pads.

"Al. We need to act," Nomad said.

Forte held up a hand as if to stop time for a moment.

For a moment, he saw Larue sitting in his canoe, his back to the cabin, his cane pole over the water. The sun was directly behind him. His head was cocked slightly, as if just now noticing that Forte was there. The old man's face was backlit. A breeze carried the rotting sweetness of the swamp. The moss curtains swayed in a lazy dance. The canoe came around as if moved by a huge unseen hand. Larue's face was lit enough to show the smile in his eyes. He nodded at Forte as if they were passing on the road. Then, he whispered, and across the water, the message came to the yellow-eyed man at the window.

"Just do the next thing, cher. Don't fool yourself, boy. We can't know everything about everything. The next step is all we got." Then he did the closest thing to a smile that Forte had seen.

And disappeared.

Forte studied the others, then spoke to Martin.

"I'm going to ask you to do something. It will be hard but you have to do it."

"Just tell me. I'll do whatever I need to do to get my son back," the younger man said. All hesitation and weakness were gone from his face.

"You need to report in to Chug. Tell him you will be there tonight. That everything is on course."

"He won't believe me."

"Make him believe you. You have to."

Martin looked down at the table, then back at Forte. "I'll do it."

Nomad was at the door, holding it open. In the distance, an alligator swam slowly away from the cabin, its heavy tail undulating behind him. "And where are we headed?"

Forte drained the last of his coffee.

"We are going to break a few dozen laws," he said.

Nomad nodded as if his friend had suggested a picnic in the park.

"Sounds like my kind of party," he said.

Chapter 35

The instant he opened the door of his apartment, Forte sensed a presence.

He pulled out his Glock and eased into the narrow hallway leading from the entrance. Like always, he had opened the door quietly. Years of habit made it automatic. There was a chance whoever was here would not have heard him click the lock open.

He moved against the wall, listening. No sounds. Just the hum of the air conditioner vents, the buzz of the refrigerator. He passed the opening to his kitchen, scanned it. Nothing out of place there. No drawers open a half inch as if someone had pulled out a knife and hid in the shadows.

Abruptly, a Ginny Owens song began playing on the stereo.

Directly ahead, the French doors to the balcony were ajar.

He came to the place where the hallway opened into his den. He froze there.

Someone was standing out on the balcony. The figure was indistinct through the drapes that covered the windowed doors.

Keeping an eye on the shadowy outline through the curtains, he moved to his left. Was there more than one person in the apartment? He slipped up to the bedroom door, which was open. He put his back to the wall next to the bedroom door.

He ducked through the doorway low. Like a flash he aimed the Glock at all four corners of the bedroom. Nothing moved. Nobody was there.

Instead of moving quickly out of the room, he crouched, listening. He put one eye to the doorframe. The figure on the balcony was still there.

He breathed out once, then inhaled deeply. At the silent count of three, he moved.

He sprinted across the den, jerked open the French doors with a bang.

Jackie stood there, her back still to him.

"About what I expected," she said.

She wore one of his robes. Her curly hair was damp. Her eyes were red. "I borrowed your shower," she said, as if it were something she did on a weekly basis. She walked past him, through the den and into the kitchen.

Forte holstered his gun and followed her.

"Everything okay?" he asked. Her back was still turned to him in the kitchen.

"Yes, everything's fine. Go shower," she said, above the music.

He checked the time. He had a couple of hours before his rendezvous with Nomad.

He went into the bedroom, stripped, and stepped into the shower. The glass of the stall steamed rapidly. His washed the smell of the bayou off his body quickly. He tried to keep from thinking about the woman in the next room, the tough soft woman with the smell of his shampoo in her hair. *Stop it. You have a job to do.*

When he was finished he stepped out and reached for a towel. His robe, the one she had been wearing, was hanging on the hook next to the stall. *What in the ...*

He couldn't help raising the cloth to his face to smell it.

He put on the robe and went into the den. The music had transitioned to a symphonic piece layered with strings that rolled and repeated a simple touching theme.

Jackie was not in the den. Nor the kitchen. Nor on the balcony.

Had she come just to shower, then leave?

He went to his bedroom and reached for the light switch.

"Please leave it off," Jackie said, from the bed.

Forte froze, his hand raised. A tingle ran up his spine. "Should I…"

She lay under the bed spread, her face in shadows in the windowless bedroom.

"Come sit next to me." She patted the bed.

He sat. She took his hand in hers.

When he spoke again, his voice seemed strained. *What the hell?* "Jackie, are you sick? Or tired? Or what?"

She chuckled. "The big, bad Al Forte. You calmly knocked down a platoon of bikers and you are frightened of a naked woman in your bed."

Naked? He felt his body react to the news. "I'm not scared. It's just …"

"Just what?" Her voice was laden with husky tones.

He felt her fingers tighten on his.

"You've never…We've never…"

She pulled his hand to her lips. The kiss on his palm made his toes curl. "I know we've never."

He tried to stop the moan from coming out. He couldn't.

"Jackie, talk to me."

"I don't want to talk."

She pulled on his hand. He leaned down toward her and kissed her.

Still inches from her face, he said, "Tell me what is going on here."

Her breath exploded on his face. "Men!"

Then she burst out crying.

He gathered her in his arms, helpless. He held her as her crying escalated, the gasps louder, the tears running down his chest.

Finally, the sniffs subsided. She kept her face against him.

"I start chemo next week," she said. Her voice was that of a girl now.

He swallowed hard and tried to pull away to see her face. She clung to him, keeping him close. He held her and took a deep breath as he absorbed the news. "What did the doctor tell you, Jackie?"

She wiped her face on the cloth of his robe. "Oh, they are hopeful. They said it would take care of the reoccurrence." Her face was away from him now, downturned.

After the heat of their kisses, he felt the weight of the news dragging on him.

"I'll be with you, every step," he said.

In the dim light, he could see the corners of her mouth rise. "Like I could stop you, huh."

"Damn right."

They sat in silence for a moment. Then her voice floated up to him again.

"Al."

"Yes?"

"I love you."

Her fingers caressed his again. He listened to the music. He could see the effect of the morning breeze as it fluttered the curtains over the balcony doors. "I love you, Jackie."

He was surprised at the sound of his own words. It had been years since he had said them to a woman. He had been with many and had remembered only a few. But he hadn't said those words but to one other.

"We will grow old together, won't we?" Her voice was soft yet urgent.

"That is my plan, shorty."

She pulled something from beneath the pillow. It was a box. She handed it to him. "Open it."

He looked at the box in his palm for a moment, then flipped it open. Two gold bands lay on a bed of silk. "Isn't this reversed?" he said.

"I figured you would get around to it." Her voice melted a little. "Is this what you want?"

Though the light was dim in the room, the gold bands seemed as if they were lit from within. He took the smaller ring and placed it on her finger.

She did the same with the larger ring to him.

He leaned toward her on the bed, to kiss her again. Her hand pressed against his chest. He hesitated. Then he felt her fingers sliding along the fabric of the robe. They found the belt. And tugged.

The robe fell open.

"Are you sure?" he asked.

"Shhh," she said.

He felt her hand on his bare chest now, tugging at the hair. Her nails trailed lower, over his stomach.

"My, my," she murmured.

He put his right hand into her hair. The curls were still damp.

The robe slid off his shoulder. He pulled back the covers and slid under them with her.

Their lips met again. Her breathing increased as their bodies brushed, skin on skin.

Everything else faded: All the troubles of the present and the past, all his mistakes and triumphs, all his failures and the pressures of his day-to-day existence.

There was only Jackie now. And him. Together.

His rough hands ran over her as they had never before. There had been times when he had begun to touch her. Those times, she had demurred. Those times, she had never said it wasn't right. She had merely said, "You know what this means." And he had stopped.

Now, he did not stop. And neither did she. There was no talking.

There were only the sounds of love, coming faster and louder until the music was covered with cries of passion.

Afterward they lay, holding each other.

There had been an urgency about her that he had never experienced. It was gone now, satiated.

The music soothed them as the sweat evaporated. The sun had risen high enough in the morning to send some light into the cave of the bedroom.

Her breathing slowed, then became the steady rhythm of sleep. He lay for a moment, listening to her.

He pulled his arm gently from beneath her head.

She lay smiling as she slept.

Chapter 36

The church rambled over an entire acre, a collection of buildings linked by covered walkways for the comfort of its parishioners. The last of the worshippers, dressed in their most noticeable splendor, were trailing into the stylish front doors of the sanctuary. It was almost time for the entrance of the church's most renowned attendee.

At exactly 11:01 a.m., a black limousine pulled under the covered driveway behind the church. A black sports utility vehicle was already parked ahead of it, along the curb. Two men stood sentry, one ready to open the door, the other standing apart, his eyes sweeping the area.

The man standing guard at a distance gave an all-clear sign. The driver of the limousine got out and stepped away. He faced away from the vehicle toward the road from which they had come.

The man at the curb pulled open the door. A woman stepped out, followed by a teen girl. Finally, the governor of Louisiana exited the long black car.

The entire group went into the cool darkness of the church, leaving the driver in the heat and light of summer.

"Y'all go ahead. Got to take a pit stop here," said Governor Barreaux. Without a word, the women kept walking, their heels clicking on the expensive marble floors. One of the bodyguards went with them.

The other stood at the door of the bathroom as his boss did his business.

Once inside, the governor stood at the urinal, relaxing as he relieved himself. *Sad that this is one of the few times I can get some peace and quiet.*

Then he felt the pistol against his head.

"Shhh," a voice hissed in his ear. "One word, you are dead."

Nomad stepped close so Barreaux could see his face. "And put that ugly little thing away."

The governor's face flushed, first with embarrassment, then with anger. "You son of a…"

Nomad stuck the gun in his face. "The people who kidnapped your daughter will kill her if you don't cooperate with me."

Before he could hide it, Barreaux's expression morphed to fear in a flash.

"Your phone is going to ring," Nomad said.

On cue, the governor's cell phone rang. He answered it.

"Tell your bodyguard you have to go. Tell him your driver will take you home. Tell him to go sit with your family in church. Do it," said Forte on the other end of the phone.

Barreaux hesitated. "You are crazy."

Forte's voice was calm on the cell phone. "No, but I'm not too sure about my friend. Don't make him kill somebody today."

The governor glanced at Nomad. He was grinning, his eyes hard.

Barreaux hung up, walked out of the bathroom, delivered the message to the man on guard, then walked out the back door of the church.

The limousine was idling there, the driver in his seat.

He climbed into the back.

Forte turned around in the driver's seat and said, "This won't take long."

The stocky man chuckled without a hint of humor. "Y'all are crazy. Do you have any idea how long you will be in jail for this?"

Forte just sat there, the engine still running.

Nomad got into the back seat, next to the governor.

"Howdy, Governor Shorty," he said. To Forte, he said, "To the opera, James."

The limousine sped away.

Within ten minutes, they were at an abandoned factory. Broken windows encircled the very top of the building. A pile of threadbare tires half-blocked the driveway where the empty guard shack stood.

The limousine pulled through the rusted open gate and kept going to the back of the building. One of the lower loading docks was open. He pulled into the building.

Forte stopped the car.

After the brightness of outside, the interior of the factory seemed gray. The smell of chemicals hung in the air. A rusty metal staircase led up to a higher level of the building.

"Get out," said Forte.

The governor cursed. "You crazy bastards. If you think I'm going to…"

The hard slap across his face came so suddenly he groaned with the impact.

Nomad had already drawn back his hand again. "He said get out, shrimp."

Through watery eyes, Barreaux glared at him. A thin trickle of blood came from his split lip. He got out.

Forte was standing by the stairway. "Follow me."

He went up the stairs quickly. The governor followed, glancing behind as Nomad trailed.

The landing at the top opened up to a huge area where equipment had once been bolted to the hardwood floors. Heavy posts spaced every dozen feet came up through the floor and extended to the ceiling. The floor had rotted out man-sized holes in several places.

"Watch your step," Forte said.

They kept walking to the far corner of the building.

There, two chairs sat next to a large industrial sink.

In one of the chairs sat Rosalind Dent.

The governor stopped when he saw her. "What the hell is this..."

The *shickkk* sound of an expanding combat baton ripped through the silence of the warehouse.

Nomad hit him across the butt and the back of his legs, places where clothing would cover the bruises.

The shorter man went down, cursing loudly. He scrambled to his feet and lunged at Nomad.

The ex-SEAL dropped the baton, feinted left, and slapped Barreaux three times quickly.

The governor swung a wild roundhouse. Nomad dodged it easily and punched the other man in the stomach. He went down. Dust flew up into the air.

"Enough," said Forte. "Over here."

Nomad already had the baton back in his hand. He tapped the governor on the chest with it.

Barreaux moaned but got up. He stumbled over to the corner and sat in the chair.

"So, you are in this too, huh, bitch?" he said. He spat blood at the FBI agent.

Forte slapped the man hard now. "You shut the hell up now. And listen." He nodded at Dent.

Rosalind opened the leather binder on her lap. She pulled a pair of reading glasses from the vest pocket of her jacket. "Governor, I have here some transcripts of conversations you had in the past few months. Any guess as to what they might be about?"

Barreaux's head was bowed. Blood dripped from his nose to the floor. With each red drop that hit the floor, a tiny plume of dust appeared.

The agent continued as if he had answered. "They show that you have authorized the misuse of funding to your state by the Department of Homeland Security. Governor. Do you have any idea what the penalties are for doing that?"

The governor's head remained down for a moment. When he looked up, he was grinning, his teeth pink and ghastly. He spat blood on the floor. "That's it? You kidnapped me to talk about some screwed up paperwork?" He carefully studied each of their faces. "You know that each of you will spend a lot of time in prison for this."

Nobody spoke for a moment. A bird flew through one of high broken windows. It perched on a rafter, regarded the people below for a moment, then flew back out. Shafts of light cut diagonally through the room, giving the dusty air a surreal shimmer.

"We have you connected with illegal weapons. With arms smuggling," said Dent.

A flicker of doubt passed over Barreaux's face. "Sure you do. Let me see that." He reached out.

Nomad tapped his hand lightly with the baton. "Tsk," he said.

Dent continued to study her paperwork as she spoke. "We know some of the people you dealt with, Governor. But we don't understand about the children."

The man opposite her frowned. "Children?"

Rosalind Dent leaned forward, her face closer. "Do you know how it will be, even in a country club prison, for a man involved in a child sex-trafficking ring?"

Barreaux's mouth gaped. He began to stand up. "You are wrong. Guns are one thing. I wouldn't hurt kids." Nomad pushed him back to his chair.

"Governor," the agent said, "why do you think Forte was requested by your daughter's kidnappers?"

"Hell, I don't know. I just wanted my daughter back."

"But she really wasn't in danger, was she?"

"I didn't know that, at first." The governor stopped, a look of regret on his face for what he had said.

Rosalind leaned toward the man slightly. When she spoke, her voice was softer, almost pleading. "Governor, if you tell us what you know, we can cut a deal with you. But we have to know quickly."

Barreaux let his eyes flick to each of the three people around him. He looked up at the ceiling for a long moment. When he lowered his head again, he seemed resigned. "What kind of deal?"

"You can resign quietly. No jail time. But you have to tell us right now what you know."

Barreaux bent down and spat again between his knees. The bleeding had stopped.

"It started with security contracts. I massaged the bidding process to award them where I wanted to," he said. "Happens all the time. The guy was a big contributor. Then he wanted some import restrictions lifted." He spat again. "So I did. A few times."

"Who is it?" Both Nomad and Rosalind asked the question simultaneously. Forte leaned against the paint-chipped wall.

"I want our deal guaranteed. No persecution. And I want extra security on my wife and daughter right now," Barreaux said.

"I guarantee it. Governor, we need to know the name now. People are going to die if we don't stop this."

His face was stone now. "No, make the call about more security."

She did it immediately. "Now tell us."

"Brock Randall."

You would be astonished what I know. The sound of Randall's voice echoed inside Forte's head. He had come to the funeral just so I would remember it after the fact. Forte felt a slow burn starting deep inside.

Rosalyn began to punch in a number on her cell again.

"Hold it," said Forte. "Let me make one call first. The FBI Hostage Rescue Team is the best. But Randall knows about them. He will be looking for them to come in making a lot of noise."

The agent stopped. "One call. Fast."

Forte dialed. "What did you find out?"

On the other end, Poochie said, "Was just dialing you. See, Al, we are on the same wavelength."

"Just tell me."

"Okay. I got you a name. Brock Randall."

"We just got that from another source."

Poochie chuckled. "Yeah, I can guess who that be."

"Details. Give me details about what they are doing."

The drug dealer's voice lost all lightness now. "It's bad. I'm on my way out of town right now."

Forte felt his stomach lurch some. He kept a straight face for the other three nearby who were straining to understand the conversation without hearing the other speaker.

"Tell me."

"It's bio weapons. Some bad shit, Al. It does nothing inside your body for 24 hours, then…bam, you disintegrate."

"Thanks. I owe you again."

"Al," said Poochie. "There's more. This is bad."

Forte braced himself.

"They are using kids," Poochie said. "Smuggling them in. They gonna infect them and ship them all over the country." He gave the location of the docks where the children would be coming into the port.

"Okay, thanks." Forte felt his face betray him.

"Oh hell," said Nomad.

Rosalind Dent knew, too, that the news was bad enough to cause Forte to look as pained as he did now. "Just tell us."

He hung up the cell. And told them.

"Sick," said the governor. He looked stricken. "I had no idea...if I would've known...I would've..."

Forte held up a hand. "That's over. We need a quick plan here."

Rosalind stood up. "Tell me what you have in mind."

Chapter 37

Brock Randall pushed away the half-eaten plate of Eggs Benedict. He was a creature of habit. A Sunday brunch suited him, and he made a point of enjoying the same menu whenever he could. His private chef was too eager to please, however, and the portion was more ample than he required. He patted his tummy, another habit of his whenever no one was around. *Power to the fittest.*

He hadn't felt too hungry this morning. He was too excited about the venture tonight. All the pieces were coming together perfectly.

"Hi there, Killer." The voice was so sing-song and fun-loving that the words seemed less deadly.

Randall slowly swiveled in his chair. "Well, hello there, handsome. Come see daddy."

A parrot immediately flew to his shoulder.

To a new visitor in his home, that simple act of obedience seemed endearing. The men around Randall knew that it was the result of dozens of hours of training, as were the phrases the bird could utter.

The man took a piece of toast and held it up to the parrot's beak. The bird took it from his fingers gingerly. "Thank you, Killer," it intoned.

Randall returned the bird to its perch.

He sat at his computer. After a flurry of clicks, a screen popped up.

He typed in: We are on schedule.

A response came back immediately: I know. I see all.

Randall typed: You are omniscient. I never thought otherwise.

No response for a full minute.

Then: The first part of your money will be transferred when the carriers are unloaded at the dock.

Randall: As we agreed. We will communicate later.

The box closed.

Carriers. The client refused to call them children.

He opened a browser and clicked an icon on the toolbar. Another window opened, then divided itself into four squares. Four different video streams were there, each stopped at a freeze-frame. He clicked on one and the live digital video stream started.

It showed a ship edging to the dock, workers scurrying around the deck. On the left of the screen, a dock crane was already lowering its boom toward a trailer-sized white container with red X's stenciled on every side.

He clicked a zoom command and the camera gradually moved closer to a man on the dock. The man was young and wore a hardhat over his close-cut black hair. In his brown hand he held a clipboard. At that moment, Martin Bailey looked up at the camera as if he knew it was there.

The young man on the dock, however, had no clue he was being viewed.

Such a perfect ending to a long-range plan, Randall thought. He had not even known Martin Bailey before the shooting of Forte's wife seven years earlier. He had merely set up the shooting with Chug and let him decide how it would happen.

Throughout his years in prison, Chug had never told a soul about Randall's behind-the-scenes involvement in Ruth Forte's murder. And for that he was rewarded – with money and responsibility.

Martin Bailey, on the other hand, was awarded with a job at the docks three years earlier. A new life, in a way. And the young fool never even knew who was responsible for his good fortune. Randall had been like a puppet master, jerking strings – and his puppet never realized he was a puppet. Like a deep undercover spy who didn't realize he was one, Bailey had worked in his job, taken night classes, and raised his young son alone. The killing of the woman at his hand had eaten away at him, destroying his self-belief and confidence for a while. The young Bailey had been satisfied to load the trucks and sweep the dock. But a couple of promotions had come along, giving him a sense of independence and the hope that, yes, maybe he could turn his life around.

Then Chug had shown up at the jobsite a couple of weeks ago.

The very sight of the man had caused Martin to literally lose his lunch over the side of the pier. Randall had seen it from his secret surveillance camera.

Chug had filled in the young father on the secret life Martin Bailey never knew he was living. Without revealing Brock Randall's identity, Chug basically laid out exactly what had happened: That the murder of Ruth Forte had never been an accident, that Martin Bailey's job had materialized because his secret benefactor had made it happen, and that Martin would be required to look the other way just one time.

It was the least that Bailey could do to show his gratefulness for his new life.

And if he refused? Chug had been brutally descriptive about what would happen not only to Martin but to his precious little snot-nosed son, Freddy.

"What a day for a daydream, Killer." The parrot's singsong voice brought Randall back to the present.

Randall snapped himself out of his reverie. He realized he was smiling. He was reminded how much joy he got from the satisfactory outcome of an intricate plan. He had long ago become bored with merely achieving the objectives of his customers, whether they be the legitimate protective service his company offered or the murder of an enemy. For him, it was not just the end – it was the journey and how that journey was planned and executed. His mind drifted again.

He had learned as a child the joy of putting together puzzles. Hours and hours of fitting them together had taken his mind to a different place, a place disconnected from the pain he had felt at the hands of those men, the nasty boyfriends. He had graduated from two-dimensional puzzles to 3-D, and then to more demanding mind puzzles and games that required strategic thinking. Finally, he had discovered chess. He had become a master at an early age.

And he used the same strategies to plan his first murders. At first, it had been simple and required little planning. After observing how the police investigated the death of even a lowlife like that first scumbag boyfriend of his mom's, he decided he needed to take more time planning the steps. Gradually, he learned to remove his anger from the equation and to think of each murder as a game he designed. He realized how intensely pleasurable it was to see each component of a plan click together like the parts of the models he had built as a child. The actual murder itself was almost a letdown for him because it meant the game was over.

But there was always another game.

As a teenager, Randall was never seen as a bad boy. He made the honor roll. He excelled at sports. He dated the prettiest girls.

When he would come home from school, he would endure the drunken false accusations from his mother. "You pussy boy, you think you have everyone fooled, don't you?" she would scream.

"But you can't fool me. I know you. You are just like your father – a bum, a weakling. You'll never come to any good!"

On his 18th birthday, he had killed her. More accurately, he had allowed her to be put out of her misery – and his. She had been a person to be pitied all her life, but he had never realized it because of his own abuse as a boy. Only later, when he became strong enough and smart enough to control his surroundings, did he see that she needed relief from her own ignorance. It was a thing of beauty, the way she had left this existence. The trip out from the beach at Fort Morgan, the catamaran skimming along with the breeze. His mother criticizing his every move. The look on her face as she sunk beneath the waves, her life jacket filled with a wonderful substance that transformed into a concrete-like weight when it made contact with the water. *Thank you, chemistry class.*

He came out of his daydream again and found himself staring across the back yard, once again, at the guest house.

The boy came out on the balcony again. He looked worried.

It reminded Randall of the entire sequence of events that reached all the way back to the party at his home. The party where Al Forte had dismissed him so curtly.

He had spent a great deal of time studying up on Forte for an entire year before that party. The man's missions were given the highest marks by both his superiors and his fellow SEAL team members – no small feat to accomplish. Randall had come to the conclusion that the strength and single-mindedness of the man was exactly what he needed for his company. In fact, he believed that Forte was the person to take over the reins when he was no longer able to lead or when he decided to step down.

It had been no casual coincidence that he happened upon Forte in the sunroom that day. He had known the instant the two SEALs had arrived on the grounds of his mansion. He had tracked the man while pretending to give a damn about the politicos and bigwigs in the room.

I just don't see myself doing the kind of things you do. He could still remember the words coming out of Forte's mouth. Worse, the look on his face had surfaced to disturb him over the years. And those yellow eyes.

The sheer blunt honesty in those eyes had shamed him.

And anyone who shamed him so forcefully would be made to pay. Just as others had paid.

He glanced at a clock on the wall. The preparations were underway at the docks for the final move of his game.

He looked forward to wrapping it up and then proceeding to some sunny rest and relaxation.

Chapter 38

The fumigation truck slowly backed up to the warehouse. A few of the workers still in the area glanced at it, then went back to their welding or cutting or loading materials onto forklifts. There were plenty of things to exterminate on the waterfront. It was nothing unusual to see one of the trucks there.

Men in full decontamination suits got out of the truck and immediately began cordoning off the area. Warning signs were set out around the perimeter of the building. Awnings of opaque plastic were constructed and tunnels were formed coming from the two doors of the building. One tunnel led straight to the back of the truck.

The other led to the white cargo container with the red X's on it.

When the men began to bring out ominous-looking chemical tanks, the workers began to find excuses to work in another area of the docks.

Chug took in the activity through the smoked glass mask of his space-age decontamination mask. It was working just as his boss said it would. That Randall was a crazy asshole, but he knew how to plan an operation.

Chug had been suspicious of the white man when he had first approached him seven years earlier. He remembered thinking he had died and gone to heaven when he had been brought out to the big house in the Garden District. He had been suspicious about the man, with his prissy ways and his proud physique. Chug had never worried about padding his own vanity. Brock Randall had treated him with respect, however.

That first meeting had opened the young gang-banger to a whole new world.

Of course, the prison time was not part of any of their plans. But Randall had even turned that experience into something good. Chug hadn't particularly worried about protecting himself; he had already hurt plenty of people older and more experienced in the tough life he lived. He merely didn't want to spend more time for killing another prisoner in such a fish bowl environment. Randall's protection had extended inside the prison walls. Chug had made several specific contacts, at Randall's direction, that were being used in this very operation.

The sun, orange and ripe, was lower in the sky now than when they had first begun setting up at the warehouse. Everything was on time and everyone was accounted for.

He pushed his helmet off his head. He pressed a speed-dial button on his cell.

Two hundred yards away, the call buzzed the phone of Troll, one of Chug's bodyguards. The big man tapped the Bluetooth device on his ear. He shifted in the leather seat of the Humvee. Mmhmm, he spoke into the phone a few times, his voice a rumbling growl. Then he clicked it off. Most of his life was spent in waiting. He had no problem with it. This particular job was the strangest of his life as a thug. He was glad to be away from it a bit, guarding the perimeter.

Four hundred yards away, on the other side of the warehouse with the exterminator truck, the other bodyguard Pea sat in a twin of the Hummer. He received the same call. Yes, everything is clear. No, I ain't seen anyone even looking in our direction.

Chug put away his phone, slid his helmet hood back over his face, and went inside the warehouse. The interior looked nothing like the typical dust-filled metal building on the waterfront, at least the part that could be seen from the doorway where the sealed tunnel was being constructed.

It was actually a room within the larger space of the warehouse. The room had been carefully constructed so that it was sealed from the rest of the building – a low-ceiling room within a room. Then, another wall and ceiling had been built 30 inches out from the outside of the room, making it, in effect, a room within a room within a room. The space between the rooms was filled with a constantly-circulating anti-germ agent that would kill every trace of virus in the air.

The inner room was spotless, gleaming white with a wall-length metal shelving unit on one side and a row of glass-front refrigerated storage units on the other. Two men in the same type of hazardous material suit Chug was wearing busied themselves with something at a high workstation in the center of the room.

Chug stepped closer to the workstation. It was composed of a table with a thick clear-plastic enclosure rising from every side of the tabletop. The clear box was two feet tall, eight feet long, three feet wide. On each side of the clear cube were plastic tubes leading to gloves. The men had inserted their hands into the plastic and were handling something inside the case.

Chug had been briefed about the process but he wanted to see it for himself. Three-inch vials, two dozen of them, were slotted into a tray. Each vial was half filled with green liquid, translucent and sealed with a cap. Next to the first tray was another tray, also with 24 vials. These were half full of red liquid. At the end of the enclosure lay a tray with empty vials.

One of the men carefully lifted the top of a green vial. He inched it over to the end of the clear cube to the empty vials. He tipped the vial in his gloved hand until the green liquid transferred to the new one.

Everything was happening in slow motion, it seemed to Chug. Yet, he felt none of his usual impatience with slowness. He looked into the face of the man handling the green vial. Even through the hazmat mask, the sweat showed on the man's brow.

Then, the other lab worker repeated the process with a red vial. He poured his into the same vial, mixing the green and red together. Instead of producing a brown mixture, the resultant liquid was a bright blue color.

Chug could tell the man was nervous, in spite of dozens of drills that Randall had insisted on. His fingers shook slightly, but he spilled none of it. As he returned the empty vial back to the red tray, his breath fogged the mask for a moment. Then it cleared.

One down, 23 to go, Chug thought. He realized that he had been holding his breath during the transfer.

Randall had been amused slightly at his underling's rapt admiration during the explanation of what the concoction would do once it was released.

Chug, easily annoyed at any criticism, had felt nothing but awe for what Randall had planned.

And now it was actually happening.

Once released into any population, the virus contained in the mixture would spread rapidly through the air, through bodily contact, through fluids. But first it would be injected into the carriers, the children in the big white container on the dock.

Carriers. Chug was not totally unaffected by the plan to use kids to spread the bio-warfare weapon. At first, when Randall revealed the plan, he had wanted to balk. He thought of his nieces and nephews, just little kids who hadn't had the chance to turn out bad like him.

Bad like him. He shook his head. Then he shrugged.

Randall had told him that the children came from hopeless places. They would never know anything but disease and pain – and death. They would welcome the relief. And they would have something they had never known – or ever would know—in their miserable lives: A purpose.

Chug didn't personally subscribe to any particular religion or cause, other than what pleased him. But he also didn't judge those terrorists that had wreaked havoc at the Towers or other places in the world. They had a message they wanted to tell. Hell, let 'em tell it however they could get away with it.

He reluctantly stopped heeding the tedious process the lab technicians were performing. In the corner was a small desk. A laptop was open. Video feeds from inside and outside the building showed on the small screen.

Chug sat and leaned close. He could see himself on one of the small windows. He looked around the room until he saw the camera in the ceiling. He clicked a key and a menu appeared. He switched to another screen, then commanded it to take up the entire monitor.

Now he could see the children inside the big shipping container. Most of them were lying in the special bunk beds bolted to the metal walls. Chug could see their heads, mostly dark-haired, on the pillows. They had been made as comfortable as possible for the journey from Central America to the Port of New Orleans.

One little boy, however, was out of his bunk. He was looking directly at the camera.

Chug could see the boy's eyes clearly. They were red from crying.

He knew the boy couldn't see him. But he felt as if his soul had been invaded.

He closed the laptop and pushed away from the desk.

He swallowed then reopened the laptop.

He tapped another key. Another video window opened.

It showed Martin Bailey walking along the pier, outside the perimeter of the warehouse operation.

The sight of the man made Chug feel better. He would enjoy seeing the man destroyed. He had refused to keep his mouth shut during the trial that sent Chug to prison. So his justice would come tonight.

And before he died, he would witness his only little son injected with the deadly serum in the vials.

Chug had acted like he believed him earlier when he said that Forte had captured him. The story he told of being questioned and not revealing any details of Randall's scheme was delivered with passion. And Chug had gone along with it.

It was exactly what Randall had planned, to draw Forte into the area tonight.

Chug didn't know why his boss hadn't just killed Forte when he had the chances over the past few days.

The man loves his games.

Chug got up from the desk again. There was work to do.

Chapter 39

The men loading the boat could have been professional wrestlers or NFL players just planning a little jaunt down the river. They were dressed in cutoffs and tee shirts with rude sayings appropriate for oversized boys with overpriced toys.

The giant carrying an ice chest under each arm wore the slogan "When I Want Your Opinion I'll Beat It out of You" on his. He and his two buddies had been trading good-natured insults since they arrived at the boat. Others along the dock just grinned and occasionally laughed aloud at the most clever of their insults.

Two women in bikinis strolled past them on the boardwalk. One was carrying a baby.

"How about a ride out on the water?" one of the men called out to the women.

They ignored him.

"Smooth move, nimrod," the man in the Opinion shirt said loudly. "You'd be changing diapers all day, all night, and all day tomorrow. All the way to Jamaica."

They all laughed loudly and drained their beer cans. They kept loading the boat with beer and sleeping bags and duffels.

When they went below deck, their smiles abruptly switched off.

Once out of the late sunlight, everything became serious.

A fourth man was unpacking one of the ice chests. Instead of cold beer, the container held scuba masks. A duffel lay unzipped next to him, the barrels of a pair of Colt AR-15 semiautomatic assault rifles poking out of the opening.

At a table in the center room below deck sat Forte and Nomad. Two maps were spread out. One showed the stretch of waterfront from where they were back to the point where Randall's boat had docked – about five miles away. The other map, more detailed, showed the area around the warehouse where Martin Bailey said the children would be brought. Every alley in the vicinity was marked clearly.

"It would be nice if we could wear a chemical warfare suit," said Nomad.

"What would be the fun of that?" Forte said. "Wimp."

"Smart wimp."

They bumped fists then went over the plan.

"We snorkel in with the mini-subs, take out the sentries, lock the kids back in their box, then secure the bio weapon lab, all before anyone sticks anyone with a needle. Piece of cake," said Nomad.

"We will have ten minutes before the FBI team swoops in and blows the place out into the Gulf of Mexico."

Nomad continued to review the step-by-step of the plan, pointing to the maps on the table. Forte listened but part of him was elsewhere for a few seconds – back in bed at his apartment.

He had always been able to focus on the challenge at hand, forcing everything else from his mind. That ability had saved his life many times on missions throughout the world. No matter what else was falling apart in his life, he had not let it distract him from his work. People would have died if his diligence lagged, even for a half second.

Yet here he was, thinking of Jackie back in his bed. And it wasn't just what they had done there that distracted him.

It had surprised him, her decision to be with him that day. They had drawn closer over the past two years. He had learned much about himself just from knowing Jackie. He had learned there were holes inside him – in his heart, in his soul – that needed filling. He had identified the cause of his loneliness and, even though he would always struggle in some ways with the temptation to mask his pain with drugs, he knew there was another hope for him.

Jackie had gently shown him over the months how much he meant to her. But, even though they had shared affection, they had not become intimate. He had wanted it, of course, and had made his desire clear. He had not been celibate over the years since his wife's death. Those escapades had mostly been covered with the fog of drugs in his memory now. Certainly none had meant to him what Jackie meant.

All that had changed this morning.

"What are you smiling about?" Nomad studied his friend.

"Nothing. I'm listening. You were droning on about which of your knives to bring today."

Nomad snorted a curse word. "Right. You were a million miles away." Then he stopped, a look of awe on his face.

"You did it," he said.

Instead of giving his usual smart-alecky retort, Forte just rolled his eyes.

Nomad's expression became more incredulous. "Wow, you did. You got laid."

One of the men bringing in equipment glanced in their direction. He went back to unfolding the scuba outfits from a huge duffel bag.

Nomad leaned forward, whispering. "Ok, the truth. Nuns really are hot, huh."

"Idiot. She's not a nun anymore."

"Not after the total Forte experience, she ain't."

"You are still one romantic bastard, aren't you?"

"I've not heard any complaints."

"The operative word is 'heard' in that sentence."

"Anyway, back to you. I thought you…"

Forte waved away further banter. "Enough of that. We have a job to do here."

Nomad held up hands in mock offense. "Hey, just trying to show interest. You know, male bonding over a little nookie conquest."

The rumble of the cruiser's engines started up. The boat surged slightly as it moved away from the dock. They would troll along slowly, still keeping up the charade of a group of men out for some beer-guzzling fun on the water. About a mile out from the place where the smuggler's boat was docked, they would stop. The men who loaded the cruiser – all men from Forte Security or from Nomad's private mercenary team – would be above deck sunning and swimming close to the boat. In the meantime, Nomad and Forte would be clinging to their mini-subs as they were carried underwater to the dock.

"You are speaking of my future wife," Forte said. "Have a little respect."

Nomad held out his hand. "Congratulations, Al. Sincerely. She is a fine woman. I admire what you two have."

Forte shook with him. "Now let's concentrate on our work here."

The pair began to busy themselves double-checking all the equipment that had been brought below board. The men who had packed it were trustworthy to a fault, handpicked by the two ex-SEALs for the work they did. Forte and Nomad knew they could trust them with their lives.

The men on this mission, like any men, were not infallible, however. Therefore, the rule applied, as it always had for these types of missions: Measure twice, cut once. They had time during the ride out to their anchor point to recheck everything and adjust to anything that was out of place. So they did.

First, they went through the scuba equipment. The suits were checked for tears and holes. The flippers were tested for fit and flexibility. The straps were pulled and adjusted as needed. The tanks were visually checked for leaks. All gauges were rechecked and the exact pressure numbers noted.

They began to check their store of weapons. The semi-auto Colt AR-15 rifles would only be used by the team of men on the boat, if needed. Nevertheless, nothing would be left unchecked. The two leaders dismantled them, checked every part, reassembled and dry-fired them. They quickly examined the five bullet-proof vests, pulling at every seam, feeling for weakness in the structures. They moved to the Uzi machine guns they would be carrying in waterproof cases to the dock. Then to their Glocks, their knives, the flash-bang grenades – making sure each operated as they should, as much as they could determine.

Finally, they were satisfied.

Two hours before they had to gear up for their swim.

After dozens of these types of missions, the pair was accustomed to the hurry-up-and-wait nature of their work. Periods of intense preparation and focus were followed by downtime in which nothing could be done to further the mission. Then – adrenaline time.

Forte found a small bedroom away from the main strategy room. He flopped on the bed and pulled out his cell phone.

As he listened to the electronic ringing, his mind went back to the morning experience with Jackie. He could see her face, in shadows, as she lay on his pillow, sleeping. There had been something desperate in her love that had touched his soul. In the years he had known her, she had been so sure of herself and her place in the world. Never overconfident or cocky. Just sure. It wasn't as if that assurance had disappeared from her completely this morning. The way she had clung to him, needed him, in the cool of his bedroom, had shown him a part of her that he had not known.

He rubbed his thumb over the gold band on his finger as the phone rang.

As it had happened earlier when he called, Jackie's voicemail did not connect. Her phone just rang and rang.

He felt himself sink a little. Then he pushed the low feeling away. It was probably nothing. She was just sleeping the day away, off and on.

He knew he had to concentrate on the task ahead of him.

Or children would die.

Chapter 40

Martin Bailey picked up the stack of papers from the wire basket on the green metal desk. Methodically, he began sorting the papers just as he did every night. Blue duplicates in one pile, yellow in another, white in a separate stack to be filed in another file cabinet altogether.

It seemed like his life consisted of shifting useless paper from one dark hole to another, paper with words and numbers that nobody would ever heed. *Just in case, his bosses had said. Just in case.* So he did it, every night, week after week.

Tonight, he was dying inside.

After being abducted by Forte and spilling all the secrets he had about the smuggling operation, he had felt more secure than he had in the past week. Now, the nightmare of his situation was descending on him.

But he had to continue his work, just as he had every night. Things were in motion that could mean the life and death of children.

His own son could die.

And he was forced to trust the very man whose wife he had killed.

He noticed the single sheet of paper in his hand was quivering.

A drop of sweat hit the paper.

Lord, help me. He knew they were coming. He just didn't know if they would arrive in time.

"Calm yourself," he said aloud.

He realized that those very words were what his mother used to tell him as a child when he was nervous before a track meet. *Calm yourself, son.* And the words had worked.

He had used them on Freddy before a big test at school. "Calm yourself, son," he had said as they sat at the kitchen table in their ratty little apartment.

Martin bent his head until it rested on his hands over the desk. He prayed for his boy as he never had before. *Lord, comfort Freddy as only you can now. Give him Your peace as You have promised to Your children. And thank You for Your steadfast love to us. In Jesus' name I pray. Amen.*

When he opened his eyes, he felt calmer.

He went out to make his rounds at the dock. He wondered where they were.

As he walked the area, nothing seemed particularly out of place. Even the extermination truck and the containment tunnels seemed routine. Nobody was rushing around with looks of concern on their faces.

But Martin knew that people were remotely viewing the docks. He knew about the surveillance cameras that had been mounted throughout the area. He knew of the pair of mammoth guards in the black Humvees positioned on the far perimeter of the operation. He knew no one would enter the area without an alarm going off.

Where are they?

He knew Forte and Nomad would be coming from the water. It was their only possible approach.

Martin's fingers closed on the cool metal of the revolver in his pocket. When Nomad had given him the gun, he told Martin to take no action unless absolutely necessary. He hoped he didn't have to.

Just bring me my son back.

He forced himself not to gawk at the warehouse with the plastic tunnels leading to and from it. There were no noises anywhere around the storage facility, the truck, or the white cargo container with the red X's on it. No lights were visible anywhere. Martin wondered if everyone had left the area for some reason. Maybe their escapade had been called off. Maybe some part of the plan had been changed. Maybe...

"Still a pussy, ain't you?" said Chug.

He had materialized out of thin air, it seemed to Martin. He was standing to his side, in the shadows. He was wearing an orange hazmat suit but held the mask and helmet in his hands.

The shock of seeing the man stunned Martin for a moment. "Where's my son?" said Martin. His voice sounded stronger than he felt.

Chug merely eyed him as he lit a cigarette. "He will be here. You just keep your shit together. Hear?" He blew smoke at him. "Anything goes wrong, he goes with us."

Martin clenched his hand around the pistol in his pocket.

Chug grunted and the other man realized it was supposed to be a laugh. "You should see yourself, man. That uniform." He shook his head in disgust. "You woulda been better off going off to The Farm with me. Make a man out of you."

Martin said nothing.

Chug stepped closer until the slim man could smell the cigarette on his breath. "But no, you had to go and flap your lips, send my ass away, din't you? You couldn't stand up and be a man, could you?"

From a few inches away, Martin could see the distilled hatred in the man's eyes.

He saw himself taking out the gun and putting it to Chug's heart, pulling the trigger.

He shivered with hatred. *Find your peace now, find it now.* He forced his face to remain as neutral as possible. "What do you need for me to do now, Chug?"

The man in the protective suit flicked away his cigarette. "Just make sure nobody comes down this road. Keep the barriers in place." He pointed to the yellow cones blocking off the entrance to the alley next to the warehouse.

Chug walked back toward the truck, then ducked out of sight.

Martin realized he had been holding his breath. He let it out in a rush now.

* * *

Inside the lab, the medical technicians were relaxing, as much as they could, until the command came for the final phase of their duties.

They had finished mixing all of the vials in the clear case in the center of the room. When the third tray was ready with its 24 vials of blue liquid, they had taken both sets of empty vials and bagged them separately. Then they double-bagged them in specially-prepared protective bags and extracted them from the clear work station cube. The bags of used vials were taken to opposite ends of the rooms and sealed in waste containment boxes with the words "Danger – Dispose properly" stamped on every side. The boxes had been taken from the lab room by others in hazmat suits and stowed in the fake extermination truck.

Then, the technicians began the riskiest part of the day's work.

Slipping their arms and hands back into the thick plastic sleeves, they carefully moved the tray of blue vials to the center of the clear box. A switch was flipped. A panel in the tabletop opened to reveal a tray of hypodermic needles and plastic caps that fit over the needle tips.

The men did not move for a moment. They exchanged glances over the top of the clear acrylic enclosure as if seeking a calming nod that would make the next step easier. The tiniest slip of the hand would mean sure death to them.

With forced steadiness, the first man picked up one of the hypodermic needles. He saw that his hand was shaking slightly. He put it down.

He took a deep breath and released, his breath again fogging the mask of his protective helmet.

He picked it up again and moved it, needle point down, to the tray of blue vials. He pushed the needle into vial one, dipping the tip into the liquid. Holding the reservoir tube of the hypodermic with one hand, he moved the other hand to the plunger handle for the needle. With as much smoothness as he could generate, he pulled the handle up to create the vacuum in the reservoir.

Though they had practiced the procedure again and again, they both held their breath as the blue liquid filled the hypodermic tube.

It looked harmless, or even amusing, like a kid's play liquid in its bright hue, to the uninitiated.

But the men knew what it was. They knew it was pure death. One hundred percent of the time, exposure to the liquid was fatal. It didn't matter if you injected it, applied it topically to your skin, or merely happened to breathe the fumes from the blue liquid once the two substances had been combined.

They knew the entire sequence of events that would occur during the next 24 to 48 hours.

First, they would bring the tray of needles into the white trailer where the children were sedated.

Second, each sleeping child would be injected with the bio weapon. They wouldn't feel a thing. For a while. They would sleep until 3 a.m.

Third, some of the children, now sluggish from their knockout drugs, would be driven in special vehicles to Dallas, Houston, and

Atlanta. The rest would be flown in small specially-equipped planes to Chicago, Philadelphia, and New York. The West Coast would be spared the immediate impact of the scourge that would sweep the eastern half of the United States. But not for long.

Fourth, the diseased children would begin showing symptoms of the flu, including coughing and sneezing. Everyone around them – at airports, malls, police stations – would all be infected.

And those people would begin sneezing and coughing, spreading it more.

Hospitals would collapse operationally under the stress of finding a cure for it.

Fifth, within two days, people would begin dying, beginning with the original children.

The deaths would come from the literal liquefying of internal organs, causing a mass collapse of all the major systems of the body.

The lab technicians knew all this. Men who had gone awry of the law long before this night, they still were appalled at the catastrophic disease they were about to unleash. They were eager to finish this job and rush home to quarantine their own families against the horrendous plague to result from the bio tubes.

It wasn't just the fortune they were being awarded for the job. It was the protection of their families – Randall had captured the people closest to them weeks earlier and had tormented them enough that the men knew they were dealing with a ruthless, amoral demon.

Though they were unacquainted with the ways of the church, they both prayed as they continued the process of drawing the blue mixture into the deadly needles.

The low drumming of the mini-subs made for an almost soothing soundtrack for their journey underwater. Forte was feeling anything but soothed by it at this point.

Neither was he feeling particularly nervous about the mission ahead. He had learned long ago that once you knew the steps of the mission, you just went from one step to the next. If something went wrong, you performed the backup plan. If that failed, you made up a new plan – and fast.

Only half of the original plans he had ever used on missions had gone right. He was comforted, as he was pulled through the dark water, that he had the experience and ability to think and act on his feet.

To his right, Nomad followed the other mini-sub, the front of his body in its mask and black wetsuit visible from the light of the sub's headlight, the rear of his body invisible in the black water. It seemed as if only half a man was being towed through the dark sea.

Half a man.

Forte remembered the first time that phrase had struck him. It was after he had emerged from his required six weeks at the drug treatment center. He had been completely capsized by the truth of his inability to keep his life under control. He hadn't been in control of anything for a long time. His wife's murder had been the trigger on a bomb inside his existence.

He had been terrified to reenter life as he had known it, only to realize his life no longer existed. The person everyone else had known as Al Forte had never really been there. Now he had to figure out who he was to the people in his life. *More* important: Who was he to *himself?*

He had no clue. All he knew to do was to start on his "ninety meetings in ninety days," the standard advice to anyone first coming out of treatment.

"I had been a merchant marine for years before becoming a preacher," the wizened man with the Popeye forearms and bushy white eyebrows had said. He was at the podium with AA on the front of it, addressing the crowd of about twenty recovering drunks and addicts. "On the boat, when a man was sick or injured but could still work, we said we were 'half a man' down. We knew he could do some of his work most of the time, and probably all of his work some of the time. But we couldn't count on that man to be at full strength a hundred percent of the time."

The slight preacher had gazed around the room with the most piercing blue eyes that Forte had ever seen. "When the folks at my big church found out about my drinking, they fired me. Of course, I blamed them and anyone else I could for why I was a drunk. But the truth was, they couldn't count on me. I was only half a man.

"After I finally realized I was powerless to change my alcoholism by my own power, I went through treatment and sat in a chair just like you are tonight. I thought I was a whole man again. Until one day, I came so close to drinking again, that it terrified me. I realized I was not whole. Then I realized I never would be whole if I expected to do it by myself. That's why we need each other in this journey – to be the other half of what makes us whole. You can't make it without the rest of us – and I can't make it without you."

The crowd clapped roundly and Manning Laird took a seat. It was Forte's first introduction to his future sponsor.

Half a man. As a SEAL he had always counted on the others on his mission teams. But deep down he always thought he was the most important member of the team. It had pained him to understand his own pride years later, but he accepted it.

He looked over at Nomad as he surged through the water behind his own mini-sub. He gave a thumbs-up sign. Forte returned it.

He checked the gauge on the mini-sub that showed the exact distance they had traveled from the cruiser. It showed 1.6 miles. Any moment now they would be seeing the bottom of the ship that had brought the carrier children into the Port of New Orleans.

There. The keel of the ship loomed ahead. They were about thirty feet below the surface and the bottom of the boat went even lower. Both men switched their lights to an infrared beam. They slowed the mini-subs to a crawl. Forte signaled to the left and went around the front of the ship. Nomad followed and they gradually made their way to the other side.

There they moved closer to the surface. Finally, Forte's head came up into the darkness. The dock loomed above them.

To his right about a hundred yards was the white cargo container with red X's. A group of warehouses surrounded it, one of them connected to it by a plastic tunnel. The children were inside the white container.

Forte motioned to Nomad. They shut off the mini-subs.

The rest of the trip would be performed under flipper power.

They began swimming toward the ladder leading out of the water up to the dock.

Chapter 41

Freddy Bailey approached the balcony rail for the hundredth time that day. The light had faded completely now, making the house across the back garden look like it was on display, the chandeliers from the big ballroom sending brilliant rays in every direction.

He could sense something was going to happen tonight. Nobody had said a thing to him all day. The lack of communication was the biggest tip. Though they didn't say much, the guards who brought him his meals usually spoke to him, even if it was "Better eat, kid; can't have you getting sick."

He had roamed the grounds earlier, strolling through the maze of paths through the jungle-like foliage. No one seemed too aware of him. Despite the evil man's promise that he could leave whenever he wanted, he knew from looking around that it wouldn't happen. There were too many cameras and wires strung through the lush garden for him to easily escape.

Besides, the man had said his father would die if he tried.

Still, he took notice of all three gates in the wall that led to the outside street. He memorized the placement of the guards – there were four of them. And he noted the movements of the man – Brock Randall – in his big house on the other side of the courtyard from his balcony.

The man had not been mean to Freddy. He hadn't even raised his voice.

But something about the man terrified him.

When he looked into his eyes, he saw a nothingness, as if he had started falling into a hole with no bottom, one where he would just keep falling and never touch the sides.

He shivered despite the heat. He avoided looking at those eyes whenever the man spoke to him.

Several vehicles had left the grounds a few moments earlier. And nobody seemed to be moving around the house, though every light seemed to be turned on. Freddy wondered if something was happening that had drawn everyone away from the house.

And where was the evil man?

Freddy went back inside. He picked up a comic book and began thumbing through it without really seeing it. Restless, he walked back to the balcony.

The only movement in the garden was from one of the guards. The man made his way through the twists of the path until he came close to the sunroom in the big house.

He stopped and pointed his gun toward the windows of the sunroom. Freddy followed the man's line of sight.

A woman was standing in the sunroom. She was smoking a cigarette, backlit by the lights in the house behind her. The haze of smoke radiated out around her creating a halo effect. She was wearing a dress. A purse was hanging from her shoulder.

Freddy dropped down on the balcony and peeked from between the rail posts.

At the sunroom, the guard still had his gun extended. He stepped to the door and said something to the woman. She seemed to be laughing. She took another drag off the cigarette and gestured with her hand as if she were at some party instead of looking at the barrel of a gun.

The guard came closer, still apparently questioning the woman.

The woman remained in a relaxed stance with one hand on her hip, the other holding a glowing cigarette near her face. She laughed again.

The guard came closer.

He lowered his gun slightly.

Then, action exploded.

The woman's arm shot out toward the guard. Small flashes of electricity flew from a device in her hand.

The guard tried to twist away, then convulsed and dropped to the floor.

The woman picked up the man's gun, kicked off her heels, then took a pair of running shoes out of her bag. She slipped them on and ran out into the garden, disappearing into the shrubbery.

Freddy shrank back, stunned. He realized his hands hurt from gripping the rail posts of the balcony so hard.

Who was the woman?

He continued to scope out the scene but nothing was moving now.

No other guards came running to the sun room.

No movement anyway. Had they all abandoned the house, leaving behind one guard?

Freddy went back into his room at the guest house.

He agonized. Is this my only chance?

He ran out and down the stairs into the garden area.

He darted along the path, then stopped, listening.

Was the woman coming after him? Who was she?

* * *

Forte stopped at the bottom of the metal stairs leading from the water up to the dock. The water lapped against the side of the ship. From somewhere in the distance came the sound of a crane unloading cargo. Other than that, no other noises seemed out of place for the pair of men in their black wetsuits. No alarms had gone off, no spotlights reflected off the water.

Without speaking, the men slipped off their flippers, discarded their scuba masks, and unzipped the waterproof holsters for their Glocks. They slipped the pistols into built-in holster pockets in their wetsuits.

Forte unclipped the nylon rope attached to the waterproof duffel he had towed through the water. He looped the duffel's strap over his shoulder and went up the ladder.

At the top he checked for movement. Nothing.

He waved up Nomad.

Once both men were on the dock, they moved to a covered area next to pile of tires. Crouched in the dark, they silently prepared for battle. While Forte guarded against any roaming guards, Nomad pulled his equipment out of his bag: the submachine gun, Kevlar vest, rubber-soled shoes, flash-bang grenades, and light-weight helmet.

Lastly, he pulled out a sheathed 10-inch combat knife. He kissed the handle of the knife, then strapped it to this thigh.

The men switched roles as Forte retrieved his equipment.

Forte whispered, "Ready?"

"Always," said his mission partner. "No matter what."

They had studied the map enough to know the layout of the area. Their plan was simple: Take out any guards silently, then stop the attack on the children. After that, the FBI teams and bio weapon containment teams would descend on the area. Forte knew that Rosalind would have them all in position close enough – but well hidden – to secure the deadly scourge that Randall had smuggled into the country.

The two men left their hiding place, hurrying in opposite directions.

Forte stayed close to the dock's edge as he darted from behind dumpsters and discarded boxes heaped behind the buildings. The white container was not in sight. He kept moving.

When he reached the next warehouse in line, he saw it. The corner of the white cargo holder. The edge of a red X was visible, two buildings away. He scanned the area. Still no movement.

He heard a cough somewhere above him.

He silently counted to ten. Whoever was coughing would have shot him by now if they knew he was there.

He tilted his head until he could see straight above him.

A man with a shotgun was standing on a metal grid platform at the second floor level of the warehouse. From where Forte stood he could see the bottom of the man's boots, the shotgun held at a 45-degree angle so it was pointed away from the building.

He could also see that the observation platform was contained by a waist-high protection rail.

Forte moved out from beneath the platform slightly. He shot the man twice with his pistol. With the silencer, the shots sounded like coughs themselves.

The guard slumped against the wall of the warehouse and slid to the platform floor.

Forte listened for the sound of anyone running toward his area of the dock.

Nothing.

He kept moving.

To his right the ship was mostly darkened except for a light up high in the captain's pilot room. No one milled around on board. The crew was probably out on Bourbon Street. Randall had probably made sure of that.

Randall. He found himself hoping the man would be at the dock. He forced the thought from his mind. It isn't about revenge, he had told his men many times on various missions, it's about saving the ones who needed rescuing.

Would he take his own advice?

He kept moving until he could see the temporary plastic tunnels leading from the truck to the warehouse and to the white container.

A man in a bio suit was standing at the corner of the truck. An automatic rifle was in his hands.

Forte ducked back around the corner of the warehouse.

It was a good sign that the guard was still in position. It meant the children had not yet been stuck with the needles.

He circled back around the building, found a door, and ducked inside. The only light came through the high windows, but it was enough for him to make out the metal beams of the ceiling and the newly constructed room in the center of the warehouse.

He moved toward the room, stopped abruptly, and dropped to a crouch.

Another guard had come around the side of the room. He was dressed in a bio suit also and his rifle was dangling from his left hand.

Forte didn't hesitate. He raised his Glock and fired a shot from 20 yards away.

The man dropped to the concrete door with a noise louder than the shot had produced.

Again, Forte waited, listening. No sounds.

The place seemed so undisturbed. Were they too late to make a difference?

* * *

Freddy crouched in the bushes off the path, listening. It unnerved him that everything was so still in the tropical garden within the walled yard of the mansion. Where was the woman who zapped the guard?

He felt a hand slip over his mouth. He gave a muffled scream and struggled until he heard the voice.

"Freddy, it's okay. I'm here to help you." It was a woman's voice.

He stopped. She knelt beside him. "I'm Jackie Shaw. I work with Al Forte. You know him, right?" Her mouth was slightly upturned in a smile. Her eyes, however, were serious.

The boy nodded. "Where's my daddy?"

She put a finger to her mouth. "Shhh. Keep it quiet. I'll take you to him. Let's go."

She had the taser in one hand and a nine-millimeter Glock semi-auto pistol in the other. She led him back through the jungle plants to the wall at a spot exactly between the spotlights that were mounted. The wire had been cut along a three-foot section at the top. A heavy canvas pad had been draped over the wall itself in that spot, covering the jagged glass that had been embedded in the concrete there. A rope ladder hung from the top.

"Up and over," Jackie said. "Just drop to the other side and run. I'll be right behind you."

Freddy didn't hesitate. He scrambled up to the top. When he turned to drop on the other side, he looked down at her.

"You coming?" he said.

In the dim light, her smile was barely visible. But it was there. And it didn't seem to fit into the danger of the night.

"You just run, Freddy. It will be okay. Just go."

He dropped out of sight.

Jackie crouched in the mulch among the plants in her black dress and running shoes.

Within five seconds, she heard the heavy footfalls of men.

She fired at the first shadow weaving through the bushes. He went down.

The running of the others stopped. A shot came from her right, then one from her left. She rolled to the ground and came up firing, back and forth, keeping the shooters at bay.

After five minutes of the back and forth, a shotgun boomed. The blast took out the branch above her head, which missed her. She fired rapidly in the direction of the blast.

Finally, her Glock clicked. Empty.

She called out, "Out of ammo. I'm coming out."

A voice called out to her far right, away from the shooters.

"Don't shoot her," Brock Randall said. To her he said, "Throw out your gun."

She tossed the automatic out into the clearing.

"Now come out," Randall said "You know the drill."

She stepped out, hands atop her head.

Randall came out of hiding. "You think you've done something heroic, don't you?"

She merely smiled at him.

The sound of a helicopter thrummed in the distance. It was coming closer.

"Smile all you want, Jackie Shaw. I'm sure it won't be funny for your friend, Al Forte, when he sees the video of your next few hours."

The helicopter descended, making the leaves shiver all around them.

"Throw the bitch into the chopper," Randall said. His tone had lost all its smooth lightness.

Chapter 42

Forte moved toward the door of the special lab room. The man he shot was prone, moaning, near the door. Forte picked up his rifle, ejected the cartridge, and set the rifle away from the man.

He pointed his gun at the man. "Take off the mask."

The sentry moaned louder and raised his hands.

Forte reached down and tore the man's helmet from his head.

"No," the injured man gasped. "That stuff inside, if it gets out, we are all dead."

"Shut up. Where are they? Where are the needles?"

The man gasped in pain. "The kids..."

Suddenly, Nomad was at his side. He was wearing one of the guard's gas mask helmets. He shrugged. "He wasn't using it."

"Let's go," Forte shouted.

He shot the lab door's security panel. Nomad yanked the door open and went in high. Forte went low.

"Clear," Nomad yelled, his voice muffled through the mask.

The room was empty except for the clear glass mixing table at the center and a desk in the corner.

A laptop with video screens sat atop the desk. Forte could see the inside of the white container room.

A pair of men in hazmat suits were bent over one of the beds. Children were in bunks everywhere in the room, asleep.

Nomad shot out the door panel of the door leading to the plastic tunnel. Forte ran past him at a dead sprint.

In the distance, he registered the sound of a helicopter. From the tops of warehouses, a barrage of gunfire erupted. The chopper swerved above in the darkness.

Bullets began ripping through the plastic tunnel. They kept charging ahead.

The white door of the container was just ahead.

Without slowing, Forte raised his Uzi and blasted the door knob. He leaped and hit the door with both feet.

As he rolled into the room, none of the children stirred.

The two men in suits, however, froze.

Through their masks, Forte could see the horror and surprise on their faces.

One man had a hypodermic needle full of blue liquid poised over a sleeping girl.

The other held the tray of 23 other needles.

Though it was only a matter of five seconds, the action seemed to slow by a hundredth.

Forte shouted, "Stop and we will let you live." His gun was pointed at the man with the needle. His left hand was raised in the air, fingers spread.

The man with the tray of needles twisted around at the noise of the door shattering. He stumbled. The tray began to drop.

"No!" both men in the suits screamed.

The tray fell toward the floor. Forte had stopped his forward motion and stood with his feet apart in a shooting stance. To generate the speed to catch the falling tray was beyond him at this point.

His mind flashed the deadly information about the liquid in the syringes: Will kill by injection, by topical application to the skin, *by the release of its fumes into the air in a room.*

What a way to die, he thought.

Then his mind registered a blur at his left side.

Nomad was diving toward the falling tray.

His forward motion had not slowed since they came through the door.

He slid across the floor, hands out.

The man who had dropped the tray had averted his face.

Just inches before the tray of syringes shattered on the floor, Nomad caught it.

He slid to a stop. None of the syringes had broken or spilled.

For a moment it was as if all the air had been sucked out of the room. Then everyone exhaled and filled it back up.

Everything seemed still for a moment before all the sound and the motion speeded up again. During that split second, Forte took in the room full of bunk beds with the slumbering children – faces of brown and yellow and pink all peaceful now after a trip of unknown despair.

He felt a pleasant relief. All the pain is worth this moment, he thought.

He spoke into the radio mic clipped to the fabric on his shoulder. "We stopped it. Move in."

Immediately, Rosalind Dent's voice came back. "Ten-Four. We're coming."

Sirens began blaring within five seconds. Trucks full of SWAT team members and bio weapon rolled into the area.

Forte motioned to the two men in the bio suits. "Take the trays back out through the tunnel. Carefully."

Both men had their hands in the air. One of them took the tray. "Like you have to say 'carefully'."

Nomad put his hand on Forte's shoulder. "Just another day at the office, huh?"

"Bucking for a raise?"

"You mean I get paid? For having this much fun?"

Forte led the way out of the white cargo container. Once out in the plastic tunnel, he took out his knife and cut a hole between the ribs of makeshift hallway. The group of four people stepped out.

The area was lit up now. Men in black gear and gas masks were dragging two of the men in hazmat suits to a truck. A heavy white truck was coming to a halt about 100 feet from where they stood. Four people in white hazmat suits with red crosses on them jumped out of the truck before it stopped moving. Each had a medical case. They rushed past the group of four and went through the gap in the tunnel to attend to the kids.

A smaller white truck rolled up to them. Emblazoned on the side were the words "Danger – Hazardous Material Carrier." The back doors of the truck opened and a man in an FBI hazmat suit stepped out with a box that resembled a high-tech ice chest. He walked up to them, set the chest on the ground, and opened it.

He took the tray of needles and set them gently in the complicated web of stabilizing supports in the box. He closed the lid. It hissed as it depressurized to seal the chest. He walked it back to the truck, climbed into the back of it, closed the doors. The truck sped off.

"Whew," said Nomad. "That was some nasty stuff."

A group of six SWAT men marched the two lab technicians away toward a van.

Forte felt himself relaxing.

He saw Rosalind walking toward him wearing a black windbreaker with FBI in blocky white letters. A rifle was hanging from the crook of her arm.

"The kids, where will they go?" he asked her.

She seemed impatient. "They will be quarantined in a children's hospital until they are well again. Then they go to foster homes."

She hesitated. "Al..."

He interrupted. "And what about Freddy, the Bailey boy?"

Her face was strained as she answered. "We've got him. He is safe."

Something in her voice yanked his attention away from the cleanup operation all around him on the waterfront. "What is it, Rosie?"

Her mouth was set in a tight line. Her eyes, however, were shining. "It's about Jackie."

Forte felt the blood drain from his face. "What has happened?"

The agent pulled a folded sheet of paper from her pocket. Without a word, she handed it to him.

He took it but didn't unfold it. A dread began to fill him on the inside, somehow weakening his legs. "It's the cancer, isn't it?"

Rosie put a hand on his arm. "I'm so sorry, Al. Please just read it. She made me promise you would read it as soon as the children were safe."

Forte reached out and squeezed the agent's hands. A tear ran down her cheek. She gently lay the rifle at his feet, turned and walked away.

He unfolded the paper.

Dear Al,

If you are reading this then you are alive and I'm probably not. But I'm in a better place by far. Rejoice with me, my lover.

Forgive me for lying to you today. I wanted to be with you as your wife with no sadness hanging over us. It was the most beautiful moment of my life.

Here is the truth: My cancer has returned more aggressively than before. It has metastasized into brain cancer. There is no cure. I've been tested three times more than necessary. I've given the doctors permission to show you the tests so you will never wonder about my decision today.

Even with chemo or radiation, I would be dead within six months, probably less. And the death wouldn't be a clean death – for me or you or anyone else seeing it. I saw what it did to my mother. I would lose my ability to walk, to feed myself, and even to raise my hand and touch your face. The cancer would eat my brain away until I was a babbling vegetable unable to tell you I love you.

I do not choose to go that way.

The last few years with you have been the most joyous of my life. I plan to go out with a purpose.

I think you would choose the same for yourself.

I love you now and forever. Soon I will be free and with Jesus.

Your Jackie

P.S. If you see me again, you will know what to do. You know my heart.

Forte read through the note three times, absorbing it, feeling the chill come over him in the sultry summer night. He calmly folded the paper, put in his pocket.

He sat down on the concrete dock.

If you see me again, you will know what to do.

He had known something was wrong that morning, that there was more to what Jackie was telling him. The news had been bad enough. But their union had been sweet.

Now this.

I think you would choose the same for yourself.

There was no doubt in his mind. He would have done the same thing. He would have chosen to die doing what he loved best rather than waste away and let the cancer conquer him. What was she planning?

The thrumming of a helicopter made its way into his consciousness. He assumed it was a medical chopper coming for the children.

Then he heard the amplified voice of Rosalind Dent come through a bullhorn. "Stand down, agents. He has a hostage."

A hostage? The haze lifted from Forte's thoughts. He looked up.

The helicopter hovered above the deck of the ship directly across from him, two hundred feet away. A spotlight on the dock showed every detail of the chopper.

The side door of the chopper was open. In it stood Jackie Shaw with a gun to her head.

Behind her was Brock Randall, holding the gun.

Chapter 43

Above the dull drumming of the helicopter, another noise, a high-pitched ringing, penetrated Forte's consciousness.

It was his cell phone.

He inserted the phone's headset into his ear.

The voice of Randall seeped out of the ear bud.

"You thought you had beat me, didn't you?"

Forte could see the edge of Randall's head as he used Jackie as a human shield. "Beating you was only an afterthought, asshole. The kids are safe."

Randall chuckled. "Tsk, Mr. Forte. True, the children are safe now. Well done. However, I have a bigger prize now, don't I?"

It was the most beautiful moment of my life.

Forte listened to the stereophonic effect of the chopper's blades twirling through the phone's headset.

"I bet you wish you would have joined me back when I first asked you, don't you, Mr. Forte?" Randall's voice had taken on an edge, making it easier to hear above the motors.

"Would it have made any difference in how insane you are, Randall?" Forte's voice sounded tired to him.

Again, Randall laughed. "Touché, Mr. Forte. But then again, we are all crazy in a way, aren't we? What I meant was this – if you had come to work for me, instead of insulting me, I might not have had your wife Ruth killed."

Forte felt his fingers close around the barrel of the rifle on the ground next to him.

He picked it up.

Randall continued. "And I might not have killed your girlfriend here either."

Rejoice with me, my lover.

"Don't worry, I'm not going to kill her right now. And I'm not going to kill you either, even though I could. I'm going to send you a nice video of all the fun my crew and I will have with her." Randall laughed again, a maniacal sound over the cell phone.

"And there's nothing you can do about it."

Forte raised the rifle. Through the scope he could see one of Randall's eyes, barely visible behind Jackie's head.

She was smiling.

Forte lowered the gun. The look on her face had stunned him. It was the most peaceful expression he had ever seen on anyone in his entire life.

It was the face of an angel.

Randall's voice on the phone was teasing now. "You won't shoot. Put down that gun. You know that if the chopper moves an inch, you will kill poor Jackie here instead of me."

Across the waterfront, nothing moved except for the whirling of the helicopter blades.

I plan to go out with a purpose.

Forte raised the rifle again. From the pit of his sadness inside another sensation began to rise. He couldn't identify it.

Randall's voice came through his ear piece again. "Sadly, if you somehow managed to bring me in for trial, it would never stick. You don't think the governor is the only official who found himself in my pocket, do you?" The man's voice was derisive now.

Forte now knew what the unusual feeling that had settled over him. It was peace.

The face of his friend and mentor Manny Laird flashed before him, then his words replayed inside his mind. "All we are guaranteed in this life is the very breath in our lungs at the moment. And the promise that God never abandons His children, no matter how things seem."

When he read the letter, it seemed as if the very air around him had become a solid mass of quicksand, covering him, dragging him down.

Now, the heaviness was gone. Everything seemed clear.

Mourning would come, he knew. But not now. Now was a time for mercy.

"Randall," he said into his phone.

"Yes, dear boy."

"You once told me I would be astonished at what you know."

"Yes."

"Right now, there is something I know that you don't."

Through the scope of the rifle, he could see the edge of Randall's face, still hidden behind Jackie's black hair.

He let the scope travel over her face. She was still smiling at him. Her mouth was forming the words "do it... do it... do it."

The scope traveled lower to her chest.

Her fingers had formed a circle around her heart.

You know my heart.

At this angle, the bullet would travel through her and continue through Randall, killing them both.

He put the crosshairs inside the circle.

Soon I will be free and with Jesus.

Forte began the steady pressure of his finger on the trigger.

A shot rang out.

But not from his gun.

Through his scope he saw the two bodies tumble out of the helicopter, down into the black water.

The helicopter rose into the dark night and sped away.

From out of the shadows across the dock, a figure walked out with a rifle. It was Rosalind Dent.

When she drew close, he could see her cheeks were wet.

"She told me," Rosalind said. "She made me promise to take care of it if you couldn't." She stepped close and hugged Forte, then retreated into the shadows.

He walked to the edge of the dock. Without hesitation he dove into the water below. He swam over and pulled the woman's body to the side.

There, he cradled her in his arms as the sirens droned above.

Chapter 44

I'm a little mousey, mousey, mousey.

Freddy hid behind the barrier, wondering which direction his enemy would come from this time. He had outlasted the other two; this one had proven more difficult.

Running through the housey, housey, housey.

From his vantage point in the corner he could see directly along the only two corridors the enemy would come from. He took a deep breath and let it out slowly.

You've been in worse places, he told himself. And this time you have a gun.

He held the pistol straight up. His back was pressed into the corner. He swiveled his head back and forth only slightly, taking in the two pathways, looking for a shadow that would give away his opponent.

His breathing was controlled. He felt relaxed.

Then he saw it. The edge of a shadow slowly moving around a column about ten feet away.

He slipped around the other side of his barrier. The blaring music easily hid his footfalls. When he had circled around behind his opponent, he slowed.

Freddy crept forward slowly. He peeked around the column where he had seen the man following him.

He was there, walking in a crouched stance to the corner where Freddy had been standing.

Freddy raised his gun. "Hey," he shouted.

The man whirled and tried to level his gun.

The boy shot him in the chest. The man fell to the floor, moaning.

A burst of red covered the man's chest.

Freddy went over to examine him. He bent over and pulled the man's mask off.

"Daddy," he said, "you goofy goof. It's just paintball."

Martin Bailey pulled his son on top of him, they both giggled.

Forte and Manny sat a plastic table in the corner of the arcade as the father and son played paintball games.

"They seem to be okay," Manny said. "And, the children in that steel box, the newspaper article said they've been returned to their homes, the ones who had homes."

Forte set down his coffee mug. "The ones who were already orphans have been placed in orphanages and foster homes all over the country. The publicity brought plenty of support for The Refuge and for those kids."

Manny let the noise of the paintball battles nearby fill the gap in their conversation.

Finally, the older man asked, "And you. You okay?"

Forte shrugged. Manny sipped his coffee and continued talking as if his friend had responded. "So they never caught up with Chug and his bodyguards? What did the newspaper call them – Pea and Troll? Now they were a couple of rhinos."

Forte focused on his friend for a moment. He looked away. "They disappeared. The feds are tracking them." He brushed a hand over his hair absently.

Manny leaned closer. "And Rosie, how is she? How long will she be officially off-duty pending the investigation of the shooting?"

"No idea, really. We haven't spoken much. I don't expect she will be reinstated to Agent in Charge of the FBI in New Orleans. It was a bad call on her part, that shot."

The old man's blue eyes remained fixed on Forte's face. "It was an act of mercy, you know that. Jackie knew what the cancer would do to her. A horrible way to die. She chose to go out exactly how she wanted to go."

Rejoice with me, my lover.

Forte stared down into his coffee. "I know."

Manny put a hand on the younger man's shoulder.

"No need to try to make sense of it now," the old preacher said. "If you need to talk, you know where to find me."

Forte studied his friend's face, taking in the wrinkles and blue eyes and shaggy eyebrows. "Yes," he said. "I'll find you."

He reached out and squeezed the man's arm.

He got up and walked out of the arcade. His motorcycle was parked in the alley. He cranked it and sat, letting the Fat Daddy warm up.

"Which way?" he asked the bike.

On the river, a ship's horn bellowed in the distance.

"West it is."

Forte mounted the bike, revved the throttle, and rode into the setting sun.

❧ The End ❧

Acknowledgements by the Author

No author finishes a book solely on his own power. Two people have worked tirelessly to help make SNAFU a reality: Peggy Carlton Jones and Mary Beth Vitale. Their steadfast belief in this book and this character – and their hours of production and promotional efforts – have brought us to this point. Thank you, friends. In addition, first readers Ellen Aregood, Christy Embrey Grissom, Charlotte Carlton, and Matthew Funk gave invaluable feedback in the early stages. And, finally, my wife Kathy deserves more credit than my feeble words can express for her creative input and her faithful love.

About the Author

Glen C. Allison and his wife Kathy claim the land of The King of Rock and Roll — Mississippi — as their home base. They range out from that point by camper and motorcycle and make frequent trips to the New Orleans streets of Forte. Glen is author of the Forte books and *Still Standing*, the story of the Williams Brothers' gospel group, published by Billboard Books. His short story, "The Christmas Monkey," appeared n the December 2008 release of the book, *Christmas Stories from the South's Best Writers*, by Pelican Publishing. Glen has written for Guideposts, Memphis Magazine, Mississippi Magazine, Ford Magazine, the Mississippi Business Journal, among others. He is the creator of the successful PR for Nonprofits conference and an award-winning writer/producer of promotional videos and other marketing communications.

Contact him at glen@netga.com
For ongoing news about Forte and other books by Glen, go to
http://www.torturedhero.com/

YOKE
PRESS

torturedhero.com

Want more Forte?

Check out the first two books in the Forte series:

MISCUE

(book 1 of the Forte suspense series)

An abortion doctor is murdered in the Big Easy. And despite his disgust with the dead doctor's tactics, Forte is forced to track down the killer. Why? Because the doctor's young daughter has been kidnapped. Forte tracks the kidnapper from Chicago to the Caribbean — and even he is shocked at what he discovers. (240 pages) Signed copies available through http://torturedhero.com. Also available in eBook for Kindle, Nook, and Smashwords.

NETBLUE

(book 2 of the Forte suspense series)

Someone's tracking down pedophiles and murdering them. Ordinarily, Forte would applaud the guy. Except for a simple fact: The murderer has inadvertently put a foolish teen girl in danger. Throw in the New Orleans crime family threats and Forte has his hands full as he tracks the killer — and the pedophile — through the swamps of the bayou. (256 pages) Signed copies available through http://torturedhero.com. Also available in eBook for Kindle, Nook, and Smashwords.

www.ingramcontent.com/pod-product-compliance
Lightning Source LLC
Chambersburg PA
CBHW070307260626
47160CB00003B/755